secrets of the wildflowers

Sarah Talbert

Endless Threads Publishing

Published by Endless Threads Publishing

1104 NE Industrial Blvd

Jensen Beach, FL 34957

www.sarahtalbert.com

Ebook ISBN: 979-8-9902456-3-1

Draft2Digital ISBN: 979-8-9902456-0-0

Print ISBN: 979-8-9902456-2-4

Ingram Spark ISBN: 979-8-9902456-1-7

Scripture quotations are from the New International Version. THE HOLY BIBLE, NEW INTERNATIONAL VERSION®, NIV® Copyright © 1973, 1978, 1984, 2011 by Biblica, Inc.® Used by permission. All rights reserved worldwide.

This book is a work of fiction. Names, characters, places, and incidents are either products of the author's imagination or used fictitiously. Any similarity to actual people, organizations, and/ or events is purely coincidental.

Cover design credit: Alexander von Ness of Nessgraphica

Addressed to those with whom I've had the privilege of ministering. To those who have asked challenging questions about the Bible and of the God it portrays. Your inquiries have motivated me to seek answers and walk with you in the challenging moments. This book is crafted with you in mind.

To my family and friends who have allowed me to share my enthusiasm for subjects such as Gilgamesh, The Dead Sea Scrolls, and the Ancient Near East, thank you for your support and excitement during this entire journey.

"And with truth comes beauty and with this beauty a freedom before God."

— Francis A. Schaeffer

chapter
one

"Heaven and earth!" sixteen-year-old Miu shouted, throwing her stylus and clay tablet down, shattering it on the jewelry room floor. Her father, Badak, stormed in with a look Miu knew all too well. She knew he would scold her, but that was nothing new. Heat rising in her cheeks, she stared him straight in the eyes, ready to take what he said head-on. His nostrils flared, his hair wild beneath the leather band on his forehead.

"If you don't finish our inventory, you will not attend the festival tomorrow, Miu." His large, angry hands opened to her, the calluses proving years of hammering bronze and gold. How could those same large hands be nimble enough to create the finest necklaces and bracelets worn by the city's elite priests and priestesses? "Now, get to work!" He turned on his heels and stomped out.

If it weren't for the possibility of missing out on her favorite festival, she would have stormed off in a fit of rage. The love she had for the festivals far outweighed the hatred she carried for her father. Though sitting in the back room surrounded by precious stones and metals, Miu could almost smell the freshly-baked festival bread dripping with honey. She pictured the well-adorned priestesses strumming on their lyres to the gods and goddesses while children frolicked through the streets. To Miu, the festivals were more than a celebration. They brought order to her unpredictable world. They marked the constant of seasons, the movement of time, and the planting and harvesting of crops over her sixteen years. She embraced everything the festivals offered, except the worship of the gods.

Today her mind was distracted by thinking of the excitement outside her father's workshop, and she hadn't focused on the numbers. Her wandering mind cost her free time. She took a deep breath, willing her eyes to focus on the tablets arrayed on the table before her. Flinging her unruly hair in a knot on top of her head, the way her mother despised, she set to work.

While most of her girlfriends learned to weave and make pottery, Miu spent those years with a clay tablet and stylus rubbing calluses on her own fingers. As she grew, her father took advantage of her other abilities, a mind to understand numbers.

"Father, it's time to order more hammers from the blacksmith," she'd yell. Or, "Father, have we set aside the funds for the new shipment of lapis lazuli?"

And he'd watched her skills closely. She also kept watch over the employees to ensure no one was stealing from Badak, and she knew when to smile at an unhappy customer.

Though most girls Miu's age were married by now and taking orders from their husbands, Miu lived at home with her father, mother, brother, and sister. She was a master accountant in her father's jewelry business, a skill her father bragged to all his friends about. And because she didn't find numbers difficult, it infuriated her that accounting was the reason her stingy father sent her to school in the first place.

Exhaustion and frustration crept in whenever he asked her to do anything. She dreamed of having her own business where she could keep track of the accounting for herself. Could she own a business where the numbers and accounting gave her the control to say who was hired when and what shipments would be sent off where? She had ideas and lots of them. If she controlled the numbers in her own business, then she'd make sure everyone could rely on each other.

Last night she had lain in bed whispering to her little brother, "What if the farmers harvested wheat using bigger tools?"

Zigan rolled over facing the wall.

"Zigan, what if we had a way to bake bread in larger quantities? What would that do for Ur?" she wondered as she heard him snoring.

She loved numbers, but she also loved giving people like her brother and sister new ways to see the world. And she felt suffocated in this back office. She wanted to escape and run through the wildflowers outside of Ur's city walls. That's where she felt alive while her mind raced with new ideas–in the wildflowers where she could run free. If Miu had her way, she'd take her brother and sister on a journey to the edges of the world. They would see the places her father traveled and beyond. If she had her way, she'd trick the gods into letting her control her own life. She wasn't sure how, but she'd break their rules and prove to everyone she could run the accounting and see the world.

She needed fresh air. She reached for the curtain separating the office from the back alley and pulled it open. Dull. Lifeless. A little bit of stale air floated inside. Tucking her tunic under her legs, she sat down again. Setting her jaw, Miu picked up her stylus again and tried to get back to work.

"Enough daydreaming," willing herself to focus. She had to finish these numbers, because she had to see Jara. She had seen her last week and wondered when they'd see each other again. Shifting in her seat, she began gnawing on her stylus. She needed to speak to her by the end of the week.

Jara had been allowing Miu to sit with her and observe a woman running a business. It was rare, but Ur's government allowed god-honoring women to own certain businesses like taverns and wool-making shops. Jara allowed Miu to sit in on conversations with patrons.

"Always smile, Miu," she'd say. "It doesn't matter if they're man or woman or child. You make eye contact. If it's a man, you face them. You may bow to them with respect, but you are not to show weakness. Do you understand me?"

"Yes," she'd said. But it wasn't in Jara's words that Miu learned. It was in her actions. She'd watched her speak to high ranking military leaders the same as she would a small child. Eye contact. Smiling. Relaxed. Miu wondered how she ran this business with such order. And her curiosity couldn't stay quiet long.

"How do you do this without a husband? You run this all alone!" Miu stated.

Turning to face her with a jar of olive oil, "Miu, you must understand, no one does things alone in Ur. I have dear friends, connections, and even some family I rely on. You cannot do business, or life, without a community. Do you understand this?" Her kind, dark eyes smiled at her, piquing Miu's curiosity as if she knew something Miu did not. Her worn and bronzed hand reached out to take Miu's in her own.

"Then why...?" She begged her for answers, but was interrupted.

Miu had watched her for years. Finally, on their last encounter, she had gotten up the courage to ask her this question, that is, until the shepherd walked in.

"Flies are bad this year. Got any of that linseed oil?" he said, shrugging. Miu would have stormed out if it hadn't been Abram. Gripping her hands into fists, she waited, but she watched. She watched how Jara interacted with a man of such wealth.

"That they are, Abram," Jara responded with a smile that peaked a little higher on one side, handing him the jars he requested, her iron-bronzed hands, strong and firm. Jara even treated Abram the same.

Miu had to leave before Abram did that day, but she knew on her next visit she'd ask how Jara had tricked the gods into letting her run her own business without the control of the priests or of men. That would be her way out of her father's control. The pressure was high, and if she didn't get this work done, she'd miss more than the festivals tomorrow. She'd miss her chance to talk to Jara.

"Hurry up!" Miu's younger sister, Hulla shouted, bursting through the back curtains. She jumped up and down in her new wool tunic, careful not to get it dirty.

"I can't yet. I have to finish these numbers or I won't be able to go at all," Miu grumbled. Instead of leaving, Hulla grabbed Miu's hand, attempting to pull her out of her seat.

"Not now, Hulla!" she huffed. When Miu didn't budge, Hulla sulked away.

"When wasn't she sulking?" Miu thought to herself. Tomorrow would be better. Tomorrow she'd find out if there was a way to trick the gods and escape her father's control.

Today though, Miu put her head down. She was going to finish no matter what.

EVENING WAS SETTLING INTO UR, and Miu's family was gathering around the table for the family meal. Hulla placed cups of goat's milk around the table, while Zigan placed the dishes of barley cakes with mustard and dill. Their mother was finishing the fish over the fire.

Crash! The sound of metals breaking against pottery in the back room startled their preparations.

"I've made what you asked, now pay what you owe," Badak's voice was like thunder and louder than the destruction from his hands. Something hadn't gone his way, and Miu watched her mother's shoulders drop lower and lower until the smell of burning fish hit their nostrils.

"Mother!" Miu shouted. "The fish!" She ran to her mother and took it off the fire while her younger brother Zigan darted out of the living area in fear, hiding every time their father yelled. Even though he never hit them, his voice rattled their insides.

Miu didn't search far before finding him tucked in his favorite corner of the house with a blanket covering his head. Sighing deeply, Miu knew motherly affection didn't come easy to her, but she also knew their mother would never step in to help. She'd sit in silence, weak and crying. Kneeling down to check on Zigan, she put her hand on his blanket, careful not to startle him. Lately, Zigan cowered more often than normal, and Miu wondered if it was the stupid boys at school again or the overly-zealous teachers. "I could strangle them," she mumbled under her breath.

Feeling her blood begin to boil, she pulled the covers back, feeling him flinch. "It's just me, Zigan. Come help me with dinner," she pleaded, hoping that by giving him a task he could take his mind off his fear.

Zigan was a strong boy, brimming with quiet confidence. His dark eyes sunk into his face like their father's, only Zigan's eyes glowed like a full moon. His hands stayed dirty from playing in the streets with his friends, and his voice hadn't gotten deeper yet like older men's voices. To Miu, Zigan was a perfect mixture of strength and peace. He was the one who would sit with Miu in the wildflowers for hours. Together they'd walk through any field, and he'd tell Miu what plants were growing and if they needed water or nutrients. He had a keen sense for determining when a farmer needed to let the soil sit fallow, often before the farmer was even aware. But Zigan preferred to keep his thoughts to himself unless someone prodded him. He might not need her for some things, but he did need her to defend himself against bullies, at school and at home.

"You've got to stand up for yourself, Zigan," Miu demanded. "Teachers and other kids won't stop until you make them. Father's loud voice shouldn't make you hide like this."

If it weren't for Miu, Zigan wouldn't stand a chance in the real world, she was certain. But as much as Zigan tried the last few moons, he failed to speak up to their father. "I don't like making jewelry, father, what I like is working with the olive trees," he tried to tell their father a few nights ago.

"You can like whatever you please, but your hands will do a jeweler's work," he demanded.

Miu knew Zigan tried to make her proud, but fear kept his mouth silent.

Tonight, he pulled the blanket off himself and gave Miu a hopeful look, silently requesting her assistance in setting the table for the meal. "His mood will improve if we can feed him," Zigan said wryly.

"It's time to eat. Daddy! It's time to eat!" Hulla shouted as if nothing had happened tonight. Zigan and Miu made eye contact with each other, grinning at Hulla's innocence and boldness.

Gathering around the table, Miu's father shuffled his feet to join them, looking unaware of how his shouting disrupted the order in the room. Miu caught a glint in his eye. Tonight something was different, something was wrong. But she noticed Zigan saw it too and chose to keep her questions to herself. When her father reached the table, everyone sat down.

The silence fell heavy in the room, and their mother shifted in her seat. "How was work dear?" she questioned. Miu knew she was trying to brighten the room to make him feel better, but why must she ask him questions to infuriate him? Didn't she hear him yelling only moments before?

"A shipment was stolen," he blurted, his eyes dark. He rubbed the back of his neck and then passed the barley cakes without taking any.

"What?" shouts Miu, infuriated that someone would steal from their family.

"Be quiet, girl," he demanded. "This has nothing to do with you."

"It has everything to do with me," slamming her fists on the table. "It puts food on our table, and I spend most of my waking moments ensuring everything you have is accounted for. And now something gets stolen? How does that affect the ..."

"I said quiet!" he thundered. "We now have more dues to pay, and I will not be told what to do by my daughter. You will do as I say!"

Miu's mother reached a shaking hand and laid it on Badak's arm. "What about another sacrifice, Badak?" she whispered. Miu rolled her eyes.

"That's never worked before, and this entire family knows it!" she shouted. Aware of Zigan's fear mounting, she checked on him, then on Hulla, unsure of how much they understood. Hulla was dipping her barley cakes in honey and seemed unfazed by any of the conversation. Then she smiled at Zigan, but concern was etched on his brow. He shook his head. It was up to Miu to fix it, again.

"Another sacrifice?" She lowered her tone for the sake of Zigan. "Father, we've sacrificed everything we know to do. And the gods are stealing from us. Why do they need more?" Now it was her trying to hide the desperation in her voice. Turning to her mother, "How can you allow us to sacrifice more? If this keeps going, you know we have nothing left to give."

Her mother shuffled the food around on her plate, never looking up. Was she avoiding Miu, or did she know something Miu didn't know? The shock of anger ran down her chest and arms and into her fingers. She gripped the seat beside her, willing herself to sit still for Zigan and Hulla.

"Lapis lazuli is harder to come by," her father raged, desperation weighing in his voice like a thick fog. "New sacrifices, creative sacrifices. Maybe the gods are bored," he said, throwing his hands in the air. His voice held more guessing than knowing. Then came the verses he often quoted from a scribe in Ur:

> *What in one's own heart seems despicable is*
> *proper to one's god!*
> *Who knows the will of the gods in heaven?*
> *Who understands the plans of the under-*
> *world gods?*

Where have mortals learned the way of
a god?

A TEAR SLIPPED DOWN his cheek, as he picked up his fork to eat. "No one knows," Miu wanted to shout. What was the point of trying to please the gods if no one knew what they wanted? Now more than ever she needed to find a way to take care of herself and her siblings. She'd never seen her father so restless, so desperate. And then she saw something in his eyes, something that flickered and changed deep inside him, something dark. Then the silence in the room shifted to weigh heavier than his earlier shouting. She couldn't tell exactly what it was, but Miu wasn't sure she wanted to find out.

Tomorrow she would find Jara at the festival. Maybe she would help her make a plan.

chapter
two

"Did you finish Miu? Did you finish?" Hulla asked, bolting in the back office.

Miu sat her stylus down and smiled at the excitement radiating out of her sister's bright eyes. "Full of life," she admired, to herself.

"Yes, I just finished. Are you ready?" she asked, standing to her feet and stretching her back. She had spent most of the night by the fire trying to make the numbers work. Her hands were covered in clay, clay that would never get out from under her fingernails.

Before every festival, the girls had a tradition of going down to the wildflower patch outside the city walls. It was Miu's favorite place to be in the entire city. She loved the subtle sweet smell of the flowers when the sun first hit them, and her mood changed every time she walked through them. Why did they get all the freedom? Why did the gods give her such restrictions, while these wildflowers could grow in their beauty wherever they pleased?

Taking Hulla's hand, they skipped down the streets of Ur. It was early, and the city had a low buzz of commotion. Only the merchants selling food were out making preparations for the evening festivities. Everyone else was still at home resting or

getting their clothes and homes ready for what Nanna may give to the city this year.

"Leaving the city, we have to ..."

"Be careful," Hulla rolled her eyes. "Shepherds and farmers can be just as scary as sailors," she quoted, as if she'd said it one hundred times.

Safety lay within the walls of Ur, but adventure and freedom lay outside them. But Miu knew what to watch out for, and her path bypassed them into a patch of wildflowers no one bothered to visit.

Ur was surrounded by high city walls which were surrounded by a ditch of water. Like many cities Miu's father had told her about, the water and walls kept out intruders. But they also needed food and supplies cultivated beyond their walls. So the government built bridges to cross the trench and access the fertile land located outside. It was one of these bridges the girls crossed.

Hulla let go of Miu's hand and looked at her. "What god is the festival for tonight?" she asked.

Miu remembered being young and wanting to know all of the gods. Now that she was older and had seen them demand that her father give away half his flock to the temple, she would prefer never to talk about them. But her sister had more hope in them than she did.

"Today is for Nanna, the moon god. Remember him?" she asked, trying to keep the cynicism out of her voice.

"How is he different than Enlil, Miu?" she asked as they stepped off the bridge and onto the grassy plain surrounding the water's edge.

"Nanna is the moon god, creator of the universe. He chose Ur to be his home, Hulla. He made our city great by giving us a calendar to predict the seasons for growing crops like these," she said and pointed to a field of barley growing in the distance. "Farming helped humans stop wandering the earth without order and purpose," she said, kind of grateful she didn't have to question where her next meal came from.

Hulla attempted to run ahead on the path, and Miu allowed her to do so before calling her back. She liked letting her feel the wind on her face and the sun on her skin. It was hard to feel this free inside the walls of Ur.

"Come on back, Hulla," she called as she ran to catch up, laughing along the way. "Here's our turn."

"Turn left by the first lentil field," Hulla stated as if trying to remember the path herself.

"That's right! You're smart Hulla, if you'd pay attention," Miu teased.

"What existed before the gods?" Hulla asked.

"You go from playing to asking questions," she giggled. "When things like day and night, sun and moon, skies and land were put in order and given a name, that's when they became purposeful. Remember, Father taught us things existed before the gods, but without order and purpose, they have no meaning. The gods ordered them and called them by name."

Hulla shrugged, but Miu continued, questioning the words as she answered them from memory, "It's why Father says our purpose is to do whatever the gods ask of us. Even if those requests change from god to god." Miu finished, clenching her fists together. She wanted Hulla to know the way of Ur, and she could decide for herself if she wanted to follow. Why did the gods demand everything we owned? The conversation from last night was still lingering in her mind.

"Here we are!" Hulla shouted, jumping up and down with sheer joy. The smell of the flowers hitting their nostrils and the fear of the unknown melted away.

"Go pick your favorites," Miu said, sitting down in an open space with wildflowers growing all around her. Blues, reds, pinks, yellows. The different shapes and variations of the flowers always intrigued her. She reached out to touch them, noticing how every individual flower had its own texture and beauty. Hulla came skipping back with two handfuls of flowers and laid them in Miu's lap. Then she turned around and sat down right in front of her. Miu knew what she wanted. Untangling the wildflowers, she began braiding them in the girl's dark hair. As much as she despised the reason for the festivals, she loved the preparation for it.

She got Hulla's hair just like she wanted, and then sat back to admire her handiwork. Together they twirled around laughing, both wishing the moment would never end, except the growl in their stomachs drove them back toward their home.

"Mother will want us to have clean tunics on before heading out today," Miu said. "And don't mess up that hair before tonight. You look beautiful!"

Hulla grinned a huge grin, and they both left excited to see what the evening held.

Miu and her siblings followed single file behind their mother and father to Sin's temple. The high sun was beginning to go down, and soon Ur could see Sun, the moon god, creeping over the land. Hulla skipped in and out of the shrouds of people while Zigan led their family cow behind them.

Miu was more concerned with how her mother looked. Something in her eyes looked pained. She wanted to ask why, but the fear etched on her brow warned her to keep silent.

Her mouth watered as the smells of the barley brewing and the pigeon pies filled the air, her favorite food and drink. One may think the market was open for business because of the busy streets, but looking around, she saw the tents were temporarily closed. People from all over town were anticipating the visit from Sin. If Miu had to pick a god to worship, she did appreciate him most.

As Miu and her family walked the crowded streets, people moved out of the way. She held her head high and her chest puffed out when she was with her father. She hated his control of her, but she did appreciate the respect he brought to their family.

"Hold your head high, Miu," she'd tell herself.

Walking with her father was like walking with one of the gods. He twisted that large ring on his strong finger. Was he worried about the future? His position as the temple jeweler did give him honor, an honor he used to carry with pride. His pride showed in many ways, but most often when he'd tell stories. And if Miu appreciated anything about her father, it was his ability to tell stories, especially about the gods.

Walking with him today made her feel like a little girl again. He would sit her on his strong legs and bounce her up and down as he told stories of the chaos waters rocking his boat back and forth on business journeys. He used his booming voice to mimic Sin.

"Sin protected our crossing the waters by night," he'd say, making his voice sound like thunder. Then he'd bounce her up and down on his knee, pretending she might fall off. Sometimes he let his guard down and told silly stories. He'd cross his eyes like a goat, making fun of a farmer he met in Dilmun.

His stories were Miu's only way to see the world outside of Ur. She pictured herself as a wildflower growing wherever she wished. No roots to hold her down, crossing boundaries without control. If Miu had her way, she would create beauty and freedom instead of a world where rules and chaos reigned together to choke girls like her who had dreams and ideas.

Even though she felt pride walking beside her father today, she wondered if his pride was wavering. Losing business was directly related to losing respect in the temple, and he couldn't bear that weight. He risked everything for the gods, and if the priests didn't see blessings come soon, he may lose his position as temple jeweler. What would that do to the family? To her mother? To Hulla's opportunity to become a temple priestess? To Zigan's chances of school?

"Do you think Jara will be available today?" Miu asked, trying to redirect her father's thoughts.

"What do you want with that woman?" her father snapped.

"I just asked a question," she snapped back.

"Your focus should be on Sin, not on a woman who thinks she can run a business like a man."

Miu rolled her eyes, knowing this was a pointless discussion. She slowed her steps and let Zigan catch up with her; even the cow seemed to be moving slowly today.

"Do you want me to drag that heifer up the road?" she joked with her brother, nudging his shoulder with her own.

"No, but I do wish Mother and Father would get along."

That's what was bothering him.

"What's your favorite thing about Sin?" Miu hoped to get his mind off their parents.

His eyes lit up for the first time in a few days. "He is the keeper of time! He sees the past as the future. He knows our end because he knows our beginning. He knows our destiny! He even knows fate for death."

Dread filled Miu's stomach. Where was this coming from? The festival was meant to be happy. Pushing away her feelings, she put her arm around her little brother and pasted on a smile.

"You're right, Zigan. Every spring we gather to remember Sin visiting his father, Enlil, because that's when he gave us time. Every evening he rises to power in the sky to ensure the fertility of our crops and cattle." Miu went along with the rote story-telling. It was tradition after all, and it seemed to lift Zigan's mood.

"He's that good to us, Miu," Zigan boasted, his step quickening with excitement and catching up with their father. "That's why he travels into the sky at night for a soft full moon, then he travels to the underworld to lie down. That's where he judges the lives of the dead. Then he comes back to visit us."

Their father broke out in a song of remembrance:

"... *When you have measured the days of a month,*
  When you have reached this day,
  Your day of lying down of a completed month,

You judge, law cases in the underworld, make decisions superbly ..."

"Sin deserves respect. We will give him what he wants, no matter the cost!" bellowed Father, a smile returning to his face. As much disdain as Miu had for the gods, her father's singing calmed everyone's nerves. His voice sounded like mighty rushing waters flowing to the Euphrates River, easing the mind and exciting the soul.

Hulla danced around her father's tunic, while Miu's father sang songs of their heritage. Was this what family was supposed to be like? Joyful? Moving together with the same purpose? The feeling was always fleeting.

Hope rose in her chest, while at the same despair walked behind them. Maybe Zigan and Hulla were too young to understand their futures of working for the gods and their father. Then again, maybe she should play more like Hulla instead of worrying so much about her father's decisions.

Miu's stomach growled as the smells of festival food hit her nose. She was exhausted from last night's work and had forgotten to eat this morning. Date and pomegranate pies mingled with the smell of roasted goat and duck. She looked ahead on their path, and the sparkle of lapis lazuli mingled with gold danced across the outside walls of their temple ziggurat. Almost there.

Miu tried to soak up every sight and smell on the way because soon they wouldn't be going to the temple as a family. She, Hulla, and Zigan would eventually be working at the temple for their father. Many people in Ur would love to be in her position, but she felt a pang of dread.

But she wouldn't let the dread slow her curiosity; it only fueled it. She had questions that only Jara could answer. She'd participate today, especially in pigeon pie, she smiled to herself. But she would find her. This would be her last year being controlled by her father or the gods.

Her mind waited with anticipation. What would the gods do

this year when they traveled down Ur's heavenly tower to meet with people? What would they require this year? How did Jara run a business without the control of the gods or men?

She reached down, grabbing Hulla's hand. "Today is going to be a big day, sweet girl!"

The temple ziggurat towering in the sky like a shining mountain with its head in the heavens was meant to make humans realize their humanity given by the gods. Every clay brick stacked higher and higher. Each one stamped with precision bearing King Ur-Nammu's name. If King Ur-Nammu had built this tower any higher, they may have actually reached the gods.

Miu felt small. Her father had whispered rumors to her mother of an even larger temple being built soon. If one could be built higher and better for the gods, Ur-Nammu's son, King Shulgi, could do it. God to the people, carrying the divine in him, he had the power to make it so. He had proven his divine character to Ur's people by simply being in the line of his father. The gods gave him the ability and resources to build these temples, and it showed.

"May Sin grant King Ur-Nammu and his son Shulgi a destiny of life, a long reign, and a firm foundation," whispered her mother as they continued walking.

The streets winding through Ur were narrow. Some rolled on before them in straight lines. While other streets meandered between small blocks of houses. The shepherds chose the public gardens inside the walls since they had no stake in the city where they could watch the festivities.

"It stinks!" Hulla shouted.

"Hush!" their mother quieted her.

As they continued to the temple, the streets cracked under their sandals due to the unbaked bricks that lined them. Children kicked pieces of brick back and forth to each other, and laughter bounced off the houses. It was hard to hear over the excitement of everyone's chatter.

With Zigan's mood lifted and Hulla cheery as always, Miu

decided maybe it was safe to search for Jara now. Until her father interrupted her thoughts.

"I'll be back," he shouted to Mother while grabbing Zigan and disappearing into the crowds.

Startled, Miu wanted to follow them, but maybe he wanted Zigan to meet someone. He was always showing off his children to new priests and merchants.

"Well, it's just us," Hulla almost sang. "Let's play hide and seek on the temple stairs!"

Her voice grated on Miu's nerves, but maybe Miu could hide by looking for Jara. Plus, with her father gone, her mother relaxed a bit more.

"I'm hiding first!" shouted Miu.

"Meet us at our normal waiting spot," Mother shouted as the girls darted away.

Running after Hulla, Miu neared the base of the temple. The crowds pooled in thicker and heavier. If Miu wasn't dodging people, she was tiptoeing around the shrines at the edges of the temple. Cults of smaller, less important gods were worshipped here, and Miu didn't want to get a beating for disturbing them. Her father would surely send her home for that.

Miu took a deep breath and chose a wider street to meander first to look for Jara. She saw Mr. Bala, one of the chief soldiers standing at the corner of a main street. Most girls wouldn't make eye contact, but he frequently came into her father's store.

"How is the new bronze band you bought? Does it still fit well?" she asked.

He nodded but kept his gaze straight ahead.

Miu shrugged, assuming he had to stay focused on the crowds today.

Seeing an opening at the base of the ziggurat, Miu wondered if Jara was there already making her early sacrifices. Miu could hear her now, "Be the first to do the hard thing, Miu. Then you'll be able to enjoy the harvest of your obedience."

Miu darted inside to a less crowded area, the inner courtyards, closer to the sacrificial area. Once inside, the smell of blood hit her like a stack of clay tablets. She looked around for someone she knew, but the putrid smell overwhelmed all her senses. Covering her nose with her hand, she tried to focus on her surroundings.

Workshops and storehouses lined the inside walls. Miu knew the storehouses held grain, oil, wool, and sometimes live cattle. She could name each priest who stood watch over each storehouse. She also knew many people who supplied the temple with the contents. She saw a stall holding a few cows. This must be where her father brought their family cow today. She hoped she wouldn't see him, but it was possible. Multiple tables lay in the center of the spacious room, which Miu assumed were meant for sacrifices and the likely culprit behind the odor.

Paralyzed by the smell of blood, she thought she might lose her breakfast, if she had eaten any. The gods required a blood sacrifice, but who could tolerate this smell? She placed her hand on her chest, attempting to slow her pounding heart. Unsure which was louder, her heart or the animal's bleating, she took another step inside. Behind her, the doors were blocked with people, and she wasn't allowed to be this close to the sacrifices. She hadn't been purified to be a priestess.

She scanned the room to see the best way out. Something caught her eye.

Zigan!

What was he doing here? Why was he screaming like that?

She wasn't supposed to be here, but neither was Zigan. The smells and sounds made it hard for Miu to think.

Maybe he was bringing their family cow to be sacrificed. But he wouldn't sound like one of the lambs about to be slaughtered. *Why is he wailing like that?*

On the other side of the sacrificial table, Miu saw her answer. Her father and the high priest. In one hand the priest held a knife, and in the other hand, he was pointing to the priest to hold Zigan down on the table.

"NO!!!" Miu shrieked.

In one fell swoop, the priest sliced into Zigan's liver, and the blood from his frail body gushed onto the altar. His body lay limp, and Miu could almost see the relief on her father's face. The hope he placed in the gods to relieve his stress was now taken out on Zigan. He was sacrificed for the hope of his father's success.

Miu's heartbeat pulsed in her ears. She couldn't scream; she was paralyzed. She stared at her brother's face, weak and now lifeless. She felt herself gasp and the room began to come into focus. Her father turned toward the noise.

A voice inside Miu shouted, *RUN!*

chapter
three

Running out of the temple, through the crowds and the public gardens, Miu panted. Where could she go? Putting her hands on her knees, she paused long enough to breathe. She leaned against the city's outside walls trying to catch her breath and her thoughts.

One thing was for certain, she was never going back to her father again. As a woman living in Ur, she may not have lots of choices, but she did have some. She would need to decide fast. A girl of any age was not safe outside the city walls, but then again after what she saw, no one was safe inside them either.

Once outside, she saw Ur's harbor. The busyness excited Miu when she was little, but today the mystery was gone. She was here for one purpose, escape. Boats were coming in and out like bees to their hive, but one out-of-the-ordinary boat stuck out. It boasted a broad beam and rounded, high sides. Each end was upturned with an inward, sharp point. The back end of the boat was higher than the front in a dramatic kind of way. Miu smelled the dark-colored bitumen, commonly seen on boats in harbor.

An entire boat lined with the tar-like substance shocked Miu. Curious as always, Miu inched closer. Stuck to the bitumen-lined boat were reeds strung along the entire length of the boat. She even spotted barnacles stuck to the reeds, weighing them down.

The design and craftsmanship were alluring. And Miu's instincts edged her to speak to this captain.

Trying not to trip on the docks, Miu walked closer to this puzzling boat. Wiping her eyes, she kept searching. For what, she wasn't sure.

She looked up and saw a merchant staring at her. She avoided eye contact and kept moving. He probably recognized her, most men did. She spent her child arguing with men like this over the prices of lapis, silver, and bronze. They didn't intimidate her, but she also didn't want to be seen leaving Ur.

Miu resolved to walk up to the sailor on the alluring boat and introduce herself. She had skills in jewelry making, business, and especially numbers. If she could get away from Ur, she'd be free. "Anyone was better than him," she mumbled. No matter what kind of protection Badak had provided in the past for Miu, she'd fight for herself and her safety. And if any of those so-called gods wanted something from her, she'd rather die. Anyone with a god that needed a sacrifice of a child to be happy, was not a god she would worship.

She threw her shoulders back and made direct eye contact with the sailor.

"Hello, I'm Miu," she said, hoping he wouldn't ask about her family connection.

"Name's Zaidu," he replied.

With her shoulders thrown back, she moved forward with the conversation. "I need a way out of this city. Can you help?" Desperation made you weak, and weak was not what she would become.

"Where are you headed young lady?" asked Zaidu.

"Wherever you're going," she answered.

"Dilmun," Zaidu paused. Miu guessed it was to see her response.

Everyone knew Dilmun. And Miu loved the stories that came from the city across the waters. Even though her father got most of his supplies from there, everyone else knew their stories as well.

Stories turned into legends and legends into songs. People said it was a land that gave life to any who entered. A garden that held mystery, and Dilmun's stories coursed through the veins of any who lived in Ur.

Even the god-king Gilgamesh traveled to Dilmun to seize immortality for humans. He traveled to see the only woman Miu knew of who had survived the Great Flood. All because she built an ark that Enki, Lord of the Sweet Waters under the earth had told her to build. In an act of bravery, Gilgamesh dove into Dilmun's waters with stones attached to his feet. His purpose was to bring up the flowers of immortality.

Miu remembered the chills she got when her father jumped off the floor in excitement. "Gilgamesh grabbed the flowers! But it didn't last long." In a sudden turn of events, "He let that rotten snake eat those flowers. And that cheated us of immortality."

The story didn't end there, but Hulla's interruption rang in Miu's ears. She remembered them with fondness, holding hands and spinning in a circle, giggling with the song:

> *In Dilmun, the raven utters no cry, the lion*
> *kills not. The wolf snatches not the*
> *lamb, unknown is the grain-devouring*
> *bear. The sick-headed says not 'I am*
> *sick-headed.' The old woman says not 'I*
> *am an old woman.' The old man says*
> *not 'I am an old man.*

HULLA ALWAYS GIGGLED at the mention of old men. She never took anything seriously. While most people feared old age, Hulla laughed at it all. The thought crossed Miu's mind that she may never see her sister again, but she shoved it away. Escape was all she could focus on right now, and it was staring her in the face.

If escape led to Dilmun, she would go without question. She could handle it. She didn't need weak gods who asked for the lives of her family to survive. If Dilmun brought life, it would be her new home. Her place of independence.

"Take me where you're going," Miu stated with her chin stuck out and an air of confidence.

Miu watched as Zaidu wrapped his weathered hands around a line on the boat and hesitated. His eyes were bright, holding adventure in them. Where was he going? Dilmun? Somewhere else? Weathering a boat on the chaos waters didn't seem to unnerve him. He untied ropes and gave commands like an expert sailor. But he watched her from the corner of his eye. She guessed it was because she was a woman, but she'd show him she didn't need his help.

"I'm an educated woman from Ur," she said, sticking her nose in the air.

"I can tell. Your accent gives you away. Get on," Zaidu said, shrugging his shoulders.

Could she help him by giving advice on accounting once they landed?

Miu jumped aboard without hesitation before he changed his mind. Immediately, she looked around to see how she could help. She'd earn her ride to Dilmun, and no one would owe her a thing.

CHAOS WATERS. They haunted Miu as far back as she could remember. As a little girl, she avoided playing near the docks. The curling waves moving back and forth only intensified her struggle with unpredictability. Fear tormented Miu's thoughts like a lion circling its prey. As they pulled out of the safe harbor, her feet felt unsteady. Maybe Ur wasn't safe, but then again neither were these waters she carelessly decided to navigate. Apsu was the god of the deep groundwater, and Tiamat was the god of the salty ocean. Together they guided their boat upon salty waters to Dilmun, whether she trusted them or not. The gods Miu questioned were born in these waters.

> *When skies above were not named*
> *Nor earth below pronounced by name,*
> *Apsu, the first one,*
> *And maker Tiamat bore them all*
> *Mixed their waters together*
> *Then gods were born within them.*

SHE WAS certain the stories and songs from her childhood would forever haunt her. Miu was taught to trust most gods, but not Tiamat. She was temperamental and careless. She was violent and unstable. Miu pictured the dragon god swirling the waters beneath her, salt water caking the sides of the bitumen-lined boat. She pictured the dragon's salty fingertips brushing the shores and then her anger bursting forth without warning. Oddly, Miu did feel a tiny bit of compassion for Tiamat. The dragon did create all the gods, only to find them revolt against her.

The story goes that Marduk wanted dominion and a city on the dry land, outside of Tiamat's control. He wanted a place of his own, and Miu resonated with that as well. And in traditional Tiamat fashion, she declared war on Marduk. Marduk then summoned what he had within his control, the wind. He commanded the wind to rip and gash Tiamat's throat open with fiery arrows. Shivers went down Miu's spine as she recalled the joy her father had in scaring her and her siblings.

"Tiamat guarded the land for her pleasure. This infuriated Marduk, and in a fit of rage toward his mother, he reached into her stomach and ripped her in two!" Badak shouted as he made a ripping motion with his large, strong hands. "Then he took Tiamat's body and formed the dome we call earth. That is what today you see as the waters above and the waters below." Her father looked relieved after telling that story. If it weren't for Marduk bringing order from Tiamat's chaos, the glorious city of Ur would never have existed.

The gods were in everything that surrounded Miu, especially the waters taking this boat to Dilmun. And it was in these chaotic waters she began to wonder if order and peace existed at all. The king and the priests chanted about it, but they added to the gods' frenzied behavior. That didn't bring order. Her parents ranted about loyalty to the gods, and that didn't bring order. Especially now.

Could she escape the gods? In an act of bravery, she peered over the edge of the boat. Her body and mind felt as if she were lost in those dark waters. Was she on the edge of falling forever into a wilderness wasteland? It was so deep that Miu felt it would reach up and choke her.

As she shoved herself away from the edge, a young man about Miu's age interrupted her thoughts. "What makes you go toward Dilmun, young lady?" his voice was as gentle as a lamb.

When did he jump on board? Startled, she looked him over with caution. He bent over, his strong arms muscling the cargo in perfect stacks. The high sun shone onto his strong, bronzed legs, and Miu had to wipe her sweaty hands on her tunic.

As he stood, he made eye contact with her as droplets of sweat dripped down his brow. He didn't say anything else, he waited for her to speak as if he were in no hurry. His presence calmed Miu's anger, and her muscles relaxed for the first time since her brother's death.

Moving about like a man who was deep in thought, she noticed he was willing to help Zaidu at a moment's call. His face was plain, but his eyes were soft and understanding.

Miu hadn't thought far enough ahead to give any kind of lying answer to this stranger. So she answered as she often did, with directness and honesty. That was the best way.

"I'm leaving Ur to make a name for myself. I hear Dilmun allows women to run taverns and some other businesses."

"Seems mighty brave of you."

Miu hesitated. Brave was not what she considered herself to be. Scared, free, sad, confused. But not brave.

Stirring up conversation, Zaidu leaned toward Miu with some hesitation. "Can I help you, sir?" She asked the old sailor.

"Reckon you can help me with some accounting when we get to Dilmun?" Zaidu asked with an accent thick as barley cakes.

"I'm certain I can. I'll need help finding a place to sleep once we're there, though," Miu wiped under her eyes nervously. She was suddenly self-conscious that she still had eye makeup on from the festival. It was probably running down her face or at the very least, smeared in dark circles under her eyes. Did the sailor notice, or care? Why did she care all of a sudden? He wasn't paying attention to much of anything except the empty cargo boxes. He wanted everything neatly organized with the ropes on the boat seamlessly laid out in tight little knots.

"He seems wise," Miu thought. The sailor's hands were wrinkled, and dirt caked in their crevasses. One eye stared slightly to the left while the other looked directly ahead. He reminded her of a crazy sheep her mother had once let her raise, but Zaidu had an air about him. It let Miu take her first relaxing breath since the accident.

"How long is the trip?"

"'Bout two days."

The boat rocked her back and forth. These men seemed easy enough to fool. She'd escaped Ur without anyone questioning her. Bracing herself on the side of the boat, she sighed. What if the men in Dilmun weren't as kind as these were? What if they took her back to her father? She rolled her head around, releasing the building tension.

chapter
four

A day of travel was behind them, and the sound of waves lapping against the boat made Miu question whether her escape by water had been the safest option. She stared over the edge of the boat again as sheer terror coursed through her body. The chaos waters, never ceasing, constantly pounding, were proof all the gods were the same. Capricious.

Miu watched as Tiamat violently struck the sides of the boat, reminding her of the anger she witnessed while walking the shores of Ur with her mother. She'd stroked Miu's hand, attempting to encourage her, but her eyes had looked uncertain. "Tiamat wants her life back, Miu. Can't you understand? She tries to pull the earth back into herself, back into the waters. Tiamat's waves are uncertain, so always be cautious, Miu."

She gazed at the teeming fish swimming beneath her. It was what lay beneath those living creatures that scared her more than anything she'd seen on the dry land. Her people believed a dark abyss lay beneath the water. Miu tried to imagine the pillars that supported the earth and the dome above the sky, anything to focus her mind on something more stabilizing, something other than these wretched waves.

The day had been long and draining. The sun was unforgiving, Miu was parched, and as angry as she was at her father, she had to admit she was used to the comforts he'd provided. Only a few hours from him and she already realized she needed to suck it up or go crawling back to him. Would he chase her down? Or would he relish the idea of losing two out of three of his children? If he found her, would he send her directly to the temple? He could control her through the gods that way. The pit in her stomach grew. If he found her, all her freedom would be stripped away.

She shook off the dread before it sank into her bones, then focused her eyes in front of her. As terrifying as Tiamat was, her father's tyranny loomed heavier in her mind, crashing over every piece of sanity she had left.

She didn't want these men to sense her fear, so instead she smoothed her tunic and tied her hair back in a fresh knot. She couldn't lose her strength now. She'd trusted men before, and they stripped her of everything. If she showed herself to be strong and capable then they might offer her work. She'd ask questions. Get to know them. She'd either find their weaknesses or learn how to use their strengths for her next venture. She'd decide for herself who could be used and who could be silenced.

"Taku, do you travel with Zaidu often?" she asked pointedly, crossing her arms.

"Yeah, I'm a courier. Messages have to get from place to place somehow."

Taku's presence got under Miu's skin. He was too calm himself, while his braided hair mimicked Miu's feelings, all tangled and knotted up inside. How could anyone be relaxed on these waves?

Zaidu appeared to be a sailor by trade, and Miu was grateful that at least he skillfully navigated the helm with caution. Was Taku's calm demeanor a weakness? Miu wasn't sure. Her guess was ignorance. Taku was probably like every other spineless person in Ur, believing they had to walk on tiptoes to keep the gods happy and content. Whatever helped this guy sleep at night. Living so nonchalantly exposed one's vulnerability, and to Miu, nothing could be worse.

Both men navigated the waters with ease and grace. She watched them work hand in hand, passing lines back and forth and pointing directions to the men rowing at precise moments. Zaidu's worn and leathered hands grasped his oar with the confidence only a seasoned sailor could hold. Taku was graceful behind the oars as he worked in unison with Zaidu. His strong, bronzed muscles moved to the beat of Tiamat's unending waves.

"Do you go to Dilmun often?" Miu pressed Taku further.

"Every few months. I take messages back and forth for different merchants in Ur and Dilmun."

Miu pondered over how frequently he traveled. Taku's mild demeanor wasn't from inexperience; this spiked Miu's curiosity even more.

"Why are you so peaceful out here? It's stupid to remain so calm with Tiamat taunting our boat to Dilmun. Don't you fear what the gods will do to you?"

The wind picked up speed, and the boat began to rock harder back and forth. Salt crusted in each man's beard as the journey continued. Miu could taste it on her fingers and even felt it in her ears. Her stomach dropped, and her skin prickled. Had her curiosity angered the gods? Refusing to show her fear, she braced her feet and her nerves, gripping the side of the boat a bit tighter.

"I've crossed these waters often," Taku answered while still rowing, not the least bit winded. "I don't notice them."

She wasn't sure if his nonchalant attitude angered or calmed her. As she gripped the boat tighter, the bitumen dug under her fingernails. "Do you know how to read since you carry these messages all day?"

"I can read and write. But I choose not to write."

She wondered why not. Out of the corner of her eye, Miu noticed a gray dove in a small, wooden cage, and it dawned on her that that must have been why the men were calm. Doves in Ur carried peace. Every traveler carried a dove with them to sacrifice on the other side of their journey. With the thought, the memory of the birds in the temple yesterday made her chest tighten.

"Do you plan to sacrifice that dove once we land?" She wanted to hear him say it even if she was sure she already knew the answer.

"That's Zaidu's. Not my boat, not my dove," Taku stood, handing his oar to a sailor waiting his turn. He seemed as if he wanted to be left alone.

Miu wanted to strangle him. She couldn't get anything out of him. Why doesn't he write anymore? Why don't the waves and wind disturb him even a little? His silence was annoying and so was this trip. If something did happen while they were crossing, she had a feeling he'd be of no help at all.

※

Unwilling to let the nosy woman unsettle his peace, Taku kept to himself. He appreciated these long rides to Dilmun and back, without questions or prying, which allowed him to create stories in his mind of the gods and the people of Dilmun and Ur without disruptions. Traveling with Zaidu was great because they could go the entire trip without saying a word. It was perfection.

But now the woman's questions rattled him. It was as if she had crawled under his fingernails and was slithering around in his skin. And her questions! They rolled around in his mind. He usually pushed the sea dragon Tiamat out of his mind, but today was different. She'd ask questions he'd never considered. Taku knew sailors tried to predict Tiamat's decisions by rolling dice or reading animal organs. It never worked. She was unpredictable. Either a ship would wreck or a ship would make it across the seas; it was all up to chance. The only reason Tiamat flooded the earth in the days of Gilgamesh was because of people's incessant bickering and fighting. She was unruly, but then again, so was this woman and her questions. In a way, he kind of liked how

Tiamat's anger made Miu angry. Two peas in a pod, he thought with a smile.

"Will we sacrifice as soon as we hit landfall, Zaidu?" Taku asked, already knowing the answer.

"We must thank Tiamat for her generosity in bringing us from land to land." Zaidu smiled, staring out at the raging chaos waters. "These sacrifices build long-term relationships with the gods, Taku. The priests tell me what makes the gods happy. We must obey the priests and the king."

Taku knew that, like other families in Dilmun and Ur, Zaidu's family had their own gods. It's why he kept a small altar at the back of the boat where the men could sit and sing songs to them as they traveled. Any god that could hear them would be worshipped. Taku wished he could trust the gods as Zaidu did. He wished his loyalty rang as true as Zaidu's. He couldn't muster it up if he tried.

One time Zaidu had lost three of his ships on the seas. He had consulted the priests before leaving and made the appropriate sacrifice. Even then, a dark squall came upon the waters. No one knew it was coming, and Zaidu lost everything. Except his faith. Everyone in Ur assumed Zaidu would be furious with the gods; instead, it made him cling tighter to them. He devoted himself even more with every trip across the seas.

To Taku, it was all a guessing game to secure favor and the presence of any god. The gods didn't bring peace, they were too violent. Not for the first time did Taku wish he could be as peaceful inside as he was outside. Chaotic waters, chaotic thoughts, and now chaotic women stole any sense of peace he had remaining.

What he wanted was a time and place to write his own stories and poems to the gods. He had trained to be a priest and to write down the words from the gods, but he had taken it too far, spoken up too soon. He never should have written his poem to Nisaba. The day haunted him often.

His one-room schoolhouse had smelled of clay, earthy and full of potential. He could still hear leather shoes trudging across the palm reeds on the floor as students piled into the room in an orderly fashion. The room itself was well lit by the windows above. He'd sat on the edge of his dried-mud bench, his palms sweating, waiting to hear the next assignment. His teacher's graying hair and long bony fingers had long since sucked the joy out of his classmates, and the older man's tunic was showing signs of wear. However, he kept the tunic tied just so, always around his waist with meticulous care. The man's stony face never showed signs of curiosity, and his serious way of staring straight ahead, never making eye contact, struck fear in the hearts of anyone who dared breathe creativity outside of instruction.

"Boys, it's time to pull out your tablets and writings from last night. We will go over the words line by line," he'd murmured.

Writing fascinated Taku; he even loved making mistakes. Many of the boys in his class were bored and unappreciative of the skills they were learning, but he found he loved how words could dance off each other to create poetry dedicated to the gods. He liked being able to fix an error and replace a word to make the poem sound stronger and more robust with a simple smudge of clay. He loved being able to rewrite some of Ur's best stories like the epic tale Gilgamesh, hymns to the gods, and other famous poems. His major problem in class was daydreaming. There, his mind would race with new ideas and stories to tell that were his own.

Walking over to Taku, the teacher had reached his hand down as he stared straight ahead.

"Your turn, Taku."

Taku's arms felt weak as his teacher read through his cuneiform tablet, his cold fingers sliding across slowly, meticulously checking every line and image. Taku was supposed to have practiced some of the six hundred signs in script, however, he hadn't written the assignment. The silence and suspense felt thicker as his teacher's fingers grew closer to the end.

Taku prayed to the gods his stomach would calm down. Last

night he'd even put an onion peel under his head while he slept, hoping Nisaba would inspire him.

His teacher gripped the tablet, anger shining in his eyes.

"You did not do the assignment," his teacher had snarled, before reading aloud what Taku had written:

> *Lady of divine lapis lazuli.*
> *Lady colored like the stars of heaven.*
> *Adorn us with brilliance for writing the*
> *fruit of your beauty.*

A SCOWL SPREAD across his brow, and he threw the tablet across the room. It shattered and everyone stared. Taku felt fear, but more than that, shame. Writing that had been a risk, but he hadn't expected this kind of reaction from his teacher.

"How dare you try and redo the work of the priestesses! Only they tell us what the gods say!"

Taku wanted to yell back. He wanted to scream, "Isn't that what we're training to do? How can I learn unless I try my own words?"

Instead he sat, puzzled and shocked.

Next came the blow. The whip across his face. Then the sting on his skin ran down his neck and up into his eyes. He reached up with caution to touch it. His face cracked but his confidence cracked deeper.

"Get out!" shouted his teacher. "You'll never write in Ur again."

Taku still felt the burn on his face every time he picked up his stylus to write anything for himself. The thoughts and ideas had never stopped, but he would never write his own words again. It didn't matter anyway. Thinking for yourself meant defeat. It meant losing the ones you love. He needed to just keep silent. Do the things he was supposed to do. Do that and he wouldn't lose more dreams or more friends. Keep the peace.

Taku was roused from his daydream when Zaidu brushed past him. It was time for him to row again. Maybe the rowing would clear his mind. He could steady his world inside his mind, but now this woman was staring at him. Would she start asking questions again, disturbing the peace he had worked hard to maintain?

Zaidu's boat rocked on, a constant that Taku was forever grateful for. If it hadn't been for this old sailor, Taku wasn't sure what would have become of him. He wasn't sure about the gods, but he was certain about Zaidu.

He had Taku's loyalty no matter what. It was this woman's gaze he couldn't get away from.

chapter
five

Miu saw Dilmun in the distance and the large tower that stood on its shoreline struck her. Made from brick, its winding monument stood erect as if to say, "Here, come this way." Alluring as it was, Miu couldn't help but ask Zaidu about it, as he was headed directly for it.

"What's that?" Miu pointed.

"A lighthouse. It helps sailors find their way at night."

A lighthouse. A way for the lost to find home. For the first time since leaving Ur, Miu's muscles relaxed. Although her uncertainty about what lay ahead nagged deep within her bones, she stared ahead, determined. What could a woman of sixteen become without her parents' prestige? Women were allowed to own their own businesses in Ur, but could they do so in Dilmun? A woman without a husband was sometimes seen as scandalous or gutsy. There was no fallback plan for women like her. It was risking it all in a business or failing with no father or husband to support you.

She couldn't look back now. She resolved to plow through the next problem as it came. Her father's ambition had threatened to consume her, but her own ambition had always saved her. Miu held tight to the memories that flooded her mind during the voyage. She mulled over the times she fought for her brother and sister, and even her mother. She had fought merchants and sailors, shepherds and priests. She had myriad memories to pull from when it came to standing up to men trying to take advantage of her mind, her insight, or her straightforward manner. Sometimes that man was her father.

If he came after her, she'd have what it took to fight back. Just like the day Miu's sister, Hulla, had come dancing and twirling into their father's jewelry store. It irritated Miu, but she knew that day was special. Father had brought home a new lamb, and Hulla, along with the whole family, was ecstatic. A new lamb meant blessing. It meant Father's business was thriving, but under that current of joy also lay the truth that with the business doing well, the gods expected something in return.

Miu knew the second she heard Hulla blurt out, "We have a new pet!" that she would have to be the one to disappoint her. After all, the lamb would be a sacrifice for the gods, not a pet. She'd have to be the one to tell Hulla the truth. Sure enough, when her father came home that evening he had explained to Miu that his business had grown big enough to start another trade route to gain more lapis lazuli. The blue stones contrasted appealingly with the dull browns and dusty wools Ur was accustomed to seeing, and as such, were sought after for women's necklaces, hair ornaments, men's belts, and other adornments. The lamb was to be a thank you sacrifice to their family's god, Enki.

Miu couldn't stand to watch her sister melt with disappointment, but it was now or later. Either way, she'd have to watch her sister's beaming smile crumble into a thousand pieces. She stormed into the house with Hulla trailing behind, ready to tell Father to take the lamb somewhere else until he was ready to slaughter it.

But it was too late.

"Papa says we can keep it in the house for a while!" Hulla had rejoiced.

Appalled by their father's barbaric decision to let the lamb in the house with them, Miu could not say she had been shocked. He was often cruel, if for no other reason than for spite. He loved watching his children grow attached to something, only to smirk and steal them away a few days later. Their mother didn't have the nerve to tell the truth, and her brother was too young to care or understand.

"Hulla, that lamb is not a pet. It's for the gods."

"I love it! Father will never kill it," Hulla had wailed. "You're just saying that to be mean to me. You're jealous because Father makes you work all the time, and he thinks I'm prettier."

Miu had sighed, resigned. Why did everyone think she was mean when she spoke the truth? She had taken a deep breath, absorbed her sister's insult, and walked out of the room that day. Hulla may be hurt now, but better for her to know instead of attaching herself to a lamb to watch it die.

A gust of wind pulled Miu out of her memories as tears welled up in her eyes. The thought of never seeing her sister again and the pain from losing her brother weighed on her like the bronze armor soldiers wore to battle. The heaviness of grief welled up inside, and she wasn't sure she was strong enough to carry it. Still, she couldn't let what her father did stop her from escaping. Stop her from freedom. She'd make her heart as stone cold as the gods he worshipped until nothing could get inside. She would just keep marching. Stop thinking about them. Stop worrying about them. She must push forward in this new life or be swallowed by her past one.

The lighthouse was in clear sight now as Zaidu navigated the boat with precision, back and forth, in and around other boats in the crowded harbor. Miu noticed the air was cleaner here. Trees lined the harbor and poked up above the horizon, the brightest green she'd ever seen. White jasmine dotted the landscape as well as bright sunflowers. Compared to Ur's browns and sporadic greenery, Dilmun was heaven on earth. Maybe this could be the place where Miu made a name for herself without the help of anyone else.

Even the waters in Dilmun were more translucent and bluer than Miu ever remembered seeing before. She could almost picture Enki bringing sweet water, the source of life, here. Dilmun was where the source of life and fresh, sweet water originated. Miu had made it this far, and the beauty in front of her reassured her decision to leave Ur. She felt hope in the possibilities that came with moving forward, no matter what. That's what Miu would focus on.

Upon arriving at the docks, Zaidu and Taku quickly disembarked from the boat and efficiently secured it to the vertical poles using their ropes. Zaidu then motioned for Taku to grab the cage holding his dove. Next, they motioned for Miu to come on and follow them, and while she wasn't a fan of men telling her what to do, she was not going to sit in this boat by herself in a strange land. It didn't take long for her to weigh her options. When her feet hit the dry land, she felt certain she was still rocking.

"Keep walking, the water feet will wear off and you'll feel steady again," Zaidu assured her.

Along the shore, Miu noticed fishermen humming and singing as they mended their nets while women sorted the larger fish from smaller ones. Children were dodging through the fishing nets and laughing. They were playing games Miu recognized, and that brought comfort.

The smell of jasmine filled her senses. No wonder these people seemed happy when beauty was everywhere. An older woman looked up and caught Miu's eye and smiled. She couldn't tell if the look was pity or kindness. She found she preferred the latter. Either way, it made Miu a bit self-conscious. She wiped under her eyes and straightened her tunic. The people's accents were different, but she could make out many of the words as she passed. It must be at least some of the same language she was accustomed to the merchants using in Ur. It did make her a bit self-conscious as to how she might sound as a foreigner here. She added that to her mental list.

If she kept to her list, she told herself, then she couldn't be controlled. Speak directly. Lose her accent quickly. Sleep with her face toward the door. Find a job using numbers.

She kept her eyes forward and tried to look as if she was meant to be here. She needed to find somewhere to get a bite to eat and wash her face.

Zaidu clearly had different plans and wanted to make his sacrifice. Taku followed. All together, they weaved their way through town. Adjacent to the main road was a sunflower field, golden and bright. Miu imagined Ziusudra landing here after the Flood. He had been the only survivor after the gods destroyed the earth with chaos waters from above and below. The gods were always cruel, but that had been worse than ever. If Enki hadn't warned Ziusudra of the gods' vengeance and instructed him to build a large boat, humanity wouldn't exist today. It's no surprise that he came to Dilmun after surviving and became the first king of humans. There were many other stories Miu heard in her lifetime about the great flood, but none that left her trusting the gods.

If any of the story rang true, though, Miu could understand Ziusudra's desire to settle here after all the destruction. It must be why the sunflowers were so prominent here.

"Almost there," Zaidu said after coming to the end of one of the large sunflower fields. He turned right, guiding their small crew as if he knew this island like the back of his worn, weathered hand. The long, dirt road felt much different than the one Miu had walked two days ago with her own family to the temple. This one was less crowded, held less expectations, and certainly held less attachment to people she cared about.

Miu turned to look at Taku. "Where is he taking us?" She hated trusting Zaidu, but she told herself she could hold her own if she had to escape.

"To the temple to thank the gods for a safe crossing."

She suppressed a shiver. The temple. Panic surged through her bones and her skin, and she hoped Taku didn't notice. She should have just stayed by the boat. She wanted to run like a deer from a lion, but something made her keep putting one foot in front of the other. Maybe Dilmun's beauty would make this temple different. Maybe Dilmun has a trustworthy god. Even if the gods were the same, Miu felt she at least had time to prepare herself. She only needed to be there long enough to satisfy Zaidu. He was her way to bridge the gap between Ur and these curious people. If nothing else, she'd act pious until he finished his sacrifices.

As the sunflower fields faded behind them, a new landscape unfolded in front of her eyes. Chills ran down her spine. Multiple mounds spread across the land as far as anyone could see. Sticking out of the ground about thirty grains wide and about twenty grains high, they were the most peculiar things Miu had ever seen.

"What is that?" Miu asked, trying to hide the shock in her voice.

"Burial mounds. They're chambers for the dead," Taku said matter-of-factly, his tone grating on Miu's nerves.

"So much for a happy, pleasant people," Miu muttered. "Why do they keep them like this? Why are there so many?"

She was ignored, but Miu wasn't even sure she wanted an answer as they continued trudging uphill. From what Miu understood, temples were always on high ground to connect heaven and earth, gods and people.

Finally, they reached their destination. On either side of the temple, were small houses that flecked the sides like ants crawling up their hill. They must be temple houses belonging to priests, priestesses, lawyers, merchants, tavern owners, and scribes.

The temple itself was built of rough, gray stone, probably found locally, since Miu couldn't recognize it. She ran her fingers across the bumpy rocks, feeling a bit of relief that the temple here looked different than in Ur. The rock was held together with a mortar of small stone chippings, gypsum, and sand that she was familiar with, and the roof was crafted with palm fronds woven together to keep out the heat. The shape of the temple was a long rectangle which broadened a bit toward the back. When she made note of a curious loop on the back wall, Taku said it was a storehouse for grain and other temple needs.

Zaidu walked to the altar without stopping, passing others adorned in the blues and reds only those with prestige wore. The altar was made up of a long stone bench at the back of the largest building. It was about forty grains high and one hundred grains wide. Above the bench was a bronze bull's head mounted to a musical box in which women were playing and chanting to the music.

Pure is Dilmun
Beauty in Dilmun

WITH CARE, Zaidu sat down, placing the dove in the crate beside him. He opened the metal latch, and with pious honor, he reached in and wrapped his hands around the squawking bird. He cradled it with gentle hands as he trekked toward the singing women. Miu couldn't help but think of her father, how he would carefully place lapis lazuli into the fire with both caution and precision. Zaidu now handed his dove to the singing women, who took the dove with expertise, laying it on the altar.

Miu's stomach sank as she felt the ground shift beneath her feet, her head spinning as her lungs grew tight. Waves of memories flooded her mind from the last few days, hitting like a weight of bronze. Her father holding the dagger. The priest's smirk. Her mother's eyes. Instead of fighting, she ran again.

She ran with everything she had in her. Her armpits tingled with adrenaline. All she could hear was her feet thudding on the dirt floor as she made her way out of the temple. Out one temple of Ur and out of another in Dilmun. Running to escape her father in Ur, but today she only wanted out of the temple. Away from the sacrifices. Away from the gods.

As she approached the sunflower fields she'd been adoring just moments before, she slowed her pace. Placing her hands on her knees, she tried to catch her breath when something caught her ear. Looking around, she saw a little girl crying in the street. If she hadn't stopped running, she could have tripped over her pudgy little legs.

No older than five, Miu guessed. She wanted to ask her what she was doing out here alone. The girl's heart-shaped face looked directly at her, pleading with her. Her deep-blue eyes were like the sea Miu crossed. Pulling herself together, Miu heard her whimper.

"What's your name?" Miu asked in the kindest voice she could muster, a hand to her own chest as she willed her heart to slow down.

"Didila," the little girl whispered.

"Are you alright? Where's your mother?" Miu tried to hide her frustration with the girl's mother who let her child wander this far from town.

The little girl pointed the way Miu had come in. Only a short distance away; maybe she could carry her. She belonged to someone. Could she make a connection in town?

Miu was relieved she hadn't caused a scene in front of the locals. She was grateful that she was close enough to town to return the little girl to her mother, letting the girl's problem override any fear Miu had minutes earlier.

"Can you take me to your mother?" Miu asked, smiling.

The little girl sniffed and nodded, but when she tried to get up she instantly wailed with pain. Miu's heart sank.

"Let's find your mother right now."

chapter
six

Didila gripped her leg and winced. Her face, although contorted with pain, was striking. Her piercing eyes hid when Miu tried to make eye contact. Something wasn't quite right, beyond the hurt leg. There was no joy behind her eyes or her smile. Was it sadness? Had the girl been given a choice to romp through the sunflowers, or had she run away without permission?

Didila's young age reminded Miu of Hulla, but there was more to it than that. It was the way she looked to Miu for help. Why did it feel like people always looked to Miu for help? How did she get caught up in taking care of someone else again? Still, this was just the motivation Miu needed to jump into action. She bent over and reached for the girl with tender hands, not something that came naturally to her, but a tactic that had been bred from necessity.

Miu picked her up and carried her into town. As they got closer she'd ask more specifically where the girl's parents were.

Together they navigated through the wide streets and into what seemed like the market area. Loud voices echoed through the streets, merchants and buyers haggling over the day's fresh catch on both sides of the street hoping to make the most of their goods. Tents stretched over the tables attempting to relieve the

heat of the day. Tables were laden with fresh sunflowers, vegetables, meat, and fish. The tents and the voices reminded Miu of Ur, but it was the variety that shocked her. She had never seen such an array of cheeses, flowers, and fish. Miu hadn't realized her hunger until the smell of pigeon pie hit her, a smell all too familiar. The smell of home. Was the pit of her stomach fear or hunger? Maybe both.

As they rounded the corner, the smell of yeast and fermentation almost knocked Miu over, but she squeezed Didila trying to stabilize herself. Didila pointed to a tent at an intersection of streets.

"Home," she said nervously and began fidgeting with her wool tunic.

Miu squared her shoulders and walked toward the tavern. She wasn't sure what kind of parents allowed their little girl to play that far away from their eyesight, but Miu would find out.

"Get out of here, you little whore!" A woman shouted as Miu neared the tavern tent. The woman wore expensive clothes that hugged her slim figure in all the right places. Her hair was tousled high on her head, curls dripping around her face. Inserted in her mass of hair, pearls and gold clips asserted wealth and prestige. Her bright red lips and her kohl-lined eyes gave her a seductive cat-like appearance.

Who was this loud and alluring woman? And who was the simple, stout woman being yelled at? The shorter woman held her face in her hands, weeping uncontrollably.

"What are you waiting for? Get out! I told you sleeping on the job is unacceptable," the wealthy woman shouted, stomping her foot.

Miu almost hesitated, then felt the weight of Didila in her arms. She wouldn't leave the girl alone in this setting.

"Hello, ma'am," Miu said as she made direct eye contact with her. This woman might push other people around and intimidate them, but not her.

"Are you here for a job? Oh! Didila!" She seemed startled to see her daughter in Miu's arms. "What are you doing? Where'd you wander off this time?"

"She hurt her leg near the sunflower fields, and she showed me the way here. She's a very smart little girl. You must be proud to call her your own." Miu smiled at Didila.

"Oh, don't let her tease you. She's always into something. Running off. I can't believe you took the time to bring her here. Can I give you a meal for bringing her back? It's the least I can do?"

Miu's could feel her stomach cramp, and a meal sounded like exactly what she needed, but she hesitated. She needed to know the woman's name and if Didila would be safe before taking the woman's gift. Still, she didn't want to challenge the woman, which might leave Didila in more trouble.

Handling the next steps carefully she asked, "Is this your brewery?"

"Yes. My husband Alor and I run this tavern. Which includes managing lazy whores like the one you had to see squirm her way out of here."

If Dilmun were like Ur, Miu knew taverns of brewing were also places where men could worship the gods. And men of high esteem frequented them. The prostitutes gave themselves as offerings to the goddesses and men gave themselves to the prostitutes. It was a sickening circle Miu had observed as long as she could remember.

Miu squatted and put Didila firmly on the muddy ground beneath them. The little girl scurried off without hesitation. Her leg must not hurt as badly as she'd thought.

Miu gave a quick look at her surroundings. A clay tablet hung above the entryway to the tavern:

He who does not know beer does not know
what is good.

. . .

NINKASI. The goddess of beer was everywhere Miu looked. She was in the carved images lining the tent and the front entryway. She was in the adornments woven into the tent's curtains with ornate blues and purples, and the tavern itself was orderly. Places to sit and the wooden flagons for beer were all in tidy rows at the back wall. Upon entering the main dining area, Miu could tell this tavern was highly esteemed in Dilmun.

A shout from the back room startled Miu. She turned to see a large, clumsy-looking man stumble from behind the curtain that divided the main room from what Miu guessed was the kitchen.

"My name is Hashur. Don't stand there with your mouth open. Do you want a meal or not?" the woman asked impatiently.

"Yes, I would appreciate a meal, but since you've lost a tavern girl, do you have a job opening? I could pay you back. Maybe sweep the floor or serve your guests for the goddess Ninkasi?" Miu swallowed the lump in her throat. She wouldn't be given a handout, and she liked that this woman seemed to run an orderly tavern. Maybe she could learn a thing or two. She would earn her keep while also learning a reputable craft. She'd also be able to keep an eye on Didila's safety. Then she could make a name for herself that her father and the gods could not deny.

"I just fired my best waitress. Have you ever waited on men's tables before?" Hashur gazed absentmindedly around the room, obviously ready to get back to work.

"No. But I'm a fast learner." She might not have waited tables, but she knew how to handle men.

"Perfect. Alor!" Hashur shouted with a gruff voice. "This is our new girl. Give her a warm meal. Then show her where we keep the cleaning supplies."

Hashur faced Miu again, her beauty almost intimidating. "When you're done eating, clean off that table." Hashur pointed to a table where four rowdy men were stumbling away. "Take the dishes to the back. You'll see where they belong. Do not interact with the men. They will try to touch you. No relationships. They're here for worship with my girls. Not you. Now go eat, fill up, and then you can get to work."

Alor escorted Miu toward the kitchen in the back. His gait was awkward and his rambling incessant. She followed him through a narrow hallway with small rooms on either side, covered with tapestries. Again, Miu paid attention to the wealth it must require to have such beauty hang on the walls. The tapestries contained woven images of gods and humans in erotic positions having sex. Heat flooded Miu's cheeks and Alor roared with laughter.

"Don't you wish fertility upon your land? Those who come to this tavern are inspired to worship by these images. They stir the gods' passions, which in turn fuels Dilmun's prosperity. You can't be so naïve and still live here, girl."

In a moment, Miu remembered as a little girl asking her mother questions about similar images she saw. "What are they doing mother?"

Her mother always gave the same answer. "Women have two things in this world to call their own, Miu. Two things we can use to get what we need. Your charm and what the images show. We must use our feminine power to fascinate and conquer the men around us. It's the only power you hold, Miu. It's only then we're able to lead them, like a bull with a ring being led to slaughter."

Then she'd bent down and touched Miu's face. Her sad empty eyes staring at her.

"Do not waste your power, Miu," she had whispered.

Miu wanted to scream then, and she wanted to scream now. Her mother's response never explained the images, and even worse, her mother had never had power over the men in her life. She never controlled her husband. If she could have controlled any man, it would have been her lover. She left the family every full moon to meet with the man they'd never met. She said the gods honored her pursuits. It's what women of Ur did, seeking the comfort of other men, hoping they'd bring blessing.

Her mother's proverb floated through her mind as they neared the end of the tavern hallway: "My husband hoards money for me! My son works to keep me fed! If only my lover could skin the fish I eat!" Her mother had wished men would do many things to keep her satisfied, but Miu knew her mother would never find contentment by trying to please any man.

Miu's stomach rumbled as the aroma of food from home wafted from the kitchen, and she couldn't deny she was curious about what they would serve. Pomegranates, mushrooms, eggs, fish? She didn't care at this point. She only knew she'd inhale every last morsel they offered.

Alor pointed to a short table, customary to Ur as well. She sat down on the reed mat and crossed her legs, thankful she understood at least some Dilmun customs. A woman dressed in similar garb as the one who'd been recently fired handed her a cup of steaming, red liquid.

She smelled seafood and truffle, her mouth watering with anticipation. She took a sip, and the warmth trickled to her empty belly. She tried not to gulp and be impolite, but she took a large second sip.

Then Alor handed her a piece of warm bread with melted butter. This tavern was laden with rich foods and adorned in tapestries and gold. How important was this place?

Thinking of her mother's words about men, maybe she could try to get on Alor's good side. Charm was not her best characteristic, but could she pull it off?

"Your tavern is beautiful, sir. You must put a lot of care into it." Miu offered him a smile. "My name is Miu. I'm happy to be of service cleaning or cooking in any way you see fit."

A satisfied smile crept across his face. She could tell she struck a chord with him. He stuck his hands under his armpits leaving his thumbs sticking upward. Cocky, she thought. She could continue to stroke his ego. Being married to Hashur, she was sure he didn't get much praise. If the woman's beauty struck her, she couldn't imagine what it did to the men who came in.

"Tell me," she continued, "Where do you get such wonderful recipes for stew? I bet other than the beer, these recipes must be the main reason your tavern is so successful."

His eyes lit up. Alor sat down next to her and rattled on about recipes, going on for ten minutes about a new recipe he'd been trying, incorporating duck with apples and pomegranates.

Miu was shocked at how quickly she could learn the secrets of the trade with a little charm. Her mother had imparted some truth to her. It was obvious to Miu how Hashur was the beauty and brains while Alor held the culinary secrets. Hashur stormed into the back room shouting and interrupting their conversation. "Alor! She's here to work, not sit and listen to you all day!"

Miu added to her mental list to stay on Hashur's good side but to keep learning about the tavern's inner workings from Alor.

"Yes, ma'am. I'm just finishing up here. Alor couldn't stop talking about how you keep this place running smooth as butter, Hashur," she smiled.

Hashur's anger dissipated, and Miu felt satisfied for appeasing her ego while learning more about these new people.

Miu grasped her cup and made her way to the heart of the kitchen. With a determined spirit, she resolved to master every task, from tidying up tables to crafting the perfect brew. After obtaining every secret, she would no longer be indebted to Hashur and could potentially open her own tavern. Miu wouldn't run again; it was time to make a name for herself.

chapter
seven

Taku looked behind him to see that Miu was nowhere to be found. On their crossing, she had been opinionated about the sacrifices and gods. Too cynical for his taste. Maybe she'd just stepped outside? Her ranting grated on his nerves like strumming the wrong note on a lyre, but he knew she too felt something wasn't right with temple sacrifices. He'd watched his grandfather and father go through the rituals, day in and day out, with little to no protection from these gods. The sacrifices were meant to build a relationship with the gods, but as far as Taku could tell the gods were just like humans. Selfish, quick-tempered, and out for power. Maybe Miu was onto something.

Still, even if she held a sliver of truth, he couldn't question the gods, that would mean questioning Zaidu and his loyalty to them.

"Hold this." Zaidu handed him the crate before he walked toward the priestesses singing.

Taku set the crate by his feet. Zaidu was the only one who had shown loyalty to him; he'd taken him under his wing to teach him and educate him once the school had kicked him out. Did it matter if he wasn't a scribe? Wasn't his job carrying documents, even sacred ones, across the waters enough? Taku didn't need special attention from anyone. He learned to be content with sharing others' words, even if that meant his own needed to be silent.

He refocused on the dove sacrifice taking place in front of him. Zaidu was now praying in low mumbles as the women searched the gods for approval and blessing. It was impossible to know if they were ever truly pleased; a religious person such as Zaidu and his parents could only hope for the best. They were supposed to offer their best animals, give their best guess, and hope the gods would not curse them. As far as Taku was concerned, the gods' eyes were made of stone and their priests floundered for answers to human problems.

The priestesses slowed their singing and pulled out small knives from their tunics. They began to dismember the dove Zaidu had brought. First, they took out the fat and the organs. They then laid the liver and heart out on the altar as the gods preferred.

"Bless us. Thank you," Zaidu chanted louder.

The women chose the fat and organs because in them was the seat of all emotions, and reading these organs would give insight into the motivations of its owner, Zaidu.

"Hand me the heart," a priestess said. "Now the liver."

As she took the organs, she placed them over a blazing fire. The crackle of fats from the organs resounded louder than Taku remembered from the last time. Was that a good sign? Then the smell of dove organs reached Taku's nostrils, and his stomach rumbled. He hoped the gods would be pleased. Hopefully, they were as hungry as he was.

The women continued in songs that reverberated off the stone walls as they kept their hands steady with the work, removing the remaining organs and chopping them until they resembled a paste. Next, they grabbed a piece of bread warmed by the blazing fire and scooped the remaining organs onto their knife, before spreading them onto the bread like butter.

Taku's mouth watered; was it impolite to drool in front of the altar?

"To which god are we giving this meal?" the woman's sultry tone asked.

"Enki," Zaidu bowed again.

Zaidu always said the god of the chaos waters. It was only then that Taku noticed Zaidu's shoulders released tension, and his breathing slowed. His old sailor's hands that had moments before been gripped tightly in his lap loosened. His eyes looked up brimming with tears and hopeful anticipation.

Enki's needs had to be met before he would tend to the cosmic order and purposes of Dilmun, Ur, or anywhere else for that matter. Zaidu was a piece of the foundation, placating as he was able, and contributing sacrifices as necessary. Zaidu's relief was palpable in the room as he rejoiced in the possibility that restoration and order were maintained within every sacrifice.

Taku longed to have peace with the gods and the world around him, but his gut said otherwise.

"Keep looking."

Taku heard a whisper. Looking around, he saw the women had begun cleaning up, but they were singing, not whispering. Where was he supposed to look? He was inside the temple; where else should he look for the gods or for peace? He brushed that thought aside again and listened intently to the women chanting, hoping the sound would help him regain his composure. As they moved on to the remainder of the dove, they sang:

> *The lord brought into being the beginnings*
> *   splendidly,*
> *The lord, whose decisions cannot be*
> *   changed,*
> *Enlil, to make the seed of Kalam sprout*
> *   from the earth,*
> *To separate heaven from earth he hastened,*
> *To make the light shine in Uzumua.*

. . .

THEY CHOPPED the rest of the bird into pieces with skill and precision before they walked the final pieces of the dove to a boiling pot on the other side of the bench. Taku knew this part of the ritual well; it was his time to participate in the sacrifice. The priestesses would turn the dove into a stew that Zaidu and he would share. It was part of the relationship between the gods and humans. The smell of the stew simmering reminded Taku of his mother.

She was a frail woman, older than most mothers, but she was kind. Her nurturing way drew people to her. People in town teased her saying she would feed a stray dog if it showed up. She loved and took care of every living thing as if it were put in her personal care by the gods.

"He's got a broken wing, Taku." She'd try to convince him they needed another bird in the house. "The gods want me to care for all of the hurting animals."

And she, like most mothers, appreciated an orderly house. When she was preparing dinner, she asked Taku and his siblings to go outside and play, leaving her alone. Taku smiled to himself as he remembered how flustered she got one day when someone knocked on the door right as she was dropping the leeks and chickpeas into the stew. She loved company, but not when they interrupted her process. And Taku didn't want her to forget any of the steps that would then delay his dinner.

"I'll get it, Mother," Taku had said, trying to beat his mother to it.

Inside the clay door frame had stood a little girl with big, red-rimmed eyes. She couldn't have been more than five-years-old. Her tunic was worn, showing her life was spent in the fields. Taku recognized her as one of the children who played out by the city's wall, though normally she was full of joy. Her mother was one of the shepherdesses, rumored as unruly and wild. Why would her daughter be here, at their home?

"Who is it?" Taku's mother shouted from the stove in the backyard.

"Come, Mother." Taku's voice contained an edge of fear, causing his mother to barrel out of the back room.

She pushed Taku out of the way and walked straight to the girl. Without questions or looking around, she picked up the filthy little one and hugged her. Taku didn't understand how his mother tolerated the smell radiating off the child, but within a few minutes, the tears in her big brown eyes stopped.

"There, there, child. What's the matter? Where's your mother?"

Taku was familiar with that tone. His mother was about to take care of something.

"He hit." The little girl paused and sniffed, rubbing her nose with the back of her hand. "Momma!"

"Taku, watch the stew. You know what to do."

Taku was confident he knew how to stir the stew, and he didn't want to burn it. But he didn't argue. He would take care of his mother while she took care of everyone else.

About an hour later, Taku's mother, the little girl, and the little girl's mother came walking through the door. No tears, just smiles.

"Serve our guests some stew, Taku," his mother said, her eyes warm and kind.

"There isn't—"

"Do as you're told." Her words were a warning, though she was smiling at the same time.

She hadn't made much that day, since Taku's father was away on business. He obediently poured enough for three bowls, leaving nothing left for the little girl.

"You get this stew all the time. Give yours to the girl," his mother said.

Without thinking twice, he gave up his stew with joy, watching a huge smile spread across the little girl's face.

His mother gave a nod of approval and handed him a piece of

bread and cheese from yesterday's meal. It wasn't about having the money for food. To Taku's mother, you sacrificed what you had to help those who needed it.

"Sacrifice what's yours so others can have what they need, Taku." If he'd heard this once, he'd heard it his whole life. "Sacrifice to the gods, sacrifice for others. Give away what's yours, Taku."

Taku carried his mother's mantras with him everywhere. They were what guided his life as a courier; he would carry the words so others could continue writing. Do what they needed so they didn't have to.

The sound of the bowls dipping into the priestesses' stew startled Taku out of his daydream. They served a bowl to Zaidu first, then to him. He smiled at them, wishing his mother could see him now. He still got to speak to his mother sometimes down by the shipyard, but his father was not fond of it. If he heard his father was out of town, he'd sneak back to his childhood house just to sit with his mother for a bit. Taku was still a disgrace to the gods in his father's eyes.

Today he knew he made his mother proud, serving Zaidu and serving others.

ZAIDU AND TAKU found a place to stay for the night in town, knowing they had a long day ahead of them. Zaidu never paid for rooms with fancy amenities. There would be no women to entertain them tonight or elegant dinners of roast duck. Tonight they would sleep in a simple reed house dwelling.

The reed houses had a perimeter of holes dug in the ground with bundles of reeds placed in each hole. The holes were dug parallel to each other in a long rectangular shape, then each bundle of reeds would be pulled to meet the bundle directly across from it to form a type of roof. The only thing Zaidu ever paid extra for was to sleep closer to the doors at the end of the house. It gave them more breeze, and Taku was thankful. Both men felt trapped like doves in a cage if they slept closer to the middle of the room. If they couldn't feel a breeze, neither man would sleep at all.

Tomorrow would be another long day, including meeting with the copper merchants to see what needed to be shipped back to Ur this week. At least the day would be less draining, because there would be no temple visits. Maybe he would run into Miu. *Where did she end up going?* He pushed the thought away as quickly as it came. She was nothing but trouble and chaos, and it didn't matter if he saw her again or not. She didn't even know anything about Dilmun to run away like that.

While thinking of something more stable than the crazy woman, Taku remembered Zaidu mentioning he needed to buy a new ship soon. Taku asked him if he could potentially run a shipment on his own. He did doubt himself, and also he enjoyed riding with Zaidu, but if Zaidu needed the help, maybe it was for the best. He knew what his mother would say. "Sacrifice what you want Taku." Maybe it would give him time to think of new stories and ideas along the way. He promised to remain loyal and never jeopardize Zaidu's hard work and business connections.

Lying on the reed mat provided by the inn, he gazed up at the stars.

"Keep looking."

He sighed. There it was again. Anytime his mind began to relax, the voice came. He had felt in his gut he should keep looking for a real god since the day he was kicked out of school, but the continual searching for something else was exhausting. Gods were made of clay, and their eyes were formed by people's hands. Rocks and stones shaped to be worshiped.

The gods, the celestial beings, the cosmos. It was confusing and frustrating.

"Time for sleep, Taku." Zaidu rolled over on his mat.

"I will sleep soon," Taku whispered, watching the old man's shoulders relax.

Even though Zaidu found peace, Taku's religious life looked more like a wrestling match without sure footing. A fight where questions threw punches and answers were cloaked in darkness and uncertainty.

It was hard to watch those he loved, and even Miu, as much as he despised her, waste so much time thinking about the gods who were no better than humans. Everyone he knew had lives that revolved around the gods and their desires; they were either avoiding them or chasing them. Neither option made sense to him. They never knew if their acts of worship or acts of running away were noticed or pleasing.

Were people ever seen or known? What would it be like to look up at those stars and truly know the god that made them? Could that same god ever care about humans?

"Is there anyone out there?" Taku whispered, not wanting to wake any men in the tent.

After a moment of silence, Taku muttered, "What a ridiculous question," and rolled onto his side.

Feeling a palm reed stick in his shoulder, he flipped to the other side. He sighed heavily, hoping not to wake the others. His mind went back to the temple again, where the temple priestesses flooded his thoughts. They were attractive, sure. But that wasn't it. All temple priestesses were. They were chosen above other women for their beauty and their family status. No flaws could be seen when being chosen. Was it the prostitute worship that gnawed at him? Men worshipped the gods by lying with priestesses. It turned his stomach every time he thought much about that part of worship. He could never worship that way.

Many people Taku knew did things they knew were wrong but did so because they said the gods wanted them to. As always, if he mulled over his own questions long enough, he could process his thinking through song:

I wish I knew that these things were
pleasing to one's god!
What is proper to oneself is an offense to
one's god;
What in one's own heart seems despicable is
proper to one's god.
Who understands the plans of the under-
world gods?
Where have mortals learned the way of
a god?

THE SONG GAVE words to his thoughts.

"Keep looking."

This time the words were almost audible. Taku sat up, certain someone in the tent was teasing him. The room was only lit by the moonlight streaming in, but he could see every man was sleeping. What did "keep looking" mean? Why did that keep coming to mind? Keep looking for what? Tomorrow when the sun rose again, he would feel better.

Grab the baskets," Hashur said to Miu, as she pointed to a darkened corner of the kitchen.

They were headed to the market to pick up their order of barley. Miu saw how impressed Hashur was with her ability to learn quickly while also taking charge of some of the girls in the tavern. Anything to make Hashur look better.

"Usually I send one of the girls for a minor task." Hashur threw her chin high and her hair back. "But today the king's son is supposed to be meeting with Zu."

Zu was Hashur's favorite copper merchant, or any merchant for that matter. He was connected to riches and wealth in ways people only dreamed were possible.

Last night, as Miu was drifting off to sleep, she overheard Hashur talking to Alor about him.

"Zu and the king are becoming close friends. We have no choice but to connect with them. Can you imagine what will happen to our little tavern if the king and his family visit regularly?" Hashur had lowered her voice, but her excitement leaked through.

Miu had to admit, she was impressed with Hashur, who worked hard to keep her tavern running without interruptions.

She was competitive to ensure her prices were the best in town without sacrificing the quality of the beer her women made. She frequently mingled with the elite in Dilmun, which made her tavern more popular than others in town. From what Miu could tell, every person who came into the tavern knew Hashur, and no one doubted her ability as a woman to lead Dilmun in big ways. She was strong and effective in her work, but at the same time, no one dared to get in her way. She wasn't Jara, but she was a woman in control of her business. It was enough to spike Miu's curiosity.

Hashur was never laid back in anything she did. She never entered her tavern or went to town without being fully adorned with jewelry, styled hair, and makeup. As they were leaving, she grabbed the jewelry she kept in a pot beside her bed and put the pieces on with ease. Miu grabbed the baskets as she was asked to do. Together they hurried out of the tavern.

"We need Zu to notice that we can afford lapis lazuli and gold jewelry in abundance. Here, you wear this."

She showed Miu a hair ornament. The gold was thin and molded to look like delicate leaves. She carefully draped and pinned them in Miu's dark hair.

"It's a good thing you came to us with some jewelry," Hashur laughed.

Miu's skin pricked. If someone knew her past and her father's lapis lazuli jewelry business, she could be sent back home. The jewelry she once wore to show her connection to her father now held the potential for her downfall. She had arrived at Hashur's tavern wearing it and hadn't bothered hiding it while holding Didila. Hashur admitted later that it was Miu's wealth that piqued her curiosity that day.

Miu remembered her first night sleeping in the little back room of the tavern. She'd missed her siblings so much that her bones ached. Alor had drunk a bit too much and was stumbling around trying to find his reed mat, and instead came in to bother her. Her muscles tensed, and she was about to yell at him to go to bed when he spoke.

"Hashur only wants you for what you can give her." Alor stammered as he tripped and grabbed the curtain, the only thing shielding her from the rest of the hallway. "She was kicked out of her home city of Ur when she was only a girl. Just like you." He spat on the ground, and it landed right by Miu's mat.

"Get out of here, you drunk," Miu said with a growl.

Alor was too drunk to care and continued rambling. "Her family had nothing. They begged for food in the streets, and if it weren't for my father finding her lying in the dirt outside the city walls like a dog, she wouldn't have eaten another meal. She owes me everything, and yet ..."

He paused. Even in his drunkenness, he was careful of her. Looking around as if hiding his next words, he continued. "She walks all over me. The world doesn't care if you're poor, and now she doesn't care about me. Watch yourself, pretty lady; she'll suck the life out of you just to make herself look better." With that, he was gone.

Miu didn't know where he had gone, but now she knew to watch her back. Hashur may be a stepping stone to learning more about the tavern business and gaining her freedom, but Miu would keep her at arm's length.

The market wasn't too crowded as they navigated the dirt roads. Hashur walked fast and with purpose. There were never moments in the day when Hashur didn't have every detail mapped out. She walked and talked, and Miu learned to keep up with the pace.

"We have fifteen minutes to get to the other side of the market and pick up our barley order. Miu? Are you listening?"

"Yes, go on. I can do two things at once," Miu snapped while pinning the last gold hair piece into a braid.

"Then on our walk back we will pass one of Zu's tents. I'm hoping to run into him as he's leaving to head home for lunch. I want you to meet them both, Zu and the king. Eventually, I will need someone to keep the connection with Zu open. He alone has the power to keep our tavern swarming with the elite in Dilmun. Do you understand me, Miu?"

Why did she always second-guess if Miu was listening? Of course she was; she was always listening.

"Is Zu trustworthy?" Miu still tried to adjust the leaves in her hair, tripping over a stone in the dirt walkway.

"Zu wants fun," Hashur responded. "And we're going to use his wants to get more people in our doors."

Miu surveyed the different tents and began picturing herself in charge of one. She could see herself running any of them with ease. Dilmun might be the place she could make a name for herself. She wasn't as worried about needing Zu, because men like him were common. All men liked fun and to feel important. Thanks to her father, she had practiced this skill for years and had used it multiple times with irritable customers. She'd be the one to decide if Zu was trustworthy. She wouldn't take Hashur's word for it. Hashur was not going to control Miu's decisions, but she could see how together they could grow Dilmun to be bigger and better than it was. She smiled to herself; though to keep up with Hashur she'd have to walk faster.

As they hurried through the market, the crowds of people shouting prices and politics fueled both Hashur and Miu's energy. There was something about people fighting for something they believed in, even as small as the price of wool, that energized them. Hashur continued her endless rant about wasted time due to various reasons.

"Time is money, Miu. People don't respect you if you're poor. Speed up." Hashur demanded with confidence.

It didn't make sense to Miu, but instead of arguing, she followed willingly wanting to see the things Hashur had promised her.

Finally, they made it to the barley merchant and then quickly on to Zu's tent. "Remember, pretend we just bumped into him. Also, make sure you listen to his stories and laugh at his jokes," Hashur said.

Miu wouldn't laugh at a joke that wasn't funny, but she would listen. If Zu was as influential as Hashur said, she'd win him over on her own with her skills. As they approached, they could hear Zu laughing and talking before they even saw him.

"Hello!" Zu shouted across the crowds when he saw Hashur. His round and jolly appearance almost took over the entire tent entrance. His balding head was not something Miu was accustomed to seeing. Much of what hair used to be on his head seemed to now be growing from his eyebrows. They reminded her of two Dilmun ships moving back and forth above his eyes. She held back a giggle.

"Who's this?" he asked, as Hashur and Miu moved closer to the crowd surrounding Zu.

"Zu, meet Miu. She's my newest help at the tavern. She's smart and has learned to keep the pigeons away from my drying barley," she laughed, touching Zu's arm playfully.

"That's some of the finest stonework I've ever seen." Zu studied Miu's neck.

Miu touched her necklace and smiled. Her father might be a jerk, but he was a skilled jeweler.

"Thank you." She smiled, hoping he wouldn't recognize her father's handiwork.

"Miu came to us knowing little about the techniques of brewing, but she's a fast learner," Hashur interrupted. Her defined shoulders pulled back a bit more than usual, making her look like a peacock parading herself in front of Zu, but he didn't seem to mind.

Hashur looked up at the sun and mumbled a word of thanks to the gods they made it to Zu on time. "More recently Miu has started managing some of the girls at the tavern, and they follow her lead."

Zu's ears perked up a bit. He leaned in toward Miu, his eyebrows going back and forth. "Businessmen like myself are always looking for leaders. Those who can make other people work. Sometimes it's impossible to get people out of the tavern and into the fields or the ships."

Miu nodded.

A smile crept across his face. Was he about to make her a proposition?

"I enjoy fine clothes and roast duck." He rubbed his belly. That was obvious to Miu. "I also enjoy parties at my house or the king's. You see, I get bored easily, Miu. I'm in business because I get bored with one venture and move on to another. I always need someone to take over something I've started."

He tilted his head, and Miu guessed he was pondering the openings in some of his businesses, considering where he could use her. He opened his mouth to speak when a courier ran up to them. The man was out of breath and panting, and he reminded Miu of Taku.

Holding her hands behind her back, she gripped her wrist tightly. Why did the thought of Taku frustrate her so much? She forced herself to remain present and to hear what was being said, sensing an opportunity.

"I've come a long way with a message for you sir," the messenger said.

"Spit it out already!" Zu shouted.

The courier panted out his words. "Your ship was almost to Ur before it sank in a storm. Everything on the boat, including your crew, is in the netherworld, the Land of No Return."

The fear among them was palpable. The ground felt like it was shifting as everyone waited with dread to see how Zu would respond.

Miu gained her composure and leaned over to Hashur. "Quick, go get him a beer from inside."

Hashur did as she said, and Miu leaned toward Zu, putting her hands on both his large shoulders to get his attention. "What can we do?" she asked.

Everyone stood there waiting to hear from Zu. The pause was

long enough for the messenger to catch his breath and stand up, though even he was stunned by the lack of a response.

Then out of nowhere, Zu laughed, his belly shaking uncontrollably. He took Miu's hands off his shoulders and held them in his. "My girl, we must move on. That is all there is to do."

Miu was shocked. She knew he had lost a large amount of money as well as his people. He shrugged his shoulders and chugged the beer as if it would be his last. Then he wiped the sweat off his balding head, and with an animated glow he announced, "Follow me! We'll go drink to the gods!"

Zu wasn't concerned for his people or his ship. His boisterous laugh was insensitive, and Miu thought of Enlil. God of fates. Keeper of the Tablet of Destinies. In control of the Deluge that flooded the entire world. She didn't trust Enlil, who destroyed the world because he grew tired of the noise of humans. Who laughed at destruction, after all? She had to think. This was her opportunity to show she could make connections and help.

"I know someone," Miu blurted out. In the confusion that just happened, Miu was still constructing a plan. All eyes shifted toward her.

Zu smiled. "Come on to the house, Miu. We can chat there, my girl."

It was only a short distance in the heat toward the richer part of town. Miu remembered seeing this area when she got off the boat. The houses weren't made of reeds and clay but of stone. They were larger in comparison to anything she had lived in, and her head spun with potential and ideas. The houses here weren't as close together, and the noise from the crowds diminished, making it seem more peaceful.

Miu's heart still raced. Why did she make that suggestion so quickly? She didn't know this man. He could enslave her, or even worse, he might know her father. She had no way of legally fighting for herself as a single woman. Why was it always like this with her? Ready to take on a challenge, throwing answers out, and then deciding if the answer would even work.

They came upon a house which Miu guessed was Zu's. Upon entering, it became clear that it was anything but simple. The variety he mentioned needing just moments earlier showcased itself in every nook and cranny. His home boasted his whimsical and multitalented personality through plants, wild animals, and bright colors. Purples. Oranges. Reds. Blues.

On the walls hung the common tapestries of the gods and goddesses having sex, but these were in such vivid colors Miu wanted to stare at the handiwork. Beneath every tapestry stood statues of clay figures mimicking the tapestries. Miu had never seen anything like the bright-dyed ropes hanging from the ceiling in vibrant shades of color.

Women were everywhere, some carrying trays of figs and cheese, some sweeping the floors, while others chanted prayers in every corner of every room. The activity reminded Miu of a hive of bees, where each of them knew their role and acted it out with animated vigor.

"Have a seat." Zu motioned toward some stools in front of a very erotic stone statue. It would have made some girls uncomfortable, but Miu had been exposed to her father's customers. She was certain they had homes like this, and if they didn't, they at least acted as if they did.

Zu turned his full attention toward Miu. "So, my dear," he said smiling, those eyebrows working. "Tell me of this *someone* you know."

On the way to Zu's home, Hashur nodded her head every time the man had said anything. Miu knew she couldn't be the only one to speak and sensed Hashur had her ideas of how to help Zu, so she let her take the lead. Better for her to fail first anyway.

"We should let Hashur speak first. I believe she has an idea." She motioned toward Hashur's now-beaming grin.

Hashur's face came alive. "We should host a party together. Allow the elite to come for free. Honor the rich while the others pay a fee. They can come to watch your dancers and be in the room with the greatest in the city. This way, we can recover some of your losses while also identifying valuable connections in Dilmun."

Zu loved a party, and Hashur knew it. Today, though, his interest in Miu was stronger. He ignored Hashur and looked directly at Miu, waiting patiently for her to answer him.

Miu didn't wait for Hashur, nor did she make eye contact with her. "I know a sailor. He's skilled on the seas, honest, and sacrifices to Enki upon every landfall." Miu's insides shook, even as her gaze remained direct. She paused, knowing Zu needed to show interest before she continued.

"Tell me more." He rubbed his hands together.

"Only yesterday I heard him say he was looking to expand. I saw he was delivering copper, but I'm sure he's capable of delivering a variety of precious cargo, whatever your heart desires." An amused smile crept across her face. His interest was piqued, and she was delighted her plan was working. Men were too easy. "He's ready to go on his next shipment, but you'll have to think fast so no one else takes space on his boat."

Hashur looked impressed, but Miu could tell she didn't want to be forgotten in the conversation. "Yes, Zu. I believe acting fast and working with this new sailor would be advantageous. And my girl Miu here can help you make all the necessary arrangements."

Zu nodded. "Set up a meeting. We will talk." Then he turned to the women in the room and snapped his fingers. It was clear he'd had enough business and loss for one day.

Miu knew the seriousness wouldn't last long, but she was happy she had made her point and had proven herself connected and savvy.

"Now, on with the festivities." Zu rubbed his stomach. Instantly, women came gliding across the floor with trays of foods Miu had never seen before.

Miu felt hot breath on her shoulder. She turned to look as Hashur whispered, "Don't undermine me again."

Had she overstepped her boundaries? It was a better idea to get Zu back working again; that was best for both of them. Keep

Zu's mind moving forward with opportunities versus brooding over problems at a party. When Hashur saw what Miu had done, she would calm down.

As for the sailor Miu knew, he hadn't built a name for himself, and maybe Zaidu didn't care to do so. But Miu would use him as a building block to establish her credibility in the house of Zu, as long as she could stay in Hashur's good graces.

chapter
nine

The sunlight pouring into the tent woke Taku up. The ground still felt unsteady. He rubbed his groggy eyes and touched the firm earth beneath him, hoping to gain some stability. Some journeys to Dilmun were harder than others. His stomach and legs felt like he was walking on water instead of firm ground. He knew he hadn't drunk too much; he never drank when he toured with Zaidu. Heavy drinking led to worship, and lately, Taku was apathetic toward the gods. Maybe he needed fresh air. The breath in his lungs felt stale, and so did his thoughts.

He walked outside trying not to wake anyone. The sun was just beginning to peek around the temple at the end of the island. The temples in both Dilmun and Ur were the places where heaven and earth connected, where gods came and went as they pleased, requesting and demanding from the people what they needed. And didn't everyone need something? The gods. His parents. Even as kind as Zaidu was, he still needed something from him.

On the last trip, Zaidu had asked what Taku thought about him purchasing a new ship. "I've added up the amount of money it'd take us to buy a new one. We have enough trips planned to break even this year. We would do well together if we got a few more trips lined up," Zaidu had said. "But I need your input, Taku. I need to know if you'll take a route for yourself."

Zaidu had waited patiently for Taku to answer, even though he despised giving his opinion. What if he became responsible for the new route's success? Or what if he was wrong? Even worse, what if he disappointed Zaidu? Taku believed that it was better to remain quiet.

Zaidu could wade into lengthy silences as easily as he would wade into the waves of the chaos waters without hesitation. It was one characteristic Taku admired about him. He never rushed into things, and Taku knew he'd wait for his answer even if he never intended to give one. He thought about things, planned, and then decided what to do, and his thoughtfulness kept him out of trouble. It hadn't made him the richest sailor, but it had kept him the safest. Other sailors had tempers hotter than the sun. He'd watched Zaidu when those sailors got into heated debates about the prices they'd get for wood and ivory. He'd watch Zaidu wait it out. When a sailor's world was racked with anger, competition, and fighting, it never ended well.

Mostly, Zaidu taught Taku to avoid all of it. His calm and insightful way was refreshing, even though sometimes that trait went too far. Taku had seen Zaidu avoid ever making decisions. He'd sit on a decision for weeks until the opportunity passed them both by. But it was one of the reasons Taku trusted him like a father. Running Zaidu's ship was not writing or telling stories, but if he couldn't write about the gods or love, then there wasn't much else to write about anyway. He'd quit writing, especially since he couldn't tell Zaidu no.

Last night, Zaidu offered to send Taku to the tavern where he could find the comfort of a woman, but the thought bored him. He also didn't want the potential of running into that wild woman, Miu. It had been weeks since they'd returned to Dilmun, and he wasn't even certain if she had stayed in town. All he knew was she was the last thing he wanted to see. She made him feel like he was being chased by a pack of wild dogs, uncertain of the direction to run, just desperate to get away.

Zaidu stirred behind him, and Taku knew he'd be awake soon, along with everyone else in Dilmun. It was time to find some food and meet with the bronze merchan, even though he'd much rather stay where he was, deep in his own thoughts. Life was more manageable that way. Disruptions irked him, but he could clearly hear his mother say, "Don't rock the boat, Taku."

The sun pierced his eyes as he gave a final glance toward the temple, promising himself he'd find some more time to process taking over Zaidu's ship. As he stood to find breakfast, a woman caught his eye. She was charging in his direction. As she neared, he knew who she was, and he wanted to hide. A pack of wild dogs wrapped up inside one woman. He shook his head.

"Miu," he grumbled to himself. He folded his arms, planted his feet, and braced himself for whatever she was about to say. He could guess by the way she approached, it must be important. But then again, she seemed like the type to blow things out of proportion.

"I'm glad I found you. We have a problem and you're going to help," she said in her direct tone that Taku remembered with disdain.

"Hello to you too."

"Hello," she said mockingly. "Look, I have a new boss." She rolled her eyes as if she hated to admit it.

"Already? That was fast, especially for someone who wanted their freedom." Taku snickered a little, trying to contain the joy it brought him knowing someone else tried controlling this woman. She reminded him of the wild sea, unconfined and untameable. He wrung his hands, then wiped them on his tunic. When she wasn't around, he could find some sense of calm. Even when he crossed the chaos waters and the seas were raging, he never seemed to panic. This woman made his blood boil.

"I highly suggest you control yourself," she threatened. "I warn you, Taku. We are not to be messed with. We have work that can benefit you and Zaidu. Stop playing games. Now, where is Zaidu? He knows more than you, anyway."

Zaidu apparently heard the commotion and peeked out of the tent. Putting his hand over his eyes to shield the bright morning sun, he nodded toward Miu.

"Hello, young lady," he said. "How are things since you ran away?"

"I've brought you work. It's up to you if you want it or not though," Miu snapped.

Zaidu's lips turned up in a scowl. "I don't reckon you've learned to bite your tongue."

He watched Miu cringe.

"Are we playing a game where everyone just states the obvious? I'm here to give you an opportunity. Do you want to hear it or stand around wasting time?"

"No nonsense. I like that." Zaidu smirked, stepping into the street. "Tell me about this so-called opportunity."

Taku stood beside the old man, hoping to offer some kind of protection in case Miu got out of hand.

"I've met a very prominent man here in Dilmun, and he's lost a ship in a storm. He manages businesses all over these lands, although I'm not completely certain about everything he's involved in. I told him I knew a sailor who was honest and could get his job completed. What I do know is that he needs ships to run supplies back and forth to Ur. Do you want in?"

Taku knew Zaidu would need to think about it. He'd want to weigh the pros and cons. He'd need more information before he made any decisions. He also knew if Zaidu chose to move forward, this was the ship that would be his. This was what they were waiting for. He saw it as a good omen, one that would look out for Zaidu for years to come. But Miu wouldn't wait long for an answer.

"That's a kind offer Miu," Taku said. "We'll have to pray about it."

"What's there to pray about? The gods want Dilmun and Ur

to prosper. I've brought you both work. Gods and humans working together." She gritted her teeth. "When I came over with you a few weeks ago, you were talking about more work. I bet you're still looking for work."

"This is true, but I must seek the gods and meet with this businessman before making any rash decisions. What is his name?"

"Zu. I'm sure you've heard of him."

Zaidu nodded, seemingly a bit more comfortable with that name.

"What's the pay, and how often are shipments?" Taku spoke up, hoping to give Zaidu exact details to ponder while waiting for the meeting.

"I don't know." Miu sighed. "I set up the meeting so you can figure out the details. Meet us tomorrow morning at Hashur and Alor's Tavern." Just as fast as Miu had arrived, she left.

Taku looked at Zaidu, who shook his head. "That woman is untamed."

Taku's shoulders relaxed, and he gave Zaidu a sideways smile. He didn't care what decision Zaidu made, he really didn't. He just didn't want Miu around for any period of time. But if she was finding business, maybe he'd learn to tolerate her.

"I have many questions, but first I must pray and sacrifice," Zaidu said before he walked off in his slow, meticulous way.

LATER THAT EVENING Zaidu stared at Taku across the fire. "I can see what he meant, but I'm still not sure I trust him." he said as he picked at his food.

Taku liked Zu's fun chatter and vision for life and felt he needed to encourage Zaidu.

Children were running and playing outside the tavern. Boys were attempting to jump off the rocks in a nearby stream. A screaming child let out a wail that it caught their attention, but before Zaidu or Taku could move, the mother ran to her son.

"Now you stop it! Stop playing so rough. You'll hurt yourself!" She jerked him up and sent him on his way.

Zaidu's face was twisted in pain, as though the boy's injury had stirred something within him.

"What's wrong?" Taku had learned to follow Zaidu's lead when he was pondering something.

"My mother told me those same words when I was a boy. I had been playing that same game, to see who could jump from the highest rock. My brother was tall and handsome. All the boys wanted him on their team. I usually stood by and watched him win every game."

Taku took a sip of his beer and dipped his bread in honey. The loaves were fresh today.

Zaidu continued, "He could flash a smile, and the girls would come from everywhere. I wanted to be like him. I wanted to prove to everyone that I could be smart or brave enough. It didn't matter. Boys are silly sometimes in trying to prove who they are to each other."

A tavern woman came over and asked if they needed any refills of beer. Zaidu waved her off.

"As the game escalated, boys from all over town began climbing rocks higher and higher to jump off. 'You're a chicken!' shouted one of the boys. 'Zaidu's the chicken!' my brother shouted. He was always taunting me."

Taku smiled. He couldn't see Zaidu chickening out of anything. He was the bravest man he knew. "What did you do?" Taku asked.

"I never understood why he needed to tease me when everyone thought so highly of him." Zaidu shrugged. "But I was determined to prove them all wrong that day. I'd show them."

Taku's eyes filled with wonder and curiosity. Why didn't he know this story by now?

"All the children that day paused to watch me. I began to

climb the rocks. They felt hot and sharp and dug into my palms. I could hear the whispers from the children below, staggering my confidence. I knew they didn't believe in me, but this was my chance to prove that I was every bit as good as my older brother."

"Did you do it?" Taku asked louder than usual. Tavern customers were beginning to gather around to hear his story.

"As I stood, the sun beat on my back. Some girl shouted from cupped hands, 'You don't have anything to prove, Zaidu!' My friends below looked much smaller than I thought they would from there. My legs began to shake, but my heart was determined. Everyone else had landed on their feet. I didn't think. I didn't plan for the fall. I just went for it."

Taku leaned in, wanting to touch the old man's hands, encourage him somehow.

"I didn't land on my feet. I hit the ground and rolled right into a large boulder. There was blood everywhere, Taku." He shook his head. "Children were screaming; I scared little babies! That was the day I lost my tooth and my ability to take risks."

One tear rolled down his dusty, wrinkled cheek. "My mother paid for the doctor and the medicine to help me heal. Taking risks hurt those closest to me, and they still hold that potential, Taku. Now, I always ask for wisdom from the gods, but I also calculate the risk myself."

This venture with Zu would be no different for either of them. Taku would allow Zaidu time to decide if Zu was trustworthy. Zu had given him all the numbers willingly and was eager to get started next week. The only problem either of them could see moving forward was the tense relationship between Taku and Miu. They would have to coordinate shipments together and work closer than either was currently comfortable with. Time would tell if they'd be able to do so.

Miu hated that she hadn't been able to fight for her brother Zigan. His death had been weighing on her since her conversation with Zaidu and Taku yesterday. She'd vowed to herself to never lose another person to stupidity. She'd fight for Zaidu and even Taku to get the business they deserved, especially since they had helped her that day at the docks.

She'd also had time to think more about the gods Zaidu trusted. And she had decided, and when she decided on something, nothing could change her mind. She'd fight for those she loved, but that meant she'd never lift her eyes toward the temple. That was the motivation she needed to make a name for herself. The gods were ever present as though to constantly remind her of their control. She saw them exercise their power when it came to taking more control of the tavern. The women she had been put in charge of at the tavern were insubordinate and unruly, which was expected, but it was Hashur who acted more and more like a snake, slithering her way between thoughts and feelings. The clay sign which hung above Alor and Hashur's tavern stated: Ninkasi brings order here.

The people Miu witnessed trudging back and forth to the temple reminded her of wandering sheep hoping for direction, begging for it. Every time Zaidu meandered through the tavern, he was mumbling prayers, and every time she heard it, her blood ran cold. This tension fueled Miu into creating her own order, her heaven and earth within her.

Just as it had been in Ur, everyone in Dilmun sought order and function. It was why Enki, god of water and creation, had given every creature a name. A god or person had ultimate control when they were able to name and call creatures into order and to teach them how to grow a society using math and science. Order gave purpose, but it also gave control and power.

If a tree went without a name, it didn't belong. If an animal didn't have a purpose, it wasn't used to help society. Sometimes Miu wished she'd never been named. Being given a name at birth meant the gods needed something from her, but she wouldn't give it. She'd stiffen her neck like a bull when a plow was hooked to them. She'd not give them the satisfaction of being at their beck and call. Not in this world anyway. The gods were cruel, and the longer she lived to watch them, the more she saw their purposes were only for humans to serve them. This world needed function and rules; if the gods wouldn't handle it, then Miu would make sure she did.

She could admit the gods' layout of the cosmos and world made sense. A heavenly realm above the sky for spiritual things, and a realm here on the land for physical things. She remembered her mother's clay circle, which had sat on their dining table and pictured the world in which they lived. The dry earth stretched across the flat disc from edge to edge, which were lined with mountains that upheld the sky-dome that covered their world below. The gods could look down into their sphere to punish people based on their behavior. They used varieties of methods— hail, crop failure, or even the great flood that took place years ago, destroying mankind, all except for one man.

Above the dome were the heavens, where the gods resided in the spirit world among the sun, moon, and stars. They didn't bother coming to earth unless it was to take something they needed or to have sex with humans. The sons of Enki looked down and saw the daughters of human men, from whom they would choose wives for themselves.

It didn't take long for men like Gilgamesh to begin to rule the world with power. His bloodline still existed in kings today, but the thought shook Miu to her core. Miu's friends had giggled in hopes they would marry a man with such strength and authority.

Even knowing heaven and earth as she did didn't stop Miu's questions, it fueled them. She needed deeper meaning. She wanted the gods to answer her. If she could reach through the sky-dome and pull one down, she'd duke it out with them face to face. She wanted answers for their inability to keep order, and why on earth had they wanted her brother?

Her fists clenched, and her breathing grew heavier. She deserved an answer. It was the least she could ask for. As a child she'd stared at the sky repeatedly, yelling at the gods. She had questions, and they were supposed to have answers.

She remembered every time her sister, Hulla, would get too rambunctious in the house, their mother would shake her finger in her face.

"How many times do I have to tell you, Hulla? Do you remember anything I've taught you? The flood happened because the gods became angry with the noise of humans in their world. Don't you remember how they crushed through the sky and released the heaven's waters to flood the dry earth? Hulla! They destroyed every single human except one. Tell me, child, what holds back the waters above today? What stops them from breaking through now because of your incessant ruckus? What keeps our disc from cracking and melting into the disordered and chaotic sea?"

Hulla would run away crying. While Miu thought it was an overreaction, the one thing Miu and her mother did agree on was that order must be kept; it was the tiptoeing around the gods' reckless behavior that infuriated Miu and ruined Hulla's ability to play like a child should be allowed to.

The gods held everything in place. They held the strings to the stars and moon. They gave function to the mountains: uphold the sky. Miu loved staring into the sky, seeing the stone-cold color of blue lapis and sapphire as it stretched across, almost as skin holding the earth's organs in place. It was almost as if it kept the gods breathing and functioning.

Miu's own heart expanded, thinking of how she'd fight for those she loved. She put her hand on her chest and felt the up and down movement, inhaling the night air. Even with anger and resolve battling inside her, she always wondered if one day even the mountains could crack and fall into the sea. Humans would be left with nothing. Everything Miu was building would be ruined.

She squared her shoulders and she decided: fear or anger wouldn't push her to run away anymore. Now she'd push back when children, like her brother or Didila, were taken advantage of for cruel pleasures. She'd let her anger toward the gods push her to learn everything she could about this tavern business. Then she'd get out of here and make a name for herself.

All her avoidance of the gods hadn't come without consequence. Restless nights and nightmares had haunted her since she got to Dilmun. She'd had the same dream night after night for weeks.

She was lying mangled in the desert, not a soul around. Her clothes and skin were torn to shreds, something had been after her, and her blood was fresh enough that she could taste it. It must have been her own. Her eyes burned while her fingers moved ever so slightly until she could feel the sand between them. Life was still in her body as her breath came in before she exhaled.

As she became aware of her fingers moving, a snake appeared in the corner of her eye. The snake slithered by slowly, making enough eye contact in a way that made Miu's blood freeze. When it got closer, the creature paused for a moment then coiled herself up into a disc, as if it had the world wrapped inside its cold, slick skin. The shiny scales made Miu shrink away in horror as her breathing shallowed.

The creature was offering Miu something, she could tell by the luring look in its eyes. Although she wasn't sure exactly what the snake proffered, she was confident of the snake's desire: Miu's soul. Her mind didn't want to take what the snake offered, but her gut and desire to know more lured her closer.

The snake lowered its head, swaying back and forth. Without warning, the snake began to shed its skin. Slowly at first and then faster as it slithered toward Miu.

A snake shedding its skin was a sign of constant power and renewal, exactly what Miu craved. Power over the gods. Independence to choose her own way. In every dream, as soon as Miu tried to lift herself from the sand to take from this slithery demon, the dream would end. She'd bolt up on her reed mat in a cold sweat. In every dream, she got closer to grasping the snake's invitation.

And every night ended with Miu in a raging fit. Tonight had been no different. She grabbed her clay pot, which held her jewelry, and threw it across the tent, waking one of the tavern girls.

"Go back to sleep, girl!" Miu yelled, wiping the sweat from her brow.

Trembling, she wrapped her arms around herself and tried to fall back asleep. She wanted the gods to leave her alone. Snake or no snake, dream or no dream, she knew she would stay to fight her way to owning the tavern.

But why the snake? Why was the darkness the snake offered so inviting? The more Miu tried to push it out of her mind, the more alluring it became. The gods wouldn't control her day-to-day, even if they seemed to control her dreams.

Either way, by the gods' control or not, the dreams were probably caused by the upcoming snake festival next week. Miu dreaded festivals of any kind after losing her brother; the memories, sounds, and smells made her wish she could flee Dilmun.

Not this time. They didn't hold meaning anymore, so she

could push through. Maybe if she could prove to herself the gods weren't real, then the dreams would dissipate. As for now, she'd have to wake up in the morning and face the snake.

THE SNAKE FESTIVAL HAD ARRIVED, in all its doom and glory. Hashur was in full-on efficiency mode. She rarely sat still anyway, but this week was no exception. She had Miu run inventory four times to make sure they had enough beer to host the finest of diplomats, priests, and merchants. Many new merchants and priests had frequented the tavern since working with Zu, and she wanted to make sure they wanted to continue coming.

Hashur had purchased the tavern girls new wool tunics, all dyed in blues. They all had their hair braided the same way, in a circle around their head with wildflowers woven inside. It was Miu's favorite part of the entire day, leaving the tent to stand in the wildflower field. Even if it reminded her of her father's potential visit to Dilmun, she gladly picked as many wildflowers as her tunic could hold.

Miu left her hair as she always did, braided down the side, and hung it over her right shoulder, adding the brightest of wildflowers to her own hair. Hashur saw Miu's hair choice as a refusal to comply but ignored it. Every merchant coming to town admired Miu, and Hashur wanted to keep it that way. Miu could control men in a way even Hashur could not ignore.

As Hashur ran around making last-minute checks on the details, Miu took charge of the girls. She stationed them to brew in perfect synchrony and set up stations for men as they came in. One booth for ration cards, one for staring at the girls who handed them their drinking straws, and lastly, one for getting their beer. The girls who took names for beer rations would rotate with the girls in the back stirring the beer in the clay pots.

Miu told them all that if they couldn't handle the busyness, she'd just do it herself, and work circles around them doing it.

That was how it always worked out anyway. Managing the girls was Miu's least favorite job at the tavern, but Hashur respected Miu the most for it. If Miu planned to one day run her own tavern or take over this one, it meant the girls needed to attempt competence. Their laziness infuriated her, and so she challenged them to do better.

"It's coming!" shouted Alor, startling everyone from their work.

"Oh, you stupid man," Hashur said. "Don't be so irreverent. The snake does not bless ignorance."

Miu rolled her eyes and told the girls to get into place. Everyone dropped what they were doing and did one last check on their hair and tunics. The giggles slowed, and the solemn assembly began. The priest's proceedings began at the temple and made their way through every tent. A snake for each section of the city was sacrificed and carried through town. A community's snake was brought in a basket, carried by a priest dressed in a hat wrapped around his head.

Miu gasped. She tried not to draw attention to herself but was not expecting this.

Hashur smacked her. "Be quiet, girl!"

On the priest's hat was an eye, the exact image of the snake in Miu's dream. Here it was, staring at her. She looked down and noticed the priest's hands gripping the basket of snakes, his fingers gnarled from a lifetime of killing. His eyes were lifeless; maybe the snake had taken them from him, because the eye on his hat held a depth that was lacking in the priest.

He peered into the soul of each individual, chanting to the gods on behalf of man. Then he paused, and the chanting around him paused.

"Its body is sacrificed," he whispered.

The ritual killing and sacrificing of a snake was not one Miu ever wanted to see take place, but she stood her ground. If she were to fight these gods, she'd watch. Even if it killed her.

Beginning with the man of the household, Alor reached his

fumbling and clumsy hand into the basket, its contents Miu could not see yet, though she watched Alor with caution. Alor took what looked like a piece of snake meat and placed it on his tongue.

He bowed before the priest, who carried the basket and said, "For the protection of those in Dilmun."

"For the protection of those in Dilmun," Alor repeated.

The priest stepped next to Hashur, and Miu gripped Didila tighter. Hashur was all smiles. She wasn't interested in the ceremony, she only had eyes for the priest. He was well known in their area and was one of the finest Dilmun had for this ceremony. Hashur was excited that her tavern had evoked such emotion from the king that he sent his best. She excitedly reached her elegant and steady hand into the basket to grab a piece of meat. She then placed it on her tongue as she bowed low.

"Communion with the snake." Her eyes grew big.

"For the protection of those in Dilmun," the priest chanted with a wry smile.

Hashur's tavern only required Hashur and Alor to participate in the ceremony so they could trickle blessings down to those under their roof. The honored, aged priest moved on in a slow trod from tent to tent. When he had completed the merchants he was designated to visit, the priest paused at the end of the road.

Miu watched with curiosity and dread as he took the remains of the snake from his basket and placed it into a wool bag tied to his leather belt. Miu was certain his slow and purposeful movements meant something, but no one mentioned them or their meaning. Finally, he placed the woolen bag into a ceramic wine container one of his followers had been holding.

"Snakes that gave their lives for our protection will now be taken to the temple burial grounds. We will visit them in the coming months. Every woman in Dilmun will bring curds and sacrificial food to the snakes," Hashur said in hushed tones. "Its venom is known to give power over life, and we will thank it for giving its life in our place."

"Humph," Miu said. "Open the doors so we can start serving." A shiver went through her entire body. She had to keep moving. Hashur didn't care if Miu worshipped or not, as long as she kept her business running smoothly. So that's exactly what she did.

Miu squatted and looked Didila in the eyes. "Let's go pass out some beer."

Didila giggled while a thought popped into Miu's mind. What if the snake in her dream had the keys to the freedom she craved?

chapter
eleven

Miu glanced around the tavern, taking a mental inventory of ingredients. The baskets of legumes were in place, and beside them were new cheeses from the local farmer. She wasn't sure of the time, but she was certain exhaustion was taking over.

Earlier she might have dozed off if it hadn't been for Alor, the clumsiest man she'd ever encountered; he tottered through his restaurant like a newborn calf trying to stand. He and everyone else hid in tent corners and behind barrels of beer whenever Hashur entered the room, waiting for her to lose her temper. Now, Alor startled her awake as he dropped two clay tablets, shattered into pieces with this month's inventory carved on them.

"Alor!" she shouted. "Get out of here."

Miu used the new technology of clay tablets for accurate record keeping just like the other business owners in Dilmun. Hashur had been the one to teach her how to use the tablets specifically for inventory. "Wet them, rub off the previous writing, then write a new list of needs or rations."

Miu didn't mind the thin, clay coating her hands displayed. When she first started working with the inventory, she'd tried to rub it off, but now it was just part of who she was. Besides, if she were going to leave here one day and start her own tavern, clay tablets would forever be part of her life. Lately, they'd used the tablets for beer rations and recipes and to send messages to other merchants locally.

Hashur noticed Miu's competence almost immediately and put her in charge of inventory along with the women she managed.

In Dilmun, as it was in Ur, beer was the drink of the gods. There was no separating the drink from the goddess herself. Ninkasi was in everything Hashur, Miu, and the girls did, whether Miu approved of her or not. She attempted to keep her thoughts to herself on the subject matter, but everyone knew where she stood. Miu smiled to herself. It was probably obvious when she rolled her eyes or threw things across the room. It wasn't difficult to tell what Miu thought. She considered Ninkasi alive but didn't hide her disdain. She was there to learn what she could, not to lift her eyes to a god.

Miu continued counting the inventory, notating that they needed more beer straws since there were only twenty left. She wiped the wet clay off her fingers onto her tunic and sat. Sweat dripped down her forehead, and she sighed. She had been trying to figure out a way to get out from under Alor and Hashur, because she wouldn't rely on them much longer. They were stepping stones to where she wanted to go, like steps up the ziggurat to the gods. Miu would use them as steps to a kingdom she'd build for herself.

The connections she had been making with Zu were good resources for her, but she hadn't figured a way out on her own yet. She did know a lot about the jewelry business Zu was involved in; maybe she could make her own pieces for merchants. She'd made sure to keep in Zu's good graces either way.

Zu's jolly demeanor and propensity for a fun time led most people to trust him, or at least want to be around him. He laughed easily and made quick business decisions, while also trusting Miu's instincts. Because of this, their friendship formed quickly and naturally. Zu even seemed to appreciate her straightforward approach to his own business, something Hashur found threatening. He never had to guess what she was thinking because she said it, always without hesitation.

"Zu, your numbers are off, and it's because you trusted that idiot with them. If you don't double-check things, you're going to lose a lot more money," she had told him last week, knowing that he wouldn't double-check himself. He might ask her to help.

Sometimes her comments made him mad, and other times it caused him to think. He spent an exorbitant amount of money on exquisite meals near the temple and the finest clothing, and like her father, he liked jewelry to adorn almost every part of his body. In that way, and in his storytelling, he reminded her a great deal of her father.

Miu often wondered if the two knew each other. Was he the one her father bought his lapis lazuli from? Miu's shoulders tensed as she thought about the possibility of her father finding her in Dilmun one day. If he did, he had every right to drag her home if he wanted. Knowing him, he'd probably force her to work in the temple, and the entire law system would allow it. A man with his status always got what he wanted. She'd be careful sharing any personal information with Zu, or anyone else for that matter.

When people asked how she got to Dilmun, Miu would respond that she had been orphaned. Her aunt had placed her on the ship to Dilmun in the hope of a better life. Orphans were often given to the temple to serve the gods or the disgusting duties of cleaning up after festivals and sacred prostitution. No one really questioned her about the story, so she kept it simple. Lies could stay hidden when there were fewer details to get mixed up.

When Miu wanted to get serious and understand how the business worked, Zu would laugh and lightly slap her shoulder as he always did. Then he'd tell her to stop being so serious, and, "For goodness sake, girl, wipe the scowl off your face." Then he'd begin a long, drawn-out story about a farmer who forgot to plant crops or an oil presser who never removed the seeds from the olives before making oil.

She'd first thought these stories were a waste of time, but she stood in the heat and listened. Sometimes she'd get just enough insight into where he was shipping jewels or who his next business partner would be. The stories were his way of teaching Miu, and she soaked it all up like a lizard in the sun, helping to warm its body enough to get to work.

The story he rambled on about yesterday was still nagging at her though.

"One day a group of shepherds decided to leave their herd to go into town for some breakfast, salted fish, bread, and beer."

"The best of breakfasts," Miu teased, encouraging him to continue.

"As they were walking back to find their herd, they noticed the sheep had moved to a new pasture from where they left them. This is common for sheep because, without a shepherd, they wander. They frantically begin to look for them. The sheep were found about a mile outside the city, and the men began to run. Very undignified, I might add." Zu stood and flailed his arms.

"They found their flock running toward a cliff. As soon as the sheep reached the edge, they jumped."

"Heaven and earth!" Miu said, shocked.

"Hundreds of them jumped to their death. There was no way to stop them. One shepherd fell to his knees and wailed. Another shepherd ran toward the sheep screaming and waving his arms around, which only proved to scare more sheep to their death. When the chaos was over, the shepherds took the long walk around the hill to the bottom of the cliff. They had one thousand sheep in total, and do you think any survived?"

Miu stared in amazement at how stupid sheep could be. She just shook her head.

"To the shepherd's astonishment, four hundred and fifty had died at the bottom of the pile. This left five hundred and fifty sheep who were saved." He laughed his belly laugh. "As the white, fluffy pile became higher and higher, the sheep who jumped off the cliff landed on a warm, soft bed and were saved. Never leave your sheep to get your breakfast." Zu laughed heartily.

Miu smiled then, but she couldn't stop thinking about the sheep. They just kept jumping off without a question. She'd never be that blind. And even if she had to jump through hoops or off a cliff, she'd wait and watch. She'd be the last to jump. She'd jump off the backs of the idiots before her and save herself, if that was what it took.

People. She rolled her eyes. She'd never be like sheep. She'd never be her father, Hashur, or Taku. She'd never blindly follow anyone. She refused to follow the gods to her death or be told what to do. She'd get out of this dark hole of a tavern and lead this community in a new way, somehow. She'd show the people how to be their own god. She knew her next step was to get out from under Hashur and Alor; she wouldn't stay here much longer.

Didila's giggle as she burst into the kitchen interrupted Miu's thoughts. Didila skirted around the place with pure energy and joy. The memory of her sister, Hulla, filled Miu's mind, but she pushed it aside. If she lingered on memories of her family, she couldn't handle the void and regret that followed.

Didila loved playing around the tavern with Miu. She'd hide behind the barrels of beer, and Miu would have to find her. Sometimes they'd grab a rope and see how many times they could jump over it as they swung it in circles over their heads and under their feet.

Although Miu was exhausted from both the mental energy of trying to find a way out of the tavern and the physical labor of managing the women and the inventory, this little girl brought life to an otherwise mundane job. She was the light in the darkness of the tavern's dank, wheat-smelling back kitchen. The giggles could be heard throughout, but what caught Miu's attention was something dark under the little one's eye. A purple bruise was rising to the surface.

"What happened?" Miu demanded.

Didila covered her eyes quickly and ran out of the room sobbing.

Miu ran after her and grabbed the little girl, turning her around. With less intensity this time, she asked her what happened to her eye. She sensed Didila's fear, so she relaxed her muscles, smiled warmly at her, and then tried again.

"What happened?"

"Mama hit me," she whimpered.

Miu tried with everything in her power not to grab Didila up in her arms and confront Hashur. Instead, those dumb sheep came to her mind. *Think through the situation.* Another thought came to her mind: What if she ran away with Didila?

No, running from problems was what got her here and what she promised herself she wouldn't do. Where would she even go? Back home? Her father was worse than Hashur. At least she kept her child alive. Then again, if Miu challenged Hashur, she would kick her out of the tavern without giving it another thought. She didn't have enough resources and connections yet to make it on her own if Hashur was against her.

She hugged Didila like she used to hug her sister when she fell, and a depressing and heavy thought came to mind. One that left her feeling more trapped than she ever had before.

What if she stayed at the tavern so she could protect Didila?

This decision would keep her doing the tavern duties. It would mean no independence. It would mean keeping herself stuck under Hashur's unpredictable grip. Also, Didila slowed down productivity when she wanted Miu to play her games.

Miu wanted to scream. She loved Didila as a sister, and she couldn't let this woman hurt her. Why did people always get in the way of her plans? Why were they selfish? Why did they have to be so foolish?

She wiped her hands on her tunic and squared her shoulders, knowing exactly what she needed to do next. She'd stay at the tavern. She'd fight for her and Didila to have their independence, together. It might take longer, but it was what the girl needed. She'd teach her to be strong and to ask questions.

As for herself, she'd learn as much as she could from Zu and the other merchants to ensure she'd never have to go back to Ur or her father again. Together, no matter how long it took, Didila and she would destroy Hashur. Miu would push Didila to be brave. She wasn't sure how, but she'd be patient.

No matter what, she'd protect Didila from people, people like her mother and her father. *Keep your guard up. Watch the work they do. Anticipate what's coming.* She wouldn't turn an eye away from the abuse, but she would come up with a plan to destroy Hashur's reputation and take over her tavern.

"I've got you, sweet girl. You're safe with me." She smiled and scooped the girl up in her arms before returning to the kitchen to begin preparing the girls for the evening rush.

She'd be the last sheep standing with Didila by her side.

chapter
twelve

The barmaid, Tiame, jabbered on about stories of Dilmun, as Miu stirred the beer.

"The waters surrounding the island were unique, and the residents boasted in their history. They told stories of Dilmun's beginnings of how the god of bitter waters mingled with the god of sweet waters, creating their immortality." She continued as she moved to another barrel of beer, checking its contents. "According to the city's legend, the gods separated themselves in a violent fight for rule over humanity. Even then, it wasn't until the gods made the dry land and separated the land from waters that those sweet waters flowed freely from the land to provide health and life to those who drank it." She searched Miu's face for a response. Miu wouldn't give her one.

Miu's family also shared stories of Gilgamesh, the god-king who came to the Dilmun waters looking for eternal life after the death of his trusted friend, Enkidu. Miu found the whole idea laughable, especially when she watched women, even some of the friends she had, swoon over the cool, blue water's edge.

"Flesh of the gods himself came to visit Dilmun," Tiame, the barmaid, told her the other day as her eyes lit up with hopeful anticipation that maybe these waters would bring her immortality. Her hair dangled over the water, dripping with the bath she'd just taken there. "What immortality may we find if we only keep searching?"

Gilgamesh came after traveling over wilderness and grassland to visit the city of the sun, Dilmun. He came like many others since, searching for life unending. Gilgamesh's journey was told to Miu many times by her father, teachers, and even priests.

Today Tiame recounted the story to Miu as she wiped down the tables in the tavern. "Gilgamesh visited a tavern just like we own Miu! That day, Gilgamesh visited him, and Siduri the tavern keeper asked him, 'Gilgamesh, where are you roaming? You will never find the eternal life that you seek. When the gods created mankind, they also created death and held eternal life for themselves alone. Humans are born, they live, they die, this is the order that the gods have decreed.'"

"See, that's how it goes. The gods do as they please, Tiame. I know the story. Stop exhausting me with your rambling."

"But you see," Tiame continued.

Miu kicked sand, the girl was absurd.

"After Gilgamesh negotiated with the god of Dilmun, he gifted him the secret to eternal life. The only problem was that it lay at the bottom of the sea. But in true Gilgamesh form, he left the god standing there and dove into the abysmal waters."

Tiame's breathing was heavier, and Miu could almost hear lyre music playing for dramatic effect.

"Do you know what he did, Miu?" she asked as she poured barley into a basket.

Miu relented, knowing the girl had to finish the story or they'd never get back into town with the oysters they'd already purchased for Zu's next venture. "He grasped the oyster which contained a pearl or Flower of Immortality and ripped the oyster free from the oyster bed it lay on while his fingers dripped with blood. Then, with a mighty push off the bottom of the sea, he surfaced with a large gasp of air."

"You do know the story," Tiame said with surprise as she attempted to braid her dripping wet hair and finished the story.

"Miu, he held the plant tightly because it was the antidote to the fear of death. Immortality. The story changed, Miu. It changed forever because Gilgamesh went to wash in a pond of fresh, living water later that day. It was by these living waters that a green and shrewd snake carried away his only chance of eternal life."

"Stop it! I've heard enough," Miu shouted, weary from this back and forth. She jumped and looked down to see that what she thought was a serpent was just a wave creeping over her toes. The snake was too much. It held too much power. The snake which came to steal life from Gilgamesh was also destroying her dreams.

"Miu, it's why we must keep searching. When the snake slithered away, its scaly skin began to dull and slough off in one large piece, leaving behind a living and bright snake, one that was renewed and shining as the sun."

Grabbing the basket of pearls they had purchased, she shoved them into Tiame's arms. "Get these to Zu. I'm going to get the tavern ready for the evening. Heaven and earth girl, don't dawdle!"

TAKU RESTED by the water's edge, desperate to escape the noise in Dilmun. After the snake festival, the town was on high alert, always hoping to reunite somehow with the snake. Dilmun held more hope and more beauty than any town he'd visited. Maybe it was the prestige of their gardens, but often it was the hope of immortality. The snake's ability to shed its skin, to leave the creature glowing and new was what every human hoped for. Get rid of the old hatred and selfishness and reveal a new life. It just wasn't possible. Humans always did the same things to each other.

The hype of the festival had interested him. As much as he loved crossing the waters, he was curious to dive beneath them. This afternoon seemed like just the right time. He pictured Gilgamesh's strong muscles swimming beneath the waters to dive for the pearl. Men did this now for their work, so Taku could do it too. Taku took his sandals off and waded into the warm waters up to his knees.

He wasn't in a rush, but alert, looking for the freshwater springs to bubble up below him. Fear pricked his skin, but he pushed it away. He wanted that nagging voice to leave him alone. "Keep looking," it kept saying. So here he stood, looking. It wasn't like him to argue with the gods, but this one didn't seem to argue. It seemed like a still, small voice. It was almost as if it cared about him, as if it were trying to show him something. Maybe this god would show himself in the waters below.

There was more, Taku knew it deep down. The endless wrestling humans had with the gods for immortality was futile. People wanted to defy the order the gods had given to the world, but the gods were immortal, and humans were not. In his mind, it was as simple as land separating waters.

Taku reasoned with himself that it was why people created writing. They could hold a tablet and write something as if it were true. It could be passed from family to family. A story written on the heart or told around a fire now became a fact for future generations. No one defeated death, at least no one that Taku had met. It took the young, the old, the women, and the men. No one escaped it. And yet men still built houses and ships, ziggurats, and temples. They stored their treasures, created families, and built towers to defy the gods. These waters would one day show them how they would contain their bodies in the underworld.

If Gilgamesh couldn't achieve eternal life, then what was the point for Taku, a simple courier turned sailor? Either way, Taku wanted to see if he could get the nagging voice to leave him alone. He craved peace inside himself and was willing to do anything for it. So, there he was, wading in the same waters Gilgamesh had.

Earlier that day, he had sat across from Zaidu as they munched on figs and cheese. "I'm going to search for pearls by the waters. We can sell some back in Ur."

Zaidu had shrugged, and Taku had taken that as his friend's

silent approval. The trip was more than a search for pearls. He was seeking peace.

The water rocked back and forth on his legs, a reminder of his instability, but the warm sun on his back calmed his racing heart. He paused and took a deep, purposeful breath as he wiggled his toes around in the sand before he walked a bit deeper. There was an oyster in front of him.

He reached into the water with hesitation, keeping his toes planted securely around the shell. He felt the cut on his toes, and he lifted it out of the water. A smile spread across his face, and he pulled out the knife hanging on his leather belt. It felt like he was doing some awkward procedure on the shell, like what he saw the priests do at the temple. Prying open the oyster was no small task. He peeked into the shell of the oyster and there it was, a pearl staring back at him.

Snake eyes. That's what they called them. Eyes to see who could inherit eternal life.

"Hey, Taku!" Miu strode across the coast right toward him. He had been so entranced in this search for the pearl that he missed a chance to avoid her. She looked angry as always; poor Didila trailed behind her, careful not to get too close to the water. The girl was so skittish.

They had spent many days and nights together recently working out a deal with Zu and Zaidu. There was always a fight or an argument, and it was exhausting. But Miu thrived off conflict; it seemed to help her think better.

One thing was for certain, he did admire her sheer grit and determination to get a deal settled. She wouldn't let either side lose, which caused all three men to admire her once the deal had been settled. He had never seen a woman with the ability to challenge a man to do the right thing in the way she proved herself.

As much as Taku hated to admit it, they made a great team. He could see where both men were coming from while simultaneously Miu challenged them on their own viewpoints. She could force anyone to her viewpoint, but she handled that ability with caution. She wanted both men to choose what they wanted and then fight for what they wanted, even to the bitter end.

"Hey." Taku quietly stared, still entranced by the pearl in his hand.

"What do you have there? A pearl?"

"Yeah." He refused to let her know he had been searching because a voice in his head told him to do so.

"My dad used to get pearls from Dilmun. He said they were magic and connected you to the gods. It's asinine if you ask me," she said. "But do as you please; they make pretty good money. I just sent Tiame, the maid, to Zu with a basket full of them we purchased."

"Hello, Didila." Taku bent down and smiled warmly at her.

The little girl looked into his eyes and immediately looked down.

"Speak up." Miu nudged her closer to Taku.

Didila's eyes brimmed with tears. Her poor face looked swollen from crying.

"Go easy on the girl, Miu." Taku felt an odd connection with and a need to protect the child.

"I'll handle her. You handle yourself."

As much as Taku tried, he would never get over how Miu could turn from warm to cold, just as the sweet water could turn to bitter water.

She sighed. "My frustration has a cause. I need a way to protect Didila. Hashur has been beating her. What can we do about it?"

Taku wasn't shocked. Many parents beat their children when they got in the way. It's the reason he was with Zaidu now. He felt compassion for the little girl, but at the same time, she wasn't his responsibility. He also didn't like how Miu disclosed the information in front of Didila and said she had been hit. Some things should be kept quiet.

"Maybe we can meet up later and talk about this?" Taku asked, hopeful Miu would be quiet.

"It's like you to put things off. She's being hit by her mother, and I won't take it. I have a plan, but I need to know you've got my back." She put her hands on her hips and tapped her toes on the sand.

Taku waded up out of the water, wishing he could still feel the waves lapping his toes and silencing his inner voice.

Miu could rock the boat even when there wasn't one. Today though, as he caught sight of Miu's eyes, he saw something was different. She was still shouting orders at the little girl and was more guarded than normal, but today something was resolute. She had taken this little girl that she seemed indifferent to and brought her to safety, if even for a little bit. She did care about something.

"I'm impressed that you care this much, Miu," Taku said hesitantly, uncertain of how she'd take a compliment.

"Isn't that what we all should be doing? She's hurting, and I won't sit around and do nothing while someone takes advantage of her. That's why I'm here."

"How can I help?" Taku almost believed he had something in him that could be of service. And then another thought came to mind. How did she see something in him? That challenging and harsh exterior actually was calling out some potential in Taku. He almost believed her.

"I don't need someone to watch her; she follows me around like a stray dog. But I have a plan to take over Hashur's tavern. I'm going to run that woman out of town. It's the least I can do."

Taku's eyes widened, and doubt filled his insides, making him feel like he'd eaten a rotten pomegranate.

"Don't freak out yet." She rolled her eyes. "She's been hiding how much beer she's rationing off to the priests, and in turn she's making more money than the temple tavern. I also overheard she wants to poison the temple tavern so she's the only one in business. My plan is to go along with it."

Taku's insides squirmed. He wanted to wade back into the water, but with the little girl by her side, he had to be brave.

Miu continued, "But to prove her poisoning plan is going to take some strategy. We want her to be the downfall of her own greed. What I need from you is eyes and ears open. If you see anyone speak of her tavern, let me know, especially anyone coming and going from Dilmun. My hope is someone starts talking about her."

"That could take years. Do you really think people are talking?" Fear crept into his throat as he tried to make excuses.

"If someone is getting more beer than is rationed to them, word will spread fast. If you hang out around any tavern in Dilmun, you're likely to hear something incriminating. Especially if they've had too much to drink. We're not going to just take over, we're going to destroy her. Every connection. Every person she loves. We're going to utterly get rid of her peace." She laughed.

Taku swallowed hard and took a hesitant step forward. He'd rather side with this wild woman than with an abuser. "I can listen. I'm always watching people anyway because ..."

"Because what?"

He knew she wouldn't let this one slide. "Because I like writing stories about people and places in my mind. Like the story of Gilgamesh or other places like Ur and Dilmun. I get inspiration from the people I see and meet."

"Whatever. Do what you want. Just pay attention if you hear any gossip about Hashur or Alor. We need it to keep Didila safe. Right, honey?" She looked toward the little girl with big eyes full of hope.

Taku was shocked she didn't laugh at him. Maybe there was more, something deeper to this wild, crazy woman.

chapter
thirteen

The days moved slowly to Miu. Her days were full, yet monotonous. The routine of taking care of the slowest women to ever walk the earth sucked the breath of life from her. The women laid around stirring beer and chatting while Miu made sure they kept a roof over their heads. She'd escaped the wild ox, but now the wild cow confronted her. Her father controlled her before; now it was these horrid women, and she was constantly picking up their mess.

Beer suds in the pots were always overflowing onto the ground because the women couldn't pay attention. They'd get caught up in telling local stories about the shipbuilder leaving his wife for the bread maker, or how the priest's son was always the one getting into trouble with the gods. No one ever wanted to work. If they put in a bit more effort, the tavern would be a better place.

No one saw things as she did; no one was as desperate as she was to get out from under her father's potential visitation to Dilmun or away from Alor and Hashur's right hand. If the women would take her lead, together they'd be able to take over from Hashur and Alor. That's when they'd build something great.

But no, here she was, always the one making sure everyone else did what they were supposed to do.

Aside from their laziness, the way the women memorized the song to Ninkasi, the beer goddess, grated on Miu's nerves as well. Long before clay tablets, songs were the way their ancestors had learned to remember the science, math, and cooking the gods taught them. It's what gave songs their value. Remember the songs, remember the gods, and even more important: remember how to stay alive. Today the girls' singing sounded like fingernails on a clay tablet, plaguing her very thoughts.

> *It is you who bake the beer bread in the big*
> *oven and put the piles of hulled grain*
> *in order. Ninkasi, it is you who bake*
> *the beer bread in the big oven and put*
> *in order the piles of hulled grain.*
> *It is you who water the earth-covered malt;*
> *the noble dogs guard it. Ninkasi, it is*
> *you who water the earth-covered malt...*

SHE PITIED them for believing Ninkasi was the one behind their success in brewing. Couldn't they see it was their own skilled hands that had learned how to brew beer? Sure, in the beginning, Enki had come down to give humans the secrets to mathematics, science, and growing barley needed for beer. But had Enki done any of the work? Hadn't the farmers grown the barley and the girls the ones who brewed it? Not the gods.

The gods were lazy and expected humans to provide for them. Did they even try to support the pillars and dry ground from crumbling back into the sea? That thought terrified Miu.

Alor stumbled into the kitchen. Every girl scurried out to make themselves busy elsewhere. Miu didn't mind Alor's drunkenness; she'd kept men like him under control for as long as she could remember.

"What is it this time, Alor?" she asked.

"We have a banquet coming up." Alor tripped over stacks of barley. His red eyes were almost swollen shut. It was enough to catch Miu's attention.

"Clumsy, tired, and drunk," Miu muttered to herself.

She had noticed his drinking had intensified, everyone had. And if anyone knew the side effects of consuming too much, it would be Alor. Owning a tavern gave him a view of men losing control of themselves, getting into fights about things that didn't matter and sometimes things that did. He saw how men treated women as mistresses and how women loved the power beer gave them. He watched men lose their money and their rations for a single chance with a woman. Children lost their parents for one more drink, hoping for better days.

Alor should know better, but he had relented. Hashur ran things, and he had given up trying to be enough for her. It was obvious.

Even last night, Alor should have been pouring beer for customers; instead, he was reclining at tables. Girls floated around him while bowing low in front of the men sitting nearby. Sure, it made them purchase more beer, but it also kept the kitchen backed up with orders, making other customers unhappy. Hashur was furious with him. She tried to be long of nose while acting unfazed in front of customers.

"Alor, meet me in the back," she had said through gritted teeth. Everyone knew they wouldn't see Alor the rest of the night.

The tavern's reputation was of utmost importance, and Miu could tell Hashur had had enough. The night did end with the highest profit Miu had recorded since being here, but she could see success was ruining their relationship. It was changing them. Alor was shutting down while Hashur was missing her own mistakes due to pride.

"How many people will attend this banquet, Alor? I want to begin spreading the malt on the roof earlier than last time."

Miu ran through a list in her mind of what needed to be done to make extra beer. First, the malt would need to be ground into a paste. Next, she would choose a few girls to spread the paste out to dry in the sun so it could ferment on the roof. Finally, she would need an extra girl to be taken away from the regular chores of the tavern and stationed on the roof at all hours. If not, the birds would come and peck away any profit or success Miu hoped to attain. Finding a girl wouldn't be a problem, but getting Alor to commit to paying her might be.

"I don't know how many people will come. Just make extra beer, and do it well," Alor barked, rubbing his bony fingers across his temples.

"You idiot!" Miu's fists clenched and her back went rigid. This blubbering man was not going to be the reason they lost profits, and Miu wouldn't be blamed for his refusal to get the details.

She grabbed his tunic and stared him in the eyes, his breath foul. "You will find out how many people will be in attendance, or we're not doing the banquet. Plain and simple. You will do what I tell you."

Alor could barely stand from the encounter but nodded his head, relenting, then walked out.

"Another thing handled for the day," Miu grumbled.

Didila bolted through the kitchen door, and Miu couldn't stop herself from smiling. She wiped her hands on her tunic and tried to shake off the encounter with Alor. She wanted to be present with Didila, but there was always an emergency.

"Hey, my little apricot." Miu held her arms open wide.

Miu was shocked how the girl seemed to shift her mood. "If nothing else in the world brings you joy, Miu, that girl does," Tiame had teased.

"Miu, my tummy hurts." Didila looked a little pale for coming in from playing in the afternoon.

"Did you tell your mother?"

"No." She looked down with fear in her eyes. She wiggled her toes.

Didila's bruises had become more frequent but never predictable. At first, Miu had thought they'd show up after she was being rambunctious, as children often get. Then one day when Hashur slapped her after breakfast, Miu knew it happened more often.

"Oh, my apricot, I'm so sorry. Here, follow me."

Miu led the smiling little girl to the back of the kitchen. She pulled a pot down from the top shelf. Didila peered into it with a curious glance that only a child could own. Then she looked up at Miu, trusting her with whatever was next.

"What's in there?" she giggled.

Those big brown eyes melted Miu. How could someone not protect her? She tried to hide the tears that pricked her eyes. Miu swallowed hard and looked down into the pot. "Close your eyes, Didila. Take a deep breath."

Didila did exactly as she said. She grimaced, held her stomach, and then smiled.

"Now, what do you smell?"

"Mint!"

"That's right," Miu said. "Now, let's go make you some tea."

A SMALL WHIMPER woke Miu up from a deep sleep.

Didila had asked to sleep in Miu's room that night. Alor had been drinking again, and Hashur was in the middle of a meeting with a weaver. Hashur wanted a new tunic to show off her growing prominence in Dilmun.

Her incessant need to rub shoulders with the elite had given her a chance to meet the temple's main weaver and clothes designer. Her bragging made Miu's anger rage until she felt like a pot of boiling water.

Fed up with Hashur's pretending and Alor's drunken stupor, she held her tongue and went to bed. She needed to hold on a little longer. At the rate Hashur was spending money, she'd hurry the temple poisoning and hopefully make a mistake. Miu just needed to make sure she was next in line to take over.

Didila's request to go to bed early was a welcome one. The mint tea had been helping her feel a little better, but the pain always returned. Each time worse than the time before.

"What's wrong?" Miu whispered, wrapping her arms around the little girl.

"My tummy again."

The girl curled into a tight ball, and then with a violent heave, she vomited. It went all over the girl, the reed mat, and Miu. It seemed to continue until there was nothing left. And then the heaving continued even though her stomach was empty.

As the girl began to settle, Miu used her tunic to wipe Didila's mouth, then got up to clean the mess.

"Couldn't you have made it outside?" she asked, frustrated. Miu's cleaning was like a bull bolting across a field, grabbing and wiping what she could.

Didila looked like she had done something wrong. She crawled to a corner of the room trying to silence her tears.

"Get up! You can't just lay there in your vomit. Get those clothes off you, then you can rest."

As Miu finished cleaning, she saw Didila dressed in a new tunic sobbing in the corner. She felt remorse. Didn't she understand she was just trying to teach her how to take care of herself? The girl needed to know her mother and father wouldn't do it, and so the girl needed to be stronger.

"You can't just lay covered in vomit, even if you feel bad."

"Yes, ma'am."

Hands falling to her sides, Miu regretted how harshly she had spoken to her. She despised anyone's nod of approval over their respect. She wanted the girl to learn a life lesson, not fear her. Miu's anger was in the girl's lack of trying, not because she was sick. She needed the girl to respect herself enough, even though she was small, to take care of herself.

With a pained expression, she sat down and held Didila. Miu looked around the tent. The other women had fallen asleep even after that ruckus. Outside she could hear the breeze of a storm coming, while the dark and musty tent smelled of rosemary and turpentine.

As she rocked Didila to sleep, she reasoned with herself, "The cleaning needed to be done anyway." Miu looked down at the girl and smiled. Tiame would nag her tomorrow and tell her how harsh she was on the girl, but she was no harsher than the cruel world that lay outside this kitchen tent.

Miu combed her fingers through the girl's dark hair until she was snoring. Maybe one day Didila would be strong enough to take on the world with her. They could run this tavern with their eyes closed. Together, they'd have all the priests and merchants begging to dine here. And if her father ever came to Dilmun, he would be shocked at how well she'd survived, even without his prestigious name.

If Miu was going to get there though, she'd have to keep pushing Didila. "Stop whining. You have to try." She'd champion her no matter what. But before they could even take over Hashur's tavern, they had to figure out why Didila kept having stomach pains.

Where could she go? She had tried every medicine her mother had taught her. Then a thought came to her that made the hair stand up on the nape of her neck, and she tried not to tremble and wake Didila.

"I'll have to go see the asu."

chapter
fourteen

More than two hundred plants lined the shelves of the asu's tent. Another two hundred or more pots were stacked against the walls, leaving very little room to walk. Turtle shells were strewn across a low table in a corner that held dry snakeskin.

Miu shivered. "Heaven and earth! Snakes are everywhere in this dumb town." Didila squirmed a bit in her arms, and Miu bounced her in her arms, hoping the girl would stay sleeping.

A short table about three inches off the ground stood in the middle of the room. A turtle shell under it contained bitumen, the dark wax-like substance, layered with what looked like animal fat and plants from the wall. Miu was almost certain it was a concoction the asu had brewed for incense. The air was thick and caught in Miu's throat. She tried inhaling deeply to fill her lungs and noted smells of turpentine, honey, and herbs.

The smell reminded her of her mother's back room, which was full of medicine, much of which she had learned from *her* father, who was chosen as an asu. He had taught her mother to mix bouillon, fats, milk, honey, herbs, and especially animal products into something that carried the potential to heal.

In days long past, when the waters were separated from the dry land, Enki chose to pass down his knowledge and understanding to humans. Enki wanted humans to understand as he did regarding science and medicine, as if they would use it for good.

Miu had always considered humans with the power to hold this wisdom dumb on the god's behalf. Humans rarely used it to help each other, and instead their ideas were often used to hold power over each other, just as this asu did here in Dilmun. If an asu held the secrets to healing, then no one else could even guess how to please the gods for healing. This then left people desperate to do any ritual they requested.

When Miu was seven, her aunt stole a concoction for a wound she had gotten from a broken pottery shard. Common people were allowed to make healing ointments for outside wounds such as cuts and bruises because the cause was obvious. A scrape often didn't come from evil spirits, they came from just an ordinary day. A fall in the fields or a bite from an animal usually meant a person knew the reason for injury.

But if the cause of injury or pain in a family wasn't obvious, an asu would pass his duties onto an elder asu. Miu's mother often had to relinquish children and hurting mothers and fathers to these mystical men's hands. Children who, just like Didila, had done nothing wrong. This asu could seek the gods and then tell the family what the offense was. They'd tell their parents what demon brought disease or plague and then offer them hope if only they'd participate in a dreadful sacrifice and play hopeless guessing games, all without ever holding the asu accountable for losing the life of the child.

Miu jumped at any chance to prove the gods wrong or even question them, but holding Didila in her arms she found herself like many others, desperate to find the same medicine her mother would give her.

"I'm taking Didila to the asu tomorrow. She can't go on like this. I've tried every healing ointment and herb I know to do," Miu had whispered to Hashur last night after the girl had fallen asleep after another bout with stomach pain.

Didila squirmed with her eyes closed on her pallet while Miu brushed her sweaty hair away from her eyes.

"Do what you have to do." Hashur had waved dismissively. "I have patrons to attend."

Miu had wanted to strangle the woman, but at least she had gotten her permission to be here. Didila didn't concern Hashur enough to even cancel the meeting she had this morning. Miu expected just as much. If something needed to be taken care of, Miu would be the one to do so. She inhaled deeply and looked up from the girl she was holding.

"Greetings," said a man dressed in a purple-dyed tunic. Layers of beads hid the wrinkles in his neck that reminded Miu of the caves near Ur. His eyes were dark, radiating a knowledge that Miu feared. What had he done in his life that had given him the insight he would share with her? A single chill ran down her spine. He was barefoot, and she could feel a darkness clouding his presence.

"I'm here to get a mixture for this girl's stomach pain," Miu said. The last thing she wanted was for him to think she was here for incantations and sacrifices. She would be clear about her needs. "She hasn't been able to eat anything and continually vomits while holding her stomach."

"How long has she suffered from such pain?" His voice was thin yet pierced the dark air.

Didila shifted in Miu's arms. Miu sat her in a seat while still hovering over her. This man would not touch her.

"Three weeks. Last night she vomited blood, and she's refusing to eat."

"Three weeks." He paused and looked around his shop. "I believe we need to look into this a bit more before I prescribe a remedy." The asu walked over to her and placed his hands on the girl.

Miu leaned toward him, "Keep your hands away from her."

"We can't tell anything unless I feel what is going on."

"I'm watching you closely." Miu clenched her jaw while holding Didila's hand.

He stood up and folded his hands as if a decision had been made in his mind. "She's haunted by spirits in the underworld. Herbs may help the pain, but they won't stop spirits from returning. We must rid them or give them what they want."

What they want. Miu shuddered. He would not manipulate her.

"Look, this is how it's going to work. You can say whatever it is you need to say for the evil spirits to leave her alone, but you're also going to give me the mixture of poppy and mint. I'd do it myself, but my mother never taught me to cut the poppy so you can keep its medicine."

"You know medicine, my dear." He looked shocked but regained his composure. "I can do this, but her haunting will continue." He paused and stared at her with those petrifying eyes. "Until you allow me to speak to the gods on her behalf."

"Heaven and earth, just do it already," Miu said, annoyed, but looked away so he wouldn't see the trickle of fear rising in her.

The asu turned around, his slow movements reminding Miu of molasses pouring out of one of his clay pots.

"Lay her on the table. I will return in a moment."

Miu did as he said and laid Didila on the table in the middle of the room. The air was stagnant as she pulled her hair out of her face to cool her, never taking her eyes off the asu. He gathered some tools outside, which included a thin knife, a clay bowl, and what looked like a thin straw used to drink beer but cut in half long ways.

"My poppy pods are in the back," he said.

Miu took a step toward him, trying to decide if she should follow him and leave Didila or stay with the girl. She took a step backward and while wavering with her decision, he returned carrying the pod carefully in his bony hands. Hands that carried in them evil and good. Hands that brought healing, while also tottering between heaven and earth. His hands represented a darkness that Miu couldn't fully understand.

The asu grabbed some straw off a shelf and laid it in a bowl.

Next, he took the poppy pod and placed it on the thin straw he had cut in half. He made a careful and precise incision into the poppy pod. Immediately, Miu saw the cloudy, white liquid seep into the straw's opening. She watched with intensity how the scalpel did not go so far into the pod to puncture the seed inside. If the cut was too deep, the thin liquid could run out and drip to the ground before it was used. She was glad to see him use the straw method. She also observed how he didn't cut too shallow because then the pod itself would coagulate before he could harvest its liquid, one droplet at a time.

The slowly-dripped liquid flowed into the straw and then eventually into the bowl of mint before it became dark and sticky just like everything else in the place.

"It's a good time of day to harvest the pods. She will benefit from this," he said with confidence.

He repeated the straw method with two other poppy pods.

"Enough to take some home," Miu reassured herself.

He took another small straw and dipped the sticky mixture into a turtle shell. There he poured wine, saffron, cinnamon sticks, and cloves. He took the shell and placed it over the fire in the corner until it came to a simmer.

"This may cause hallucinations. You'll want to know what she sees in the spirit world and report back to me. These visions will give us insight into the suffering she's facing. Remember this, if she sees in her dream a dog, her illness will return. If she sees a gazelle, she will recover. And if she sees a wild pig, you will need to recite an incantation for her. We pray to the gods she will recover. Watch her closely."

"I'm taking her home. She won't see any of that." Miu bent down to pick Didila up.

"Also, wait a minute." He went to the back, darkest corner of the tent, and reached deep into a large clay pot. "Oh good, I'm not out."

He handed Miu a skull. She immediately pulled back in horror. Aside from not knowing how she could carry a skull while carrying Didila, she was horrified at where this skull came from. Who did it belong to? Why did he have an entire clay pot of similar items? She wanted to take it and throw it across the tent, but she noticed Didila had a warm smile spread across her face, and Miu paused. Forcing her feet to stay where they were she tried to hear what the asu was saying.

"She must sleep with this beside her. You must recognize we are dealing with evil spirits, because you seem set on dismissing the gods. If she has any chance of living, you should take me seriously, and the gods' blessing will follow. If you don't, you're going to lose her."

"Are you trying to play a game where you and the gods say whatever stupid thing comes to mind? Because I'm not participating in that. Give me the medicine we came for and we will be on our way."

"Wait."

The darkness in his voice held something evil, and Miu's feet couldn't move.

"She must sleep with this skull beside her bed for a week to exorcise the spirit. To ensure it's working, she must kiss and lick the skull seven times each night. If you choose not to tell her about this, then the spirits will haunt you next. Trust me, they won't be as nice to you."

Miu bolted forward, almost forgetting she was holding the child. She got so close to his face, she could smell his soured breath. Didila's mouth flinched, and she reached for her stomach. Angry and frustrated, Miu didn't know what else to do. She ripped the skull out of his hand and could feel herself about to crush the human skull between her fingers. Dipping her toes onto the ground of this evil, god-infested place, she reasoned with herself that he was the only person who could distribute medicine. She had to hold it together for Didila. She stormed out of the tent in a fury of anger.

Miu was not angry at the gods today, she was angry that she needed them. She was furious that even though she could build an empire for herself, escape her father's tactics, and make connections with men like Zu, there were still things out of her control. And that fact in and of itself weakened her.

"Before you get too far, you must pay for the services today." The asu raised his voice and stared at Miu with an alarming grin. Miu knew what men wanted with that look. She had seen it on her father's face and almost every man in Hashur's tavern. If she didn't bow to the gods, she definitely wouldn't to a man who represented them. She took the gold coins Hashur had given her this morning out of the pouch around her neck. She spit on them and threw them at the asu.

"The gods will hold you responsible for her spirit," he shouted.

Carrying Miu out of the tent, she whispered to her, "I've got you little one."

She would watch her hallucinations, but she'd also guard what she heard from the asu and others.

chapter
fifteen

Early mornings were the slowest time for Hashur, Alor, and Miu. The tavern didn't open until the sun was high in the sky, and the tavern girls were already set to work on their daily chores. Miu hadn't slept much the night before, keeping a close watch on Didila, but she still wanted to keep her promise to Hashur and Alor by meeting them for a mid-morning meeting. Miu suggested they take a walk outside the city to get some fresh air and perspective. She wanted to understand more about how they thought and what they wanted to do with the tavern.

"Wealth is hard to come by, but poverty is always at hand," was a saying she'd heard from her father many times. She knew Hashur craved wealth, but even more, she craved status in the community. Miu wanted to see what excited her and learn how she could one day take it from her. After watching her dismissive behavior toward Didila, Miu wanted to ruin Hashur and Alor. Today would be a good day to pull them closer to her.

The smell of sunflowers brightened everyone's mood. Alor trudged along, still hungover from the night before. His drinking had intensified, leaving his eyes and hands looking more yellow than Miu remembered.

Miu let her fingers run along the sunflower petals as if her

fingertips were tiptoeing across the field. She kept her eyes on Hashur, who kept her dark head held high. She clearly had an agenda on her mind. The rain had kept the path beneath their feet damp, but not enough to be sticky. Above their heads, the firm sky held some of the puffiest clouds Miu ever remembered seeing, promising more rain this afternoon. Miu wondered why Hashur was always concerned with beauty, prestige, and fear of falling behind. She hoped to find out some of it today.

"Thank you for allowing me to take such great care of Didila." Miu hoped to create a sense of trust.

"She's a good girl, Miu. She reminds me of my younger sister," Hashur pondered, half talking to Miu and half staring into the sky. "She brewed beer, you know?"

"You've never told me about her. What about Didila reminds you of her?" Miu questioned, hoping not to press too much too soon.

"Can we just sit here?" Alor pointed to a date tree as he shielded his eyes from the blazing sun. He grimaced and groaned in pain.

"Just sit down, Alor, and be quiet." Hashur barked. "And stop interrupting me."

Alor sat with a clunk while Hashur continued.

"Do you think he's drinking more?" Miu inquired.

"I don't want to talk about him. Back to my younger sister. She was a brilliant brewer. She taught me everything I know about brewing beer. Not many people want to be like their younger sister, and I'm much prettier than her, but she gave me the gifts of brewing the gods are still honored for."

She shifted her weight and winked at Miu. "My older brother, on the other hand, is handsome. The gods favored him with height and brawn. He could also play the flute in a way that made any woman swoon, especially my mother."

Hashur's eyes flinched for a moment, but Miu caught it. She was trying to prove herself as part of the family and compete on their terms. Hashur had enough beauty and intelligence to hold her own in Dilmun, but it seemed to Miu that Hashur never felt like she measured up to them.

"They sound lovely, Hashur," Miu said, hoping to see some of the competitiveness rise in her eyes.

"They're both lovely people and moved to Egypt about three years ago. That's when I knew it was time to start the tavern."

"Oh, so you couldn't run your tavern when they were in town?" Miu began walking toward the tree to take a respite from the sun as well.

Hashur followed, now deep in thought. "It was more about them and my parents. My mother made it impossible to see anyone else when she was around. My brother was the beautiful one, and my sister was the talented one. But then there was my father. He paraded my mother around banquets, hoping to catch the eye of the king. Her beauty far surpassed anyone in the courts of Dilmun. Her dark, slightly wavy hair caught the eye of men and women alike," Hashur said, almost pained.

"It sounds like you follow closely in her footsteps." Miu hoped Hashur would continue talking.

"It is much like myself in the tavern," she boasted. "Men flock to her and me like a moth to a flame. She had a charming way about her when she'd walk into a room. I think it was the slight smile painted on her face that allured even the most loyal of men into her company."

"You said your father took her to these festivals. What was he like?" Miu asked.

"Let's walk." Hashur bit her lip. She didn't seem to ever be able to sit still.

Miu didn't mind though. Sitting made her mind wander, and she wanted Hashur to stay focused.

"Sure, was your father handsome as well?" she prodded harder.

"Yes, and tall like my brother. He was very involved in Dilmun before he died. He would protest in the court of the king the injustice he saw happening in the back streets of Dilmun. He fought for peace in the city instead of war. The poor and rich esteemed him the same." Hashur held her chest high. "Everyone admired his charm and ability to shine joy into the dimming light of Dilmun."

Miu realized Hashur was trying to outproduce and outshine her family, if only for the slightest compliment. The thing was, compliments only lingered for a moment, then they were off like a feather floating in the wind. Words were empty, and Hashur and Miu both knew it.

"Are you proud of what you've built in Dilmun to the gods?" Miu asked. "You should be. You've worked hard."

For the first time since Miu knew Hashur, she wouldn't make eye contact. "Sure," Hashur said with an uncomfortable laugh.

"When I was thirteen, there was a girl who taunted me every time she went to the well to draw water. Miu, she had some of the best pearls Dilmun could offer, and her tunics were always the prettiest in town. Because my father spent his money to help the poor, my siblings and I often went without anything that my father called frivolous. But going without these finer things also meant going without friends." She paused. "And going without admiration."

A lizard ran across Miu's foot, and she squealed. Both women laughed, and they turned to see Alor slumped over snoring.

Hashur rolled her eyes and continued. "So, I developed a plan. I would work hard at home doing some of my siblings' chores so they'd give me some of their money. I then gathered four of the most popular girls together that played by the well. I told them, 'Whenever "pearly girl" walks by, say something nice about me. Say you like my tunic or my hair. My hair is nicer than hers anyway.'"

Miu laughed silently to herself. How insecure could she be? She could see that Hashur's insecurity would be her downfall and as she continued, Miu herself began crafting her own plan. "What happened?" Miu feigned interest.

"Well, the girls did as they promised, but the compliments

weren't the real goal," Hashur said, quick to avoid the pitying look Miu was giving her. "It wasn't money wasted. It was a stepping stone toward being in that group of girls. They were the same group of girls that helped me purchase this tavern."

"How did you end up marrying Alor?" Miu was very curious now. If a woman purchased a tavern, then why did she have to marry?

"My father gave me in marriage to Alor in hopes together we could fight for a better cause in Dilmun. I just saw a faster route than sitting with the poor and holding their hands. Poverty is no noble cause, Miu. Faster and better is the route to money. The tavern was the best way, a place where women could own a business in the name of the gods."

Miu reached over to Alor and grabbed the cow skin he carried full of beer. She took a deep chug and passed it to Hashur. The silence was refreshing before the night came with its never-ending requests from patrons and waitresses alike. They sat, both thinking, but it was Hashur who broke the silence.

"I love the fancy clothes and jewelry that come with owning a tavern that's growing in prominence, but I think there's more. There's always more to have, Miu. It just depends on what you're willing to do to get there." A wicked grin formed across her mouth. "I have an idea. It's borderline heretical, but it could work," she whispered.

Miu recognized that look from her father. How she responded to whatever was about to come out of her mouth would be her rise or her downfall. Hashur reminded Miu of a small child when she didn't get her way, throwing herself on the floor crying or stomping her feet. A child willing to say or do anything to get what she wanted.

"I'm willing to help you as much as you need." Miu knew she would twist it to her own benefit.

"We could poison the beer that's made in the temple."

Miu bolted up from her sitting position. "What?" Her heart pounded in her throat.

"Oh, quiet down. Hear me out. It's up to us to secure Dilmun. Not the priests, not the soldiers, and not the king. It's us, Miu."

Miu was grateful to hear her speak as if they were on the same team. It would help her later as she grappled with her own plan.

Hashur continued, "Even if that means selling our souls to do so. The priests make more money than they need to keep that temple running, and if their beer is infected, people will say the gods are against them. Their beer isn't strong enough to allow for hallucinations and encounters with the divine as ours does. We're already a step ahead of others, Miu. It's time for us to come into our roles in Dilmun. We may never fully know and understand the gods, nor do they want to be understood, but they do want us to create order here in Dilmun. And I believe that order is for us to be at the top."

Miu just stared at her. Poison. The downfall of the temple's brewery. It made Miu shudder. But it also could be possible for Miu to rid control of Hashur, Alor, and the gods in one fell swoop.

"Those brewers were put in place by the gods." Miu tried to push back a little.

"Those brewers are causing more chaos than order, Miu, and you know it. They're not brewing the thickest, most potent beer. They're doing this town a disservice. The gods, the priests, and the people of Dilmun deserve the best. It's up to us to be the only tavern in town. If we don't win, we lose, Miu. I refuse to lose."

THAT NIGHT, while Alor and Hashur were arguing, Miu was up again with Didila all night wishing the gods weren't as vengeful as they had shown themselves to be. If they'd show their faces, let themselves be known, then she could fight them and question them. They were always shifting, and humans were always guessing. One day they were on her side and the next they'd destroy a little girl like Didila.

The people in Dilmun craved order; to them, it meant their society was the highest, best, and favored by the gods. Order meant less war and more prosperity. Order meant roads were built that led to the temple for ease of worship, gardens that produced food in abundance, and children playing in the street without fear of war. Order was the highest form of success.

Miu had passed an angry man in the street yesterday. With his fist raised toward the sky and waters above, he shouted, "We want order!"

Miu had never related so much to another human in her life. Her anger mirrored his, and emotion welled up inside until she had grabbed his fist in her own and said, "You have to create order yourself. Stop waiting for the gods to do it for you!" Furious, she'd stormed off.

There was no one looking out for her. People had to create their own order. It's why her defiance toward the gods was growing. If they wanted order, they'd create order. It was obvious they didn't. What would it look like if the gods fought for and protected the very humans they made? Nostrils flaring, Miu despised how quickly she got angry. Weren't peace and justice worth fighting for? Not power and dominion.

Trying to fall back asleep, Miu had to get up to relieve herself. Passing Hashur and Alor's room, she overheard the two of them whispering. She leaned in, careful to not make a sound. They were discussing the temple tavern and the poison. Excitement crept into Miu's bones. Hashur had told Alor. Telling that idiot may just be the thing to leak the plan. Maybe Miu could prove their attempt together to undermine the priests.

Satisfied, Miu continued outside to find a place to go to the bathroom, then tripped over a clay jar Tiame left in the hall. "Stupid girl!" she shouted.

Hashur threw back the curtain to find Miu holding her toe

and bouncing up and down. "Oh, good, it's only you. I was just telling—"

"You're too loud when you speak, Hashur. Be quiet. We can hear you a mile away keeping us awake."

Alor stumbled out of the tent, his eyebrows drawing together. Hashur, not wanting anyone else to wake up, motioned for Miu to come into their room to finish the conversation.

"Alor, I shared this with Miu earlier today."

"She's not trustworthy."

Something flashed in Hashur's eyes. Was that doubt? She had shared everything openly with Miu earlier, so why would she trust this drunk over her? Miu needed some leverage.

"You've trusted me to handle the healing of your daughter. Do you even know what the asu prescribed? It's causing her nightmares, and she's wrestling with demons. We may lose her, and it would be on your shoulders, not mine." Miu stared them both straight in the eyes.

Hashur's head jerked back at Miu's abruptness. "You're under my care, Miu. Don't pretend to know what the gods are doing. They don't want you to know what they're doing, but we must prove ourselves to them," Hashur said, calming down.

Miu noticed blood dripping from her toe and tried to wipe it away.

"I'm not the gods, and I don't pretend to appease them, Hashur. But I am all for taking down another tavern. I want everyone to know I will not be controlled or manipulated, as I'm sure you understand. You want the praise of people like Zu, and you need me for that. You want the pearls of eternal life, and I can get those for your neck only. You want a tavern where gods and humans coexist together as they once did in Dilmun in ages past. I can get you all that, Hashur. But you have to trust me. You have to give me more control of the tavern."

Alor sat down and rolled over away from the quarreling women, trying to go back to sleep. Hashur shifted on her mat, took a deep breath, and squared her shoulders. It was late, and

Miu could tell she was tiring, but her desire to be the most admired in all of Dilmun, from the lowest shepherd to the greatest king, enticed her to continue to listen to Miu.

"Are you going to trust me, Hashur? We have the same goal, even if we disagree on the gods' abilities and purposes."

Hashur crossed her arms in hesitation. Miu waited. She'd wait all night for an answer.

Something caught Hashur's eye, and she looked past Miu.

The curtain opened fully. It was Tiame.

"What do you want, girl?" Hashur barked.

"Didila is vomiting again," Tiame whispered, her head bowed.

"I'm coming," Miu said.

But she would not leave until Hashur gave her an answer. She turned to face her again, tapping her foot.

"You've got a deal, Miu. But we have to keep this a secret. If someone finds out about the poison, it will be us, not them, that descends into the watery chaos of the underworld."

Miu rolled her eyes. This again. "No one will control me, Hashur. My father couldn't. The gods haven't. The priests of Dilmun won't." She turned and raced to check on Didila.

It was just a matter of time before Miu controlled the tavern.

chapter
sixteen

Taku's stomach sank, his knees clasped tightly together. The clay tablets felt like he was carrying The Tablet of Destinies in his palms. The words on this tablet didn't carry the future of humanity; instead, they carried his name, Taku. And according to this tablet, his future didn't look promising. The first time he'd read the words on this tablet, his instinct had been to shift the blame. It wasn't his fault anyway. He looked down to read them once more. Tracing the etchings, he felt the anger embedded deep within the complaint.

"I ordered a shipment of fine-grade copper for our chisel-and-knife set in Ur. We received your shipment within the allotted time, but it was subpar quality. I am returning all the copper you sent, with the correction needed. Send me the correct shipment. I will not be paying for shipping. Also, I trust you will credit my account for the previous shipping costs. I expect better from Zaidu's men."

Even after Zaidu had shown the complaint to Taku, Zaidu said it wasn't a big deal.

"It's going to be fine, Taku. These things happen. We have money set aside for accidents," he assured him.

Of course, Zaidu had money set aside. *This is why I never lead anything. I mess up things for everyone else.* He wasn't pouting, he was stating a fact. Things worked best if he never took responsibility for things he couldn't control.

The complaint on the tablet was a weight he couldn't carry. Zaidu had trusted him, and he had let him down. Maybe he should have handled it himself, but that wouldn't have been honest. Maybe he could go visit Miu once he was back in Dilmun.

That thought alone shocked him more than the others. Why did that woman come to mind when it felt like the mountains were quaking and the world would fall into the sea? Why her? Something about her held a grip on his life. She didn't quake with fear at small things like complaints. Instead, she saw life and tried to tame it, bend it to her will, like the bulls that now wandered the fields outside Ur and Dilmun.

His voice didn't matter much, but when he did use it, it seemed to break apart families, friends, and coworkers. Zaidu tried to show him this wasn't always true, but Taku didn't believe him.

Complaints to Taku felt like a sheep that needed shearing, weighty and hard to move beneath them. Maybe he should delegate the task of driving the boat and checking the shipments.

"Time to go," shouted a sailor from the docks, startling Taku out of his thoughts. He stepped onto the boat.

Together, the men loaded the large bags of wool heading back to Dilmun. It was just as Taku had gotten comfortable with taking shipments from Dilmun to Ur that Zaidu now had shipments going back and forth. This added to the sheer number of trips each month, requiring Zaidu and Taku to sometimes take separate boats.

The work was tiring, but Taku didn't mind it. He just didn't like the disruption from the routine. He liked knowing what time he'd wake up and what time he'd ship out. The constant change in shipments tired him more than the work itself.

Today, more than normal, he had a lot on his mind. He smiled to himself. *Maybe I think too much.*

"Time to pull out," he said.

THE PATH to Zu's house was crowded and well developed, considering he lived near the outside of town. Miu and Taku walked together, each listening to the sound of their feet on the packed dry earth beneath them. Expectations were high as they were excited to see the new barley shipment from Ur.

The air was crisp, and Taku filled his lungs with the cooler air. The conflict with the copper merchant from earlier this morning had unsettled him, and his legs felt as shaky as a rattlesnake's tail. The merchant had said he'd been cheated out of time, but Taku had the records to prove his destination was honest. He wished he'd never told Miu about the grumpy customer; he should have kept it to himself because once she heard, she forced him to face the man head-on. It wasn't as bad as he expected, but the potential loss of a customer, mean or not, weighed heavily on him.

"Shake it off, Taku. Move on already. The guy made a mistake, and he corrected it," Miu said, matter of fact. "Zu hates a foul mood, and we need him to be as happy as possible. This new barley is our opportunity to show Dilmun that we have new ways of making a name for the city, letting the gods see us. Once the temple tavern is poisoned and we have this new beer idea created, our growth will be unstoppable. Everyone will trust us. "

"The less I know the better, Miu."

She rolled her eyes. "If we don't get this work with Zu, we won't have a way to talk to the priests about the opportunity of presenting the gods with options. The priests are always looking for ways to expand."

"You don't even care about the gods," Taku replied.

"You're right, but I do care about being able to control the beer trade here in Dilmun," she said in a wry tone.

Miu shifted the basket she carried from one hip to the other. Why hadn't Taku noticed the basket she was carrying before? He had been so caught up in his own thoughts, like usual, he didn't pay attention to details.

"What's in there?" He tried to change the subject.

"The barley." She gave him that all too common look that implied he was stupid for even asking.

"Why didn't you bring enough for him to taste? There's probably enough in there for one drink, Miu."

"This is the new technique, my own idea. It's what I'll call, 'traveling beer.' A sailor or traveler can carry these tiny loaves of barley that have been baked by the sun once." She pulled back a thin cloth covering the basket.

Taku peered in to touch the loaves, almost as if they would sting him.

She shoved the basket toward him. "Boo!"

He startled, and she belly laughed, holding her sides. He was too easy, he knew it.

As always, he waited for her to calm down until he could speak. She annoyed him to no end, and yet she was smart. Her curiosity and ability to fly through the world kept Taku feeling invincible, like he could soar through any of life's challenges.

"Are you done?" he teased. "How do tiny loaves of barley like this turn into traveling beer?" he smiled as he rolled them around in his hands, impressed by her ingenuity.

"When a person travels across sea or land, they can take these smaller loaves. All you do is place one in your pitcher and add the sweet water from a local well into it. It takes a bit of time, but you can watch the beer begin to form. The barley floats to the top and the sweet beer is below. We've started with basic flavors, but we can branch into mixing more flavors as things grow. Surprise! Traveling sweet beer."

Taku was impressed. He stood back and crossed his arms. A smile crept across his face. "I've seen a lot of new inventions in Ur, but I can't imagine any that would work as well as something catering to people's love of beer." The temple for Ninkasi, the beer goddess in Ur, was one of the most beautiful he'd ever seen. No matter where he traveled, people loved beer. The plan was solid, and he was excited to watch Miu make it happen, if for nothing more than watching her smile.

Zu burst out of his front door, his arms spread wide. "Welcome! So glad you both could come."

Miu gave Taku a side glance, and they headed toward Zu's welcome arms. Entering through the front gate, Zu reached toward Taku, picked him up, and spun him around. He would have done the same to Miu, but she moved her basket of dried barley directly in front of her, holding her boundary firm.

Zu smiled with enthusiasm as he peered into her basket and laughed. "I thought you brought new beer to try, Miu. Do you think beer is a joke? You can be killed bringing lousy beer into the temple." He slapped her on the back, laughed like a hyena, then motioned for them to enter the house. Knowing Zu was joking, Taku still took a deep breath. Big personalities like Zu made Taku question if he should have even come along.

Inside, the windows in the house were open, and the brisk, salty air blew through. It was just enough to make the women's tunics blow a little more than Taku was comfortable with, while at the same time exciting Zu to shout even louder.

"Bring the breakfast!"

Taku wanted to leave. He felt like every movement and shout was draining the life out of him. All the laughter and joking made him want to go hide in the backyard until the meeting was over. But he tried to settle in and listen to Zu tell stories. The smallest fly on a windowsill made him tell a long-winded story about his grandmother, or another time it was about a new merchant connection across the world that had him laughing until he fell out of his seat. Beer or no beer, Zu was the entertainment.

The smells of breakfast wafted through the main living area, and Taku realized maybe all his jitters were just because he was hungry. His stomach growled, and he reached to touch it, hoping no one noticed.

He looked around the table while the girls brought in the feast:

melons with fresh mint sprinkled on top and figs dripping in honey. Another girl, with eyes so dark Taku's palms got sweaty, brought in porridge. It was probably made with barley, Taku told himself, trying to keep his mind on the food. Behind the girl with the porridge came a woman carrying another tray, this one lined in perfect circles with cheeses. He could feel drool puddling in the corners of his mouth.

"Where's the girl that follows you, Miu?" Zu asked, startling Taku from his thoughts.

"She's been sick, Zu. We've seen the asu and are waiting to see what happens."

"Keep an eye on her," he said flippantly, clearly not wanting to be distracted by sickness. "Now, show me what you have, Miu." Zu plopped himself down in his large, ornate chair.

Taku had never seen anything quite like it; the entire chair was covered in gold, and each arm held carvings of bulls wrapped in snakes, Dilmun's famous animals. The legs looked like tree trunks from Jordan. Taku couldn't even imagine the cost it would take for a blacksmith to do this kind of work.

Miu stood up, dismissing the food so she could focus. "This is going to revolutionize Dilmun, Ur, and to the edges of the earth. I brought this to only you, Zu, because I knew you'd have the stamina and excitement to help us get this idea to the head priest of Dilmun's temple," she said, stroking his ego. "Zu, you're capable of making connections anywhere."

Taku tried not to roll his eyes, but Zu stuck his chest out a bit. Taku almost giggled, realizing he could barely tell because the man's large stomach was in the way.

One of the girls caught Taku's eye again, but he looked away so as not to draw attention to himself. Zu had gained a bit more weight since the last time Taku or Miu had seen him. It was probably the power and prestige of money that had given him the opportunity for overindulgence in food, luxury, and travel.

"Bring me more food!" he shouted and startled Taku.

Laughing again, Miu ignored him and kept pushing forward with her presentation. She moved and stood directly in front of

Zu, ensuring he was paying attention. She took the cloth off her basket and began to walk him through the new process with precision. She moved with grace and enthusiasm, because if she didn't, Zu was out.

"Imagine being able to carry beer across the seas. Imagine how the gods will bless us if we do this for them." She leaned down and placed a straw on Zu's lap making direct eye contact. "Zu, the gods will bless you abundantly if you're involved."

"What do you think, Taku?" he asked, catching him off guard.

The women brought in trays of salted fish, disrupting Taku's thoughts even more. The copper merchant mix-up this morning still had him on edge, and he was hesitant to speak his opinion after that. Everything was rolling around in his mind. What if Miu's idea didn't work? He didn't want to be responsible. But Miu was counting on him to get this out there. She was hoping to overtake the taverns in Dilmun, and he believed she could do it.

A woman walked slowly between Taku and Zu, bent down, and offered Taku a warm bowl of porridge sprinkled with pomegranates. Taku reached for the bowl, feeling the warmth radiate through his fingers. It was just the courage he needed.

"Miu has put work into this. She's done the hard thinking and creating to make sure these loaves are stable and consistent. I think you should watch it work yourself. Try it with this meal."

Taku's attempt to take himself out of the decision-making process was best. Let Zu decide after tasting and watching the process. He probably knew beer better anyway.

"Get me a pot and some sweet water, Zu," Miu directed.

He waved his hand toward a servant woman who seemed to be waiting to do whatever he asked. She put her tray of food down on the main table and hurried out of the room. She came back in a rush and placed the pot and sweet water from the well in front of Miu, interested in what was about to happen.

Miu walked Zu through the entire process, but they all knew it came down to tasting. She had brought the fig-flavored beer today, knowing it was the most unique they'd created so far.

With a steady hand, she handed Zu a straw, and he leaned over to take a deep drink. She waited for the sticky substance from the top to glide across his tongue, then a smile crept across his face as a sweeter-than-normal barley flavor came next. His eyes got as big as the moon, and he dropped the straw into the pot in shock.

Taku waited in horror. What if he didn't like it? What would happen to Miu then?

Zu smacked his leg as if he were stunned. "Miu, I've never tasted anything like it. I could drink this whole pot. It tastes like the beer I drink at the taverns, only ..."

"Only what, Zu?" she demanded.

"Only better." He beamed.

"Zu, if you want to see a change in Dilmun, you have to create it yourself. If you want power, you have to take it. You believe the gods give us the knowledge to make beer, and that may be so, but it's humans, like you and like me, who have the ability and creativity to take control of the beer itself." She paused. Taku could tell she was trying to end this speech without giving away her ultimate plan. "Zu, if we work together, we can have every luxury the world has to offer, but we have to start with the temple and priests in Dilmun."

She had him. The look of pleasure on his face was just enough excitement to get Zu riled up. The only problem was that she'd have to keep him excited until they could get their beer into the temple. She made eye contact with Taku, and he hoped they were thinking the same thing.

For once Taku spoke up, shocking both Zu and Miu. "Zu, can you help get this into the temple?"

Instead of laughing, Zu made eye contact with Taku and said with sincerity, "I'm in this no matter what."

For the first time since coming to Dilmun, Taku noticed Miu's body relax a little. All the pieces of the foundation she had been laying were coming together. The temple, Hashur, a life for Didila. It all was beginning to make sense. Taku wished he could relax a little. Why had he spoken up? What happened to him?

What caused him to be so bold? Maybe there was some underlying motivation in him somewhere.

They finished up their visit with Zu, ensuring they would meet again to set up plans to distribute these barley loaves to the tavern. Taku noticed how calm Miu was for the first time since knowing her. As they walked the dirt path back to Hashur's tavern, Taku couldn't hold his questions in any longer.

"What is it you really want, Miu?"

"Freedom." She smiled as if that explained it.

"Freedom from what?"

"Taku, since being in Dilmun, this is the first time I feel secure. Since the day I left Ur, I have had to fight for control of my own life and freedom from my father and his life. I want freedom from the gods, freedom from my father, and freedom from the priests' evil lifestyle." Sighing, she continued. "I have to fight to stay in control, Taku. If not, he can come back to control me. Time is running out before he makes his way to Dilmun one day. But before that happens, I need my own life and rules established so he can't take anything away from me."

Taku knew there was more to her story, but she shifted that basket again, and he knew she'd said all she wanted to say today.

"Let's celebrate." He picked up his speed toward home.

Maybe one day she'd trust him enough to tell her everything that had happened to her. Until then, they had a job to do together: get Hashur to spoil her own tavern by spoiling the temple tavern.

chapter
seventeen

Exhaustion lay like a wet blanket on Miu's shoulders. She still went about her work with fervor and intensity, but lately everyone avoided her because of her violent outbursts. Her pursuit of exposing an entire temple of gods and goddesses was supposed to feel freeing. It meant she could prove to those around her that they could control the gods, and prove the gods' need for humans.

Didila also weighed heavy on her shoulders. The girl should have been better by now, and if the gods cared at all about their precious beer, temple, and priests, Miu thought they would have healed her by now. She was a child, for heaven's sake. She wasn't caught up in the power struggle of what others wanted in Dilmun.

Miu felt like she was the only one with enough thinking ability to make anything productive happen, especially in the tavern; it was as if she herself were the pillars holding up the earth. Sometimes she didn't mind, but in the last few weeks, it was beginning to feel like too much to carry. She felt like she might give in and ask the gods for help.

Didila was draining her resolve to end the temple's tavern and gain her own control. She lay awake at night wondering if it was worth it. Maybe Taku could take her and Didila away to another city he had ventured to see. One that was smaller, one the gods wouldn't be concerned about controlling, one without a temple.

Dilmun was where the world had been created anyway, through chaos and war. Gods ripped each other to pieces to stake a claim here, a land of beauty, pearls, and commodities to fill their appetites. Beating the gods at their own game was doable, but at what risk to Didila?

"Miu, are we doing dates or fig barley this batch?"

Miu's thoughts were interrupted again. She gripped her fists in an attempt not to throw or punch something. "Fig!" she shouted, exasperated.

The woman scurried away, and Miu rolled her eyes. "If people would just pay attention when they were told the first time," she yelled over her shoulder. "Then they wouldn't get yelled at!"

Miu never had a hard time knowing what to do next, but these women always needed someone telling them every step of the way. They feared her and their gods, which made them second-guess everything. She could hear them behind the drape that separated her room from the pots of barley they were mixing.

"Did you see Bo leave town today with his sheep? His muscles have gotten much bigger since he's been tending sheep with his uncle." Tiame, the maid, giggled.

"Did you hear he killed a lion?" another girl said in a high-pitched squeal.

Miu rolled her eyes. "Get back to work!" She opened the curtain just a bit. Enough for them to see her face and that she meant business.

Why did she always have to be the bad guy? Sighing, she picked up a handful of beer straws and stacked them in a round pottery container. She noticed calluses were forming in the outer parts of her forefingers and the base of all of her fingers. Maybe the same had happened inwardly.

Since childhood, she had always worked hard, but in the past, she cared about those around her more. When she lived at home, she cared about her father, even as tough as he was with her. She respected her mother. She could laugh with her sister. She knew what customers wanted, needed, and she worked hard to make their requests known to her father.

But when was the last time she laughed with genuine interest at something? She loved her brother, but his memory was too much to bear. She started to walk out of the tent before someone saw the tears in her eyes, but Didila's coughing stopped her.

Another thing. Another need. She inhaled deeply before going in to check on her.

She had been doing what the asu had asked. It wasn't Miu's belief in the gods that should heal Didila. It should be doing what the asu asked of her that appeased them, right? That's what the asu had said in his creepy, brittle voice. She shuddered every time she thought of him. A god in the form of his priest. He was meant to give answers and insight to men on behalf of what the gods wanted from humans. Guessing what the gods wanted and trying to be on the religious good side of them seemed more chaotic than just living by her own rules.

Enough arguing. She bent down and brushed the girl's hair out of her eyes. "Sweet girl, what's wrong? Can I get you something?"

Her breathing was better this week. Didila couldn't understand what was happening to her. She was too young to know she was a pawn between the priest and the gods. She should be skipping through the sunflowers where Miu had run into her. She should be playing in the streets with her friends. She should have a mother who cared whether she lived or died.

Anger rose in Miu's chest, and she gripped her own tunic so she wouldn't throw something across the room and frighten the girl more.

Miu sat and placed Didila's head in her lap. She reached for the bowl of broth that was placed next to Didila's wooden nightstand, next to her new pallet. Miu had created a special bed with sheep's wool and feathers together that was more comfortable. It gave Didila some rest from this thief of a disease eating away at her life.

Miu knew in her gut that praying to these gods was futile. She couldn't stomach it, but this frail little one's eyes were the only thing that made Miu second guess if her fight was worth it. She knew the ones she had been taught about weren't worth worshipping or sacrificing her hard-earned food and time to.

Could there be a god out there she hadn't heard about? One that was kind, one that saw her and Didila's pain? She shoved that thought away. Sometimes though, Didila's eyes caused Miu to want to say a prayer to a god she'd never heard of before.

Miu remembered her own eyes looking at her father like this. They'd sat out under the stars together one night, myriad wildflowers surrounding them. Some tickled her bare feet while others blew in the slight breeze, creating an enchanting aroma. She had dreamed of being like one of these wildflowers then. Free in their beauty and growing wherever they pleased.

Above them danced a night sky so vast and dark that it felt as if it would swallow them whole. She'd squirmed with delight seeing the sky above them and the wildflowers beneath their feet. She felt so small. But at that moment, her father's arms helped her feel grounded. She looked up at him with childlike eyes, eyes like Didila's now, but boldness in her voice of a maturing woman her father had come to respect.

"If the gods crave order, why do they create chaos, Papa? If they want us to create cities and irrigation and medicine to help our fellow humans, then why do they create pain and war among us?"

Her father had no answer. A lump in his throat moved up and down, and his eyes moved away from hers. He got up, unable to sit without answers, and led her back toward Ur's city gates.

She had perplexed him, but Miu had never forgotten that question. There had to be a god out there somewhere who wanted real order and peace. Was he too fearful to show his face among Ur's dreadful gods?

"I want to sit up," Didila whispered. "Can we sit in the sunshine?"

Miu's eyes widened. Did she hear her correctly? Her heart raced, and she grasped her chest to calm it. Didila hadn't sat up in two weeks. Of course, she could enjoy the sunshine.

She supported the girl's back and slowly pushed her to a sitting position. Nothing in Miu's world had ever made her as tender as she was with this little girl. Even with her siblings, she would push them to be better, be stronger, and although she often pushed Didila to do the same, Miu saw a gentler side of herself.

"How's that?" She checked to make sure Didila wasn't in pain.

Didila nodded in a slow movement. "Can I have more broth?"

As she tended to Didila, hope rose in her. If she could only get Didila better, then Miu would really be free to make her own rules. She wouldn't have to abide by the asu or anyone else.

Should she put things into place sooner to poison the tavern? No more Hashur or Alor. No more father threatening her in her thoughts. She'd conquer the snake's plans for her. She'd be in charge. No one telling her what to do. She'd be like the wildflowers her father had wandered through with her. People didn't force wildflowers to grow where they wanted. The secret of the wildflowers was they grew wherever they wanted, never to be domesticated by humans. That's what Miu wanted. Beauty and freedom uncontrolled.

As soon as Didila was done drinking the broth, Miu called in Tiame and asked her to sit with Didila for a bit before carrying her to sit in some sunshine.

"No funny business! No talking about boys. You sit here with her. If I'm gone and something happens to her, you will regret it."

By now Tiame understood Miu's direct and often rude comments, but she also understood she didn't want to find out if her words were a threat or just words.

"I'll be back before the tavern's evening rush." Miu was satisfied with the fear she'd instilled in Tiame as she stepped out of the tent.

She went to see if Taku was still in town. With Didila possibly feeling better, she needed to know if he'd heard anything about Hashur's plan in town. It still shocked her that Taku was the first person she wanted to tell when something good happened, but she pushed that aside and went to look for him anyway.

MIU STUMBLED upon Taku relaxing in a hammock between two trees by the sea. She could always find him near the chaos waters, something she didn't understand. What she found chaotic and dreadful, he found peaceful. Another infuriating behavior. She walked toward him with purpose.

Then she paused when she saw him up close. How could he radiate so much peace while she lacked it in equal amounts? She hated that he never showed his frustrations. Did he even have any? How could he not be frustrated living in Dilmun, Ur, or anywhere else for that matter? She shoved her confusion about him down further and plowed into his peace.

"Good afternoon!" she said unapologetically.

He bolted out of his serene space and almost fell out of his hammock. Miu laughed so hard, she bent over and held her stomach. He stood and wiped the sand from his tunic, dusting his hands together with a clapping motion.

"Leave it to you to make me fall out of a hammock and then laugh," Taku joked.

At least he wasn't sensitive. "I'm happy you're here," she exclaimed before suddenly stopping, surprised she had started the conversation that way.

"Leave it up to you to say what you're thinking," he teased her. Was he trying to get one over on her? She watched a grin spread across his face. Why did he fluster her so much?

"Be quiet!" Miu rolled her eyes. "I had a few things I needed to tell you about the tavern and Didila."

"Then tell me so I can get back to the hammock."

"You're full of yourself today, aren't you?" she teased, placing both hands on her hips.

"No, I'm just enjoying how annoyed you're getting." His eyes lit up and his face flushed a little as he teased her.

"The tavern project needs to happen sooner rather than later. No more dawdling around in hammocks. Are you still in this, Taku? We can't let the people of Dilmun throw their lives to gods that don't care for them. Just take a walk to the temple. All the snakes that have been buried in worship create mounds of burial sites. It's disgusting. A snake may represent eternal life here, but a snake does not give eternal life. And I need to know if you've heard anything of Hashur's plan," she rambled on.

"Slow down, Miu. I am having a hard time believing anything the priests say either. However, I am uncertain that poisoning the tavern in the temple is a reliable way to gain trust and improve Dilmun."

She paused. She hated it when he had comments that halted her from fixing things. "I don't need to be in charge of Dilmun, Taku. I just need Dilmun to not be so gullible. It makes us weak. And I refuse to be seen as weak. Stories are being told across the waters that Ur and Uruk are building armies. They like what we have here in Dilmun. They like our pearls, our lapis lazuli, and our copper. They want our beauty to be their own." She sighed, clenching her jaw. "And just like the gods take what they want when they want it, so do other cities. Taku, we can't just stand by and let people believe these gods will protect them when it comes time."

Taku paused.

Miu tapped her toes and fidgeted. She wanted an immediate answer, but that wasn't how Taku helped. He always needed time to think.

"We don't have time to sit around and wait, Taku."

"I'm just trying to see where we can bring Dilmun together for Ur, instead of creating more confusion. I haven't told anyone this."

Taku's eyebrows went up as he covered his mouth.

"Oh, spit it out, Taku. For once just say what you're thinking."

"I keep hearing voices."

Miu stopped tapping and fidgeting and stared him straight in the eyes. "What? Are you going crazy too?" she snapped.

"I knew if I told you this that you'd call me crazy. But I had to risk telling someone." He hung his head rubbing the back of his neck.

"You're not crazy, but what you're saying is crazy." She reached out to touch his shoulder.

"I thought telling you might help you make a better decision about supporting Hashur. I don't know if hearing voices is even the right way to phrase it. But I don't fully believe in the gods' power or their ability to even sustain the world they created." He took a deep breath and continued, picking at his fingernails. "Remember the day at the temple? The day we first landed here in Dilmun and you left?"

Miu didn't want to remember that day. Every time she recalled that day her heart raced, and she wanted to throw something. She wouldn't let Taku know how much anger that day stirred up for her, or how embarrassing it was for her to run away. "Yes, I remember." She was determined to give him only short answers.

"That day, after you left, I heard the words 'keep looking.' And since that day, whenever I slow down between the never-ending travel from Ur to here and back or Zu's relentless ideas of new ventures or your drama—" he winked "—I hear 'keep looking.' But it's always in context with my thoughts around the gods."

She felt all the color drained out of her face. She thought a few times about there being a god that no one had taught her about.

She could never reconcile the world's balance of order and chaos without imagining something else was there. She just refused to believe it herself.

She swallowed hard, appreciating that Taku noticed but didn't ask her anything. Unlike Miu, he could let someone sit while they processed something.

"What do you think that means?" She looked out toward the chaos waters that lapped at her toes.

She didn't yell at him or storm off. That was progress for her.

Taku's shoulders relaxed. "Look at you asking questions!"

Was he encouraging her? She was trying to give a little.

"I've sat with this for months, and I think maybe there's a god we haven't heard of before." He admitted.

Miu's mind flooded with thoughts of her father and the wildflowers tumbling down on her. The weight of what was happening in Dilmun and her father's potential return to take her back to Ur all felt like a distant problem. It seemed insignificant compared to the possibility of a god that cared.

In Miu's typical way, those clear thoughts were muddled with angry demands, and the question she had once asked her father came flooding out of her mouth.

"If there's another god out there, then why doesn't he show himself? If there's another god out there, then he's too weak to defeat these worthless gods who create chaos instead of order. If there's another god out there, why is Didila still sick?" She was nearly yelling now, and her breathing had gotten heavier.

Taku stepped forward and gently leaned toward her, daring to touch her shoulder. "Miu, that's what I keep wondering. But the voice doesn't go away. And you just said Didila is beginning to gain strength."

Miu's racing thoughts stopped. "If that's the case, maybe that other god needs help getting rid of the temple's tavern. Maybe that's what we're here for. Destroy that, then we might get to see him?"

Taku wasn't so sure. "I'm not saying we shouldn't keep

pursuing that, but I am saying there has to be something else going on. For once in your life, will you take a few days to think through if we should support Hashur in this?"

Miu knew he was right. She was more confused than ever. Anger was her first reaction, but somehow Taku knew how to calm that in her. She promised him she wouldn't talk with anyone about the voices he heard or Hashur's plan until she had thought through what he had said. She also needed to make sure Didila was going to fully recover. All eyes were on Didila.

Zu and Miu packed the freshly-dried beer loaves and prepared them to take the journey to Ur via ship. Taku would be by later today with Zaidu's men to haul them to the docks. Miu was excited and tried to bite down a smile that crept across her face. A sense of hope ignited deep within her when Zu promised to cover the expenses of the five shipments to Ur.

She expected the hope and excitement, but it was the guilt that confused her. The guilt of surviving. The guilt of escaping her father's grip, when her mother and sister were still there, when her brother never escaped. She shouldn't have been able to escape her father and his lust to please the gods no matter the cost.

She never should have escaped and left her sister in Ur, but she couldn't have stayed either. Hulla was probably a priestess in Ur's despicable religious system. As beautiful as she was, they probably would have moved her through the ranks. Every time Miu imagined what her sister must be doing to maintain the status her parents had promised her, her stomach churned and wanted to empty itself.

Even though Zu and Hashur had been giving Miu the opportunities she craved, the guilt of having those opportunities carried with it shame. Miu tried to stack away money for herself while, more importantly, building status and connections with Zu and his friends.

If her father had received the same opportunities, he would have given honor and thanks to the gods. Instead, Miu recognized she was the one who had worked for these opportunities. Not the gods.

The guilt she felt reminded her of the story Jara first told her. A story of guilt over survival, but also hope for the opportunities that came next. She loved that story. Miu had gone to visit her whenever her father would let her leave her responsibilities.

Jara's strong shoulders represented the strength she had inside as well as outside. She wore plain tunics instead of the well-adorned ones many women of her class and wealth wore. She said it was because there was work to be done, and gold and jewelry got in the way.

Miu was always attracted to how she lived her life differently from others in Ur, but one of the biggest reasons was that she was a woman running her own business.

"Tell me about the only human to ever escape death!" Miu said with expectancy. "I know he almost grasped immortality. Just a stone's throw away, Jara!"

"Calm down, Miu. Nothing good happens by demanding your own way." She had smiled in her calm manner as she folded her hands in her lap.

Miu wished she could be as calm as Jara, but waiting had never come easily. She took a deep breath.

"Utnapishtim was the only person to survive that great flood, but along with his survival came deep guilt. Enki, the god of water and wisdom, decided to choose his own path and go against the other gods. He ordered Utnapishtim to leave behind his worldly possessions and build a huge ship that would preserve life."

"It was made of gopher wood, right?" Miu had asked, trying to fill in the pieces of the story she remembered.

"Yes, Miu. It was made of gopher wood." Jara shifted in her seat, always patient with Miu. "In those days, the gods were filled with fury towards humans and their incessant noise, ultimately leading them to decide on the destruction of the entire earth." She sighed with a deep sadness that concerned Miu.

"Why must the gods always cause sadness or confusion?" Miu bounced her knee up and down. "There is no love or justice with the gods, is there?"

Jara smiled. "The gods are often self-serving. It's why they created us, to serve them. Back to the story, Miu. Utnapishtim was told by Enki to take his entire family along with animals onto the boat he had built. It was seven stories high."

"I can't even imagine something that large, except the temple ziggurat here in Ur," Miu said in wonder, her eyes feeling bigger than clay pots.

"Then the flood waters came from the chaos waters below and the heavens above. It was as if creation collapsed on itself. Days later, the rain waters stopped. It was then that Utnapishtim began to see the mountain tops. Then he waited seven days before sending out a dove."

"Do we sacrifice doves to give thanks to the gods, Jara?" Miu tried to connect pieces in her mind.

"Yes, and Utnapishtim waited to see if it was safe for mankind to step foot off the boat. After a time, he sent out a swallow, then a raven. All these birds represent hope to us, Miu. All those birds were sent out with the expectation that the gods had spared his life."

Now, Miu felt a similar hope while packing up the dried beer loaves. She wasn't sending out doves or swallows, she was sending out beer loaves into the chaos waters with the expectation that a word of delight would return. Those loaves bore her name and her name only. The loaves she had poured her creativity and passion into were now going to be tasted in other countries and other areas with other priests and brothers and sisters.

Maybe once those loaves were on ships heading back and forth to Ur, then she could rest. The only problem Miu could foresee was that she may eventually see her father again. The prospect of freedom that the loaves could bring to her and Didila was limitless. However, every time she indulged in thoughts of success, she was haunted by the image of his face, acting as a city wall around her dreams.

"Maybe I can prove to Father we don't need the gods."

"What did you say?" Zu laughed. "You're deep in thought, Miu. Is everything okay? Do you need some food?"

"Let's just get this done." She shook off her thoughts and tried to focus on the work in front of her.

She never wanted to dampen Zu's mood, but keeping him happy and interested was one of the harder parts of this job. She wasn't comfortable dancing around anyone's emotions, unlike Taku. She groaned at the thought of him always trying to make peace.

The only thing she could think of that scared her was her father. He was the only person she'd ever known with powers gods and kings alike would side with.

"Did I tell you I met the lapis lazuli jeweler in Ur a few weeks ago?" Zu rubbed his palms together in excitement.

Miu's blood turned cold. She wasn't ready. She wasn't established. If she ever saw her father again, she knew he'd bring upheaval to this world she'd built. He had every right to drag her home. If Miu didn't belong to a husband, then she belonged to her father. She shuddered but was quick to think of something to say.

"I'm sure he's nothing compared to you, Zu!" She winked at him.

She could tell she said the right thing by how Zu pushed his shoulders back a bit, and the right corner of his mouth went up in admiration of himself.

People didn't notice how flattery worked wonders on Zu. They'd laugh with him, but Miu had a keen sense of observation. If she had learned anything while being here it was that people couldn't be trusted. She trusted Zu with small pieces of her, but no one would see it all.

When those around could only see pieces of her, then that was all they could control. But once she let someone see her deepest dreams, desires, and fears, they'd manipulate what they could. Because life felt uncertain, this was one thing she could count on. People and gods manipulated others to get what they wanted. She wouldn't be the one manipulated or controlled.

Hashur came sauntering into the work yard.

"Speaking of manipulating," Miu whispered and stood to face her.

She reminded Miu of the lizards she would watch as a little girl outside her window. They would turn brown when climbing on their mud home. Then, when one would climb the date palm outside her window, it'd turn green until eventually Miu couldn't see it. Hashur was like that, melding into Zu's world like that lizard. It was amazing to Miu how Hashur could be Zu's biggest supporter while in his presence and yet hold the same excitement for another merchant at her tavern. Miu had watched her play the part of a strong business woman when the priest would come by for taxes, and then she'd act as if she understood the plight of the prostitute asking for a job.

Miu's favorite was watching Hashur in her tavern on busy evenings.

Just last night, Hashur set up a The Royal Game of Ur between two merchants. She had laid out the dice while she flirted with them both. Miu watched how both men wanted to prove they could be the winner of not only the game but of Hashur's heart. It seemed to work. They kept placing bets, a percentage of which went to the tavern. Miu wasn't quite sure how she could keep them both fully believing that she was interested in each of them.

In the end, one of the men won the game and a fight broke out in the tavern. Alor swept in and broke up the fight before he sent them both home. The tavern kept all the profits.

Miu couldn't decide if she was impressed or more concerned at how well a drunken Alor and a manipulative Hashur could keep their tavern running so smoothly. She watched her back, but after that escapade, maybe she should watch it closer.

"Which flavor are we sending to Ur first?" Hashur asked, running her fingers through her hair, catching Zu's attention almost immediately.

"Three kinds. Fig, date, and pomegranate." Zu beamed with pride.

Miu couldn't help but smile. It was nice having someone believe in her. She knew he was probably in it mostly for the new adventure and the profit, but she liked Zu either way.

"How much more is left to do? Didila is asking for you, Miu." Hashur seemed to want to be left alone with Zu, but Miu wouldn't allow that. She may have guilt for leaving Didila, but the long term result was in the girl's best interest if Miu could keep an eye on Hashur and Zu.

"We're almost done. Taku should be here soon. Zaidu put him in charge of our shipments, so all should go smoothly," Zu said with confidence.

"Have you clarified who is receiving these first shipments, Zu?" Miu asked. "It's important that the highest quality taverns get these first. There's no point in sending them to low-class taverns who won't appreciate the craftsmanship that went into these."

"Dear," Zu paused. He stopped his boyish behavior and took Miu's hand in his own. With fatherly affection, he looked Miu in her eyes and waited for her to meet his gaze. "Your interests are my interests. I know many people in Ur. You need to remember, I, too, have fought hard for you to ensure your name is known as the creator behind this invention. If I've gone to these great lengths, you have to trust I'll make sure they go to the best of the best. Plus, have you ever seen the women I bring into my home? Don't I choose quality?" He winked and walked away.

There was the Zu she was used to working with. Miu tried to stifle a giggle. On one hand, Zu never could keep a conversation serious for long. On the other hand, the women Zu brought in were the most gorgeous she had ever seen. She had thought the priestesses at Ur were dynamic, bronze, and brilliant, but Zu far surpassed Ur's women with the ones he found for his own eyes and pleasure.

Could Miu trust him? Would Zu be loyal to her if she encountered her father, in Ur or here? If push came to shove, would anyone in Dilmun fight to keep her in the city? Did she even have a choice but to trust him? Maybe having her own fleet of ships to transport goods would protect her. Maybe owning Hashur's tavern would be the better first step for freedom. If she could just prove Hashur's plan to poison the temple, then she'd be rewarded with the tavern.

She shook her head. Trying to talk herself into logic.

"Not yet," she whispered, loading the last of the beer loaves into a crate.

She had big plans, but she needed to tell Zu the truth about where she came from. If she didn't tell him, he'd eventually find out she was hiding something from him, and trust would be broken. She couldn't tell him in front of Hashur though.

"Hashur, when are we taking sample loaves to the temple tavern?" She changed the subject and caught Hashur off guard as she was flirting with the errand boy.

"We can go tomorrow." Hashur tried to look innocent.

"Perfect. Let's head home and check on Didila together." Miu grabbed Hashur's arm and started walking home.

chapter
nineteen

Why doesn't Mom want to be with me?" Didila folded her arms and furrowed her brow. She was sitting out by the well with Miu. The afternoon was warm, and the sun penetrated Miu's skin through her tunic. She hoped it was doing the same for Didila. The girl had been feeling much better lately and now kept asking to see her mother.

It made sense, but it gnawed at Miu, who had spent months nursing her back to health. She had been the one who had cleaned up the blood from vomit and wiped her mat down with oils. She had been the one to sit with her through endless nights wondering if she'd wake up again. Not Hashur.

When Miu confronted Hashur last week about it, Hashur had responded, "The girl knows I'll give her whatever she wants. But I have to keep working if I want to stay ahead here in Dilmun. You, better than anyone, understand that. If she wants a roof over her head, then she needs to understand what it takes to put it there. Doesn't she know the nice clothes she has aren't just given to her? She doesn't get the best medical treatment if I sit around and hold her all night while men stroll in and out of our tavern. We will fall if I don't keep a healthy front out in the city. No one can get ahead of us, Miu. Especially now."

She understood Hashur's desire to get ahead and stay ahead,

but something about it was different than her own desire. Miu's drive was to keep her freedom. Freedom from her father's manipulation and rules, while also having her own way when it came to the gods.

Hashur, though, was in it to be the best. No matter the cost. She'd step on whoever she needed to just to succeed. She trampled Alor's desires as she was also trying to control the temple. But worst of all, she was stepping on Didila.

Miu could tolerate her behavior until it came to harming Didila. Miu gripped her hands into tight fists as she plastered on a smile to keep from frightening the girl.

"Your mother is just busy, sweet girl. She thinks this tavern is going to fall apart without her." Anger rose in Miu's chest, and she looked away, hoping the girl didn't notice.

The sun was getting warmer, and many women had already left the well with the water they needed for the day. Miu should probably take Didila back to the tavern to get some work done before the evening rush. This journey with Didila had shown that she could love someone, fight for them, and stay with them without running away. She never realized she could love someone so much. Sometimes she would look deep into the girl's dark eyes and see her sister, Hulla.

She pushed the thought away; there was no use in being sentimental. She was relieved the girl could even walk back to the tavern, but she would likely sleep once they got there.

She had asked one of the girls to prepare a meal of barley crackers, goat cheese, and pomegranates for their return, Didila's favorite snack. She always giggled when the pomegranate arils popped in her mouth, and Miu giggled watching her. Oh, how she'd do anything for the girl. How could she not? Everyone else in Didila's life ignored her. They were all too stupid or self-centered to care or see what she needed.

If Miu was in charge, this place would be put in order. No messing around trying to get someone to care for Didila. Miu would just take care of business.

Hashur was so focused on connecting with the next rich person to walk into the tavern that even Alor began ignoring her.

Alor's drinking had gotten heavier over the last few months, no one could deny it. Miu wouldn't be surprised if he had taken a barmaid for afternoon pleasure; it was common for men to do anyway.

Hashur spent every evening schmoozing any man or woman that walked into the tavern. She would show off her beautiful lapis lazuli jewelry to women who wanted to be like her, and she'd run her fingers along any man's thigh who wanted to be with her.

Miu had never seen a woman with the ability to work a room in her favor, like a butterfly flitting from petal to petal. She held beauty by just being in the room, though she never stayed long enough for anyone to catch. Hashur's eyes held power in their depths, convincing anyone, man or woman, to do anything.

Lately, Hashur had even lured Zu into her web. Miu wouldn't let it continue, but she was watching the relationship closely. Zu had promised Miu he would watch out for her, and she felt a fatherly kind of love toward him. It was a foreign love, but she welcomed it.

Miu and Didila made their way back to the tavern just in time to wake Hashur from her deep sleep. Lately, she had been sleeping so late, but Hashur heard the news last night that a priest would let them into the temple tavern. Miu wanted to hear the details.

"Hashur, wake up. You're sleeping later and later. Your tavern will fall apart because of your laziness." Miu grinned. That would be enough to get her up.

Hashur bolted up, wiping the kohl from under her eyes. "Call a girl to get me dressed and cleaned up. Then let's talk before everyone gets here."

Didila bolted into the room. She ran straight to her mother and wrapped her arms around her in sheer excitement.

Hashur patted her on her head. "Go find something to do," she said flatly.

Hashur's coldness toward Didila shocked Miu, while at the same time she was grateful the girl had energy at all.

Tiame helped bathe and clean Hashur while she told Miu the news. "We heard from Zu the temple tavern has a rat problem. They're everywhere, and the gods find it unacceptable. It must be handled. Guess who I said was an expert in getting rid of rats?"

She paused to make sure Miu's excitement matched hers before she continued. "I told them we could show them how to take care of the rats. We've had them before, and it's an easy fix." A smile crept across her face. "But this little infestation will give us access to their beer supply."

"So, what's our first step? You're either sleeping or rubbing shoulders here at the tavern." Miu genuinely wondered if she would be the one to take care of the rats. She hated rats almost as much as she did snakes, thankful no one in Dilmun worshipped rats. She shuddered while holding her stomach; she could feel it flip-flop at the thought.

"I'll head up there tomorrow. If I'm not seen as someone who is competent, then we will fail, you're right. When it comes to putting out traps and poison, I'll send you and Tiame." She looked up at the girl braiding her hair.

Tiame's jaw dropped, but knew she had no choice. It was enough to delight Hashur, so she proceeded with her plan.

"I'll let you know where they're making the barley paste. Then you girls can sprinkle the poison into the paste. The poison itself has no taste, and no one will guess what happened. Everyone will blame the rats for the problem. When a temple is poisoned and even a highly trained tavern owner can't get rid of the rats, it often means the tavern has lost favor with the gods and goddesses. No one will suspect us, because our tavern is doing so well. It shouldn't take much convincing that the gods favor us when this is all over."

Hashur stood staring into a reflective bowl of water. It seemed she fell more in love with herself. She smiled and gently ran her fingers along her eyes, apparently loving the way they looked. Her eyes were like full moons, and men often flocked to the tavern in hopes to get a single glance.

Next, she stroked her new tunic with her slender fingers, and Miu assumed she was dreaming of her role as the lead tavern owner in Dilmun. If Hashur ever did make it as temple tavern owner and priestess, she would gain deeper insight into what the gods wanted; that was how life worked.

That in and of itself was enough to feed Miu's drive to fight her to the bitter end. She couldn't hand her that power for good. Hashur's insatiable need to win needed to be stopped. She wanted to win favor, win with her beauty and her adornments, win with her suave conversations. Miu had watched her long enough to know these were the things to make her falter.

Miu took a hard, obvious swallow. *If I don't end up strangling you first.* She smiled, and a sense of power filled her bones. She could almost taste Hashur's downfall now.

"Now, let's get on with our night," Hashur proclaimed. "Tiame, remember: when the priest of Uruk comes over to speak with me, come by and mention Zu's name. Maybe say something about how he's been asking for me. I'll ignore you, of course." She twirled her fingers in her freshly combed hair. "I'll pretend to take interest in the priest, but I need him to understand how admired I am."

Tiame nodded. Anyone desperate enough to beg for admiration was dumb enough to trip over their scheming.

"On with the party!" Miu said with a hint of sarcasm.

"Yes, let's go have some fun." Hashur gave one last admiring look at her new pearl necklace and the gold barrettes in her hair.

ONCE THE TAVERN OPENED, the drinking started and so did the rowdiness. Miu stayed busy, keeping things moving in an orderly fashion. But as always, Hashur was in the thick of it all. She beelined right to a table crowded with tall, attractive men.

Some wore bangle bracelets lining their arms, while others boasted the latest fashion accessory of belts and leather shoes. Buckles and clasps were expensive due to the intricate metalwork, and many of these men had both. Hashur was drawn to the wealth, that was all that mattered to her. Candles, clasps, and belts meant more wealth, status, and fame.

"Teach me how to play the game, boys," she teased, a flush visible in her cheeks.

On the table in front of the men was a wooden board lined with white shells, dark-blue lapis lazuli, and red limestone. The stones were all set in contrasting black bitumen. Twenty squares lined the board, each with assorted designs. Some had dots, flowers, and even eyes. The board was separated into two rectangular sections. One had twelve squares with a two-square bridge leading to a smaller rectangle holding six squares. Along the outside of the entire section lay tiles containing eyes to guard the player's moves.

One of the men gestured. "Sit here, my lady. I'll show you how the gods favor me. By the gods, I will win the game." The laughter roared across the table, and then the entire tavern. The thick scent of barley mixed with the musk of men who had worked all day in the sun hovered in the air.

Miu knew Hashur wouldn't give the men what they wanted that easily. She'd played this cat-and-mouse game for hours into the night many times before. She would keep their anticipation on high alert for the entire evening if she wished.

"We'll just see about that now, won't we?" Hashur winked at his opponent, keeping them both engaged in winning her affection. "Who goes first?"

The night wore on, and the men's hearts became glad. They hugged each other and slapped each other on the back. They'd soon turn to brawling or crying, it never failed. This was the time of the night that Miu needed to keep her mind sharp. Out of the corner of her eye, Miu saw Taku walking through the doors of the tavern.

She huffed; she wasn't expecting him. Maybe he was a

welcome face, but now was not the time. She needed to keep an eye on the table to her left. Hashur hadn't walked by them in a while, and the men were getting restless. Miu didn't flirt with the men, but she tried to give them the attention they craved until Hashur made her rounds.

"Of all nights, Taku, not now. What are you doing here?" Miu put her hands on her hips.

Startled, Taku responded, "I'm in town for a bit, and Zu said you might want to celebrate since the beer loaves are headed to Ur." He looked like a child tonight, his face holding expectation and joy for her.

Miu hated to let him down, but she had no choice. He'd get over it. "I can't celebrate until the work is done," she snapped before she turned around to head to the table of irritable patrons.

Hurt, he looked away. "It doesn't matter anyway." Taku sighed. "Trying to show you that I care is exhausting." He turned and left, his shoulders dropping.

Miu tried to shake it off, but her eye caught something he was holding in his hand. What was it? It was too late to ask. She thought about running after him to see what it was, but she'd try to find him tomorrow and apologize. He was always around and would be there when Hashur's games were over.

A pang of disappointment, foreign to her, shot through her. Wasn't she the one that wanted him gone in case anything bad happened tonight or tomorrow? He would understand that much; she'd explain later. She was protecting him, that was it. Miu had to hold on until tomorrow, until the plan would play itself out.

With Taku gone, she tried to think, tried to focus on what was happening in the tavern that needed her attention. The men bantered back and forth while Hashur kept the beer and their ration cards flowing.

Tiame patted Miu on the shoulder and pointed as the curtain to the back room flung open. Alor came sauntering out of the back with a mysterious look on his face. Miu knew Hashur had given him the job tonight of tending to Didila, which always made Alor feel resentful. Didila was probably asleep for the night, and Alor had since become restless.

Silence swept across the rowdy tavern as Alor tottered between the tables, and everyone waited to see what Hashur would do. Alor steadied himself by grabbing a waitress's arm as she passed by. She was holding a tray of straws, and they clattered to the ground, startling the tables nearby. The waitress pushed him off, and he fell back with a crash onto a table full of local leather workers.

A cold shiver ran up Miu's spine. As she gripped the barrels of beer behind her, the wood dug into her fingernails as she tried to stop herself from dragging Alor out of the tavern by his balding head. What was he doing? She wanted to quiet him and yank him out of this room. But even if she wanted to stop him, she couldn't. He wasn't her responsibility. Besides, for Hashur to stay in control, she would need to be the one to get him out of here before he ruined the night's profits.

Alor stood and tottered over to the table where Hashur sat. All eyes were on her to see how she would handle her drunken husband. He leaned down as if he were going to whisper something to Hashur. Miu held her breath. He got as close as he could, but stumbled again and caught himself on one of the man's shoulders. His breath, likely heavy with the smell of stale beer, caused the official to pull back in disgust.

"Yeah, the woman right there that you want to screw is planning on screwing you all! She's going to tavern the poison tomorrow. I mean temple the tavern." Alor paused to collect himself. "She's going to poison the temple tavern. Do you believe it?"

Miu could barely catch her breath. Normally, Alor couldn't string two words together after he had been drinking, but had he really just shouted Hashur's plan?

Rage and shock filled Hashur's face. She grabbed up her skirts that had been drawn over the priest of Uruk's lap and stormed over to Alor. In a low growl, she whispered something to him.

The color drained from Alor's face. What was Alor doing? The damage was done.

Still, Hashur was quick to the punch. "Oh, can't you tell he's drunk?" She smiled in her coy way.

"She plans on what?" one of the men roared from the other side of the tent.

Alor, too drunk to remember what he said, took the nearest pot of beer on the table and chugged it.

"Did you poison him too?" the man with the long beard and tired eyes shouted. The room stood still.

Miu tried to hold back a smile while guessing what the next move was for Hashur.

"I most certainly did not. Can't you tell he's been drinking most of the day? Ask any regular patron of mine and they will tell you I have to hold my own around here. If it weren't for me, this tavern would shut down. Then how would the gods be praised through your drinking? Tell me why I would poison him or anyone else." She squared her shoulders. "On with the music!"

Many men began to leave, some of them deciding they wanted no part of what the gods might bring down on this place if what Alor said were true. A woman who couldn't control her tavern was a woman the gods wouldn't trust.

Two of Dilmun's military officers came in without warning and grabbed Hashur by the arm. Kicking and screaming, her wild and dark hair wrapped like weeds around her contorted face as she wailed. "The gods will curse you for touching me. No one can touch me!"

As soon as Hashur was through the front curtains of the tavern, Miu bolted into action, grabbing a fresh pot of beer. She needed to look like she had control of the situation. She needed to do whatever it took and do it fast. She poured beer into the men's cups and directed Tiame to pass out fresh straws. The straws sometimes would clog, and the fresh straws were a generous gesture.

The men watched her closely, making direct eye contact with

her. They were caught off guard by her generosity, and their eyes showed it. Why was Miu giving away something that Hashur made them pay highly for? Her energy and joy flooded their drunken senses, and the thought of Hashur faded fast.

No one knew what would happen to Hashur, but Miu refused to let the night end in chaos and uncertainty.

The military officers had hauled Hashur away for treason, and the story of Hashur would spread like wildfire; once a story like this started in Dilmun, it was impossible to stop it. With Hashur gone, Miu would stand firmly in her place. Alor was too incapacitated to handle the tavern on his own, everyone had seen that tonight.

No matter, she could show the town how she'd managed the tavern and Didila. She now held everything she'd always wanted in her hands. A business to call her own without anyone telling her what to do. She could finally run things her way. If her father never crossed the chaos waters to find her again, she'd be the freest woman alive.

The night wore on, and the men in the tavern began to leave a few at a time. As they left, many whispered how they appreciated Miu's generosity and kindness.

"This is the most respected I've ever felt," said one of Zu's men. "Surely the gods are with you and favor you."

Miu began to wipe down the counters and tables. She put Tiame in charge of taking the beer pots to the back. The girl needed more work to do; if she sat idle any longer, she may never get back up again.

Miu walked to the front of the tavern to close the curtain and make sure there were no drunks left outside that she needed to send home. The night air was warm with a cool breeze, and she could see the sun peeking over the horizon lighting up the sky.

As she turned to go back in, something by the tent door caught her eye, wrapped in wool as if it were a gift. She bent down to pick it up and unwrap it. Inside was a small clay tablet attached to the gift. Her heart stopped when she read her name on it.

"Conspirators?" she questioned. "Who would want to take the tavern from me already?"

She unwrapped the rest of the wool and inside was a carved wooden ship the size of her palm. She rolled it around in her hands and marveled at the intricate details. It looked just like Taku's new ship he had built to carry her beer loaves to Ur. She picked up the clay stone that held her name and flipped it over.

"For Didila: Picture Miu's success floating across the waters."

Miu felt like she had been punched in the stomach, and she fell to her knees. Taku didn't come to the tavern tonight because he needed her attention. He came to support her. Taku had given her the gift of his friendship, to both her and Didila. She'd destroyed it with her rudeness. In getting rid of Hashur tonight, she'd also lost Taku. She had dismissed him, the exact thing everyone else in his life had done.

A flood of emotion swept over her and she wept, uncontrollably deep, heaving sobs. She had done exactly what Hashur had been doing in pursuit of her own tavern.

She now had the tavern and her freedom, but at what cost?

chapter
twenty

The breeze was warm against Taku's face, and the warmth of the sun relaxed his achy bones. Crossing the chaos waters felt more like home than when his feet were touching the dry land. People considered him crazy for not fearing the open waters, but he didn't care. Today the lapis lazuli waters lapped against his toes. He would stay here in this peace as long as he could. Something would vie for his attention soon.

He tried pushing Miu out of his thoughts, but she was everywhere he looked. This beach where they argued. The walk to the temple with the sunflowers growing in rows. She was especially in the wildflowers outside the city. Why must she need such freedom? The memory of her was even in the boat loading up her beer loaves traveling to Ur today.

This was why he had to get away from the loading dock. This shipment alone should provide him with enough money to buy a boat of his own if he wanted. But did he?

Last night when he'd left the tavern, he hadn't waited to hear her excuses. He knew she'd try to apologize for her outbursts, but he didn't care. He had spent days sitting in that hammock by the water carving that boat for Didila. The girl was special, no doubt.

Miu had a way of pushing people to be their best, and Didila was no exception. If it hadn't been for Miu, Didila would be in

the underworld. And as much as Taku hated to admit it, she brought out parts in himself that, if left to him, he would ignore.

When he saw Miu, he had ideas for writing his own stories. When they spoke, he actually had thoughts of his own. But as always, like last night, whenever Taku tried to step out and speak his mind, people abandoned him. Didn't she know how difficult it was for him to share part of himself with her?

He bent over and picked up some sand, letting it fall between his fingers, smiling to himself as a dove flew by cooing. Zaidu had rubbed off on him a little because while he may still be searching for a god Taku didn't know, he found himself watching out for doves to capture for sacrifice. Just in case.

Their cooing made him homesick. As a boy, he would fall asleep to the sound of the birds cooing outside his window. His mother had kept a cage in their backyard full of them. She fed them with the care of a shepherd watching over his herd. So much love and attention were given to those birds that sometimes Taku worried she cared for them more than him. She'd chase away wild dogs that wandered through their backyard and yell at the hawks that tried to swoop in with fierce precision to snatch them away, but always with the intention to protect her precious birds.

"Shoo, go on. Get out of here!" she would scream, flailing her arms. Taku laughed now thinking about her and the doves getting riled up when she'd wave away a hawk. He'd never let her know how ridiculous she looked running outside. Women didn't run, and they didn't yell either, but his mother handled her role in raising them with extreme care.

She never tried to sell doves on a large scale or even to the temple. Instead, she chose to sell them to neighbors for food and kept some for their families. Even though her birds weren't raised to be sacrificed, she'd always raised the best. She would visit the local temple for sacrifice, and the priests would attempt to sell her one of their spotless birds. His mother would challenge them: "Try and find one blemish on these. They're the finest doves you'll ever come across."

The priests would step aside and let her through to worship alone. She was a strong woman, and Taku admired her for that. Women from all over Ur would come to her with their problems. They'd ask her how to deal with their husbands or how to raise children who didn't bicker, and she listened to them the same way Taku felt the water listened to him.

But Taku preferred the unresponsive waters to endless chatter. The waters didn't give bad advice, and they didn't point him to an omen that never came true anyway. The waters rocked his boat in predictable ways. Even in the worst storms, Taku knew the waves were still waves, rocking and pushing him closer to shore. He'd tried to get the waves to answer his questions, but he was content with their silence. It was the nagging voice he kept hearing that was unsettling, "keep looking."

Leaving Dilmun was supposed to help him think, but he wasn't sure what to think anymore. He thought he could support Miu in her dreams. Even before that, he supported Zaidu's plans for his shipping company. He hadn't left Zaidu, but Zaidu's tasks for Taku made him feel abandoned at times. It wasn't intentional, and he knew he couldn't remain in Zaidu's shadow forever either.

He needed to take a risk sometime. He needed to decide what he wanted to do, not what someone else wanted him to do. As much as he loved his mother, her advice would be to keep helping those around him. He didn't dismiss that thought; he just wondered if he'd ever be able to write his own stories and songs. People did it. As Ur grew, more writers were coming to light.

He had read one of Ur's newest writers last time he was there, and it had given him inspiration for his own writing ideas.

> *The lord who has the decisions of heaven*
> *and earth in his hands, the Great*
> *Mountain Enlil, has made the king's*
> *fame extend as far as the boundaries of*
> *heaven.*

. . .

HE KNEW he could write like that. He had even better and more poetic thoughts. The poem he kept in his mind would honor the gods the same way any new writer had done, but the only way to show a new form of writing was to write. He folded his arms, pouting as he stared out at the horizon.

He should head to the boat soon, head back to Ur with all its hustle and bustle to intrude on his thoughts. When he got his boat unloaded, he would go see his mother. She would give him a warm meal and help him think through things. As much as he enjoyed living in his thoughts, he knew they were why his world felt out of control.

He could keep his boat on track, even on the chaos waters. Maybe he needed a guide for his thoughts; they were what ship-wrecked him far too often.

AS THE CREW navigated to the dock in Ur, Taku noted that the city looked unchanged. The men grunted as they twisted the boat in and out of the water traffic.

The crew knew the regular plan to fix the boat with its usual repairs; crossing the waters meant that the boat needed routine maintenance. Zaidu had taught him how to repair the bitumen, how to check the oars for soggy spots, and to always have fresh sails to install.

Leaving the men to their work, Taku stepped onto the rugged docks. A cold comfort swept over him. He was met with a desire to embrace the familiar, all the while knowing what he left behind with Miu. This routine was so familiar that he was able to stay deep in his thoughts as he tied up the boat.

Above the shouting of sailors all around him, a voice stood out. If he kept his head down, maybe he wouldn't be seen or questioned by the men shouting.

"Did you hear? Abram says his god told him to go to a different city."

Taku's ears perked up. Many families in Ur and Dilmun had a god for their family because choosing to worship Nanna meant they wouldn't be heard. Being ignored by a more prominent deity meant you'd find a lesser god to hear your prayers and take your sacrifices. If these men were speaking about Abram, Terah's son, then the god they referenced would have to be the god of their family, a long line of people carrying their own stories of how the world began. They had their own tablets telling of their gods that created order from chaos.

But why did this god, Abram's god, want him to leave his city? Leaving a city would cost Abram a lot more than it would Taku. He was one of Ur's largest merchants, reminding Taku of Zu because of his wealth, but not in the way he behaved.

When Taku was only a boy, he was cornered by a raging, hungry goat. Gripping the dirt wall behind him, Taku saw the goat's eyes screaming only one thing: "I want that apple." The goat began scraping his hoof, while little puffs of dirt clouded up and dissipated as quickly as Taku's breath. The goat's horns grew longer as he stared Taku down with his black, beady eyes.

Taku wasn't sure if he should run or scream or both. He glanced around at his surroundings, finding only a barrel too large for his small arms to lift, a wild dog roaming the streets, and a patch of wildflowers growing by someone's front door. Nothing useful.

As Taku tried to calm the rising panic in his chest, a man came out of the leatherworker's store. He didn't look afraid, and instead, he made eye contact with Taku and winked. The tall, handsome man reached into his tunic and grabbed a handful of round, plump figs. With precision and intention, he tossed one in front of the goat, and as soon as the goat was distracted, Taku took his chance and bolted down the street as fast as he could. He never looked back.

Taku thought about Abram often, his kindness in that

moment and the quirkiness behind those eyes. His tunic was woven with gold thread on the hem, signifying his wealth. His warm smile and large nose were what most people saw first when they met Abram, but Taku noticed more. Abram's stature was taller than other men his age, and his hands seemed as if they had no lines or wrinkles. If the rumors were true, he was almost seventy-years-old.

What was weirdest to Taku was that he didn't even have children. Maybe it's children that make adults grow older faster, Taku had giggled to himself back then. It was probably why his mother looked so old.

Taku never encountered Abram again, but he had heard stories. It was strange that Abram and Sarai were so wealthy, and yet they had no children. How did someone live this long in Ur without having someone to pass their animals and property to?

He knew enough to know Abram was not an average farmer either. His farming wasn't like his mother's hobby of raising doves. Abram had hundreds of servants. He was a skilled business-man, and his wealth was proof of that. Taku overheard his mother one day whispering about Abram's ability to negotiate with her friends. "He can talk himself out of any corner," Taku's mother had giggled.

"He needs to since every man in the city wants to steal his wife," another woman had whispered. The rumors about Abram and Sarai were nonstop. Usually, gossip was uninteresting to Taku, but the idea that a god would ask Abram to leave his city caused him to pause.

Why would a god do that? Every family had a god that belonged to them, but why did this god want a man to move his entire family and possessions?

Even Taku's mother owned small stone gods. She kept them erected on a stool in the house, with smaller ones tucked inside the blankets in the house and under the palm trees in their yard. The closer the stone images were to their family, the closer the gods were to hearing them when they needed something.

A god's presence brought security. What good was a god miles away in a temple? If someone needed a god, it was better if they were in the home. Plus, the gods in temples understood the life of stoneworkers and fishermen. And of course, if a family's god wasn't listening, then they could always try going to the temple to sacrifice to them or to a different god.

"You can't hold anything back when things are chaotic, Taku," his mother had once warned with fear deep in her voice. "Dance, give your animals away to be killed, sometimes even show your own blood. Whatever you need to do to get their attention. You worship whichever god you can reach, Taku. Our job is to serve the gods; if they're unhappy, we do whatever it takes to calm them down."

Taku began his walk to his mother's home. His insides felt like the sea he had just crossed, rocking back and forth. Taku sought what every person from Ur and Dilmun sought: order. Maybe the familiarity of home would ease his mind. He felt the thud of his feet in step with his heartbeat as he made his way up one street and across another. Dilmun and Ur were both loyal to different gods, but it had never bothered him until now.

A god could ask someone to move from their own town? This was the exact chaos everyone avoided, and yet he wondered how a person was supposed to break the cycle.

Taku arrived at his mother's house by midafternoon. He reached for the door and paused. His hand dropped to his side, and he took a deep breath. Inhale. Exhale. Then he threw his shoulders back and walked in. Once inside, the simple yet familiar sight calmed his raging insides. In the far-right corner of the room was a woven wool rug, full of blues and reds. Memories flooded him of it scratching at his legs during story time while his father told him of bears and lions.

On the rug was a short stool with the stone gods and goddesses that watched over the house. A small tray of barley sat in front of the idols, another ritual his mother kept without faltering. These rituals were her and the people of Ur's way of playing a role in maintaining order in the heavens and the dry land. The dry land and all the living things were renewed when his mother and those like her kept these rituals active.

This had also been why his mother was intent on him learning to write. Writing brought order to the gods and their creation. A society could keep track of laws and rules, and by doing so they created more order. The more order a society had, the less chaos they fell back into.

His mother and father's roll-out pallets were tucked in a tidy manner on the other side of the room. He smiled to himself, remembering how much he hated rolling up his sleeping mat when he was a boy.

"One never leaves their bed out for the dogs," his mother would say. "Order, always order, Taku."

"I'm just going to get back in it tonight, Mother," he'd fussed, stomping his feet. Eventually, however, he'd obey and would roll up his mat just so, perfectly tucked in on every corner so they stacked neatly. Whether it was a rolled-up sleeping pallet or a world of new languages, order was the most important of all.

The meaning of language, writing, and understanding of the priests' readings of animal sacrifice was understood through order. Without order, how would humans and societies begin to understand each other?

A story his father told him about a time when everyone spoke the same language came to mind. "We did not have to guess what our neighbor across the sea said. We didn't have to wonder if they meant us harm, Taku. Our language was ordered, and our government systems were organized. That is until one day humans tried to build a temple ziggurat to reach the gods, similar to the one being built in Ur. They were going to build it until its top was in the heavens, up where the gods lived."

Taku had looked up toward the heavens in wonder. How was that even possible? But he waited for his father to finish.

"They built the temple with stairs going up and down to the heavens. If we could only reach the gods, then we could control the order of our world ourselves. They wanted to run the heavens and the earth." His father's eyes were downcast, and his tone lowered.

"Wouldn't it be good if we could reach the gods? Wouldn't it be good if we could make our own order instead of the gods doing it for us?" Taku had asked with hope in his voice, wondering why his father acted like this was such a bad idea.

"Men want to captain their own ship, Taku. If the gods never gave us order and commanded us what to do, then humans would only make a mess of things. Our purpose is to take care of the gods' needs. Once humans built this large temple, it angered the gods. They separated all humans on the dry ground. It's why there are places like Dilmun and Ur. It's not what's best for us, Taku."

The questions rolling around in his mind overwhelmed Taku. If the gods created everything, why couldn't they provide for their own needs? Did Abram know about a god Taku didn't? Why would that god want to separate Abram from his city of Ur where he was already protected by so many gods? Didn't Abram's god know that people needed their city for survival?

He slumped down in the corner of his mother's house, exhausted from his trip and from wrestling with his own thoughts. He would ask his mother what she knew about Abram's god after he got some rest. Drifting off to sleep, Taku shifted his seat to get more comfortable, and the voice in his mind whispered, "Keep looking."

For the first time, the voice comforted him.

If you're doubting the gods and their choices, Taku, you'll always doubt your ability to serve them." His mother stared at him with her brows furrowed.

The sun's rays beamed in their window and bounced off his mother's face. She looked older than the last time he visited her. He tried to stifle a laugh as he watched her fuzzy eyebrows, which looked like caterpillars, wiggle across her forehead. They only did this when she was frustrated with him or his father, and they were dancing today.

"Mother, why would a god change someone's name?" Taku pressed her.

Avoiding his question, she looked down and continued kneading the dough she was preparing for breakfast.

He walked over to her and touched her shoulder.

She looked up and he thought he saw a tear in the corner of her eye.

"What is it, mother? Why does this question plague you?" he asked with gentleness.

She hesitated, then began to cut the dough into small cakes, preparing them for the fire. "Taku, a name carries more than calling someone in from the street for dinner. A name gives purpose and order. It helps the gods declare someone's future from their past." She began placing the newly formed cakes into a basket to carry to the fire.

Running her fingers along the weaving, she looked Taku in the eyes. "When the weaver begins his journey to make his basket, he takes reeds from the river and treats them. Then he carefully weaves them in and out of each other. It is not until this basket is fully complete that the weaver can place it on his table and call it a basket. Taku, the same concept applies to humans. We were named 'human' by the gods at creation. However, if a god were to change the name given to us at birth, it signifies that individual's unique responsibility and role."

Taku's mind was reeling. What could this new god want with Abram? Wasn't he established here with the role of shepherd and merchant? Take that away, and much of Ur could crumble. Not to mention almost everyone in Ur knew Abram. None of this made sense to him.

"I heard his god is going to give him a great nation," she continued, lowering her voice. "Will this new god want Abram's new nation to rise up against Ur? And how will that even be possible if Abram has no children?"

Taku found comfort in the fact that she still had questions, but those very questions made him feel uneasy. What if Abram did raise up a nation to destroy Ur? He certainly had the ability to do so with the number of men that worked for him. What if this new god was calling him to create a new army? Years ago, men from the north came to invade Ur, and while they weren't successful, they destroyed much of the order and life inside their walls.

Taku's mother handed him a piece of bread and a bowl of lentils. His stomach and mind settled down with the warm meal. Maybe he needed food. "Thank you, Mother." He spooned in a mouthful of spicy lentils.

"Don't talk with your mouth full, son." Her eyebrows wiggled again.

He laughed, his stomach and mind easing a little more with each bite. "Can I ask you one more question, Mother?"

"Of course, then I must tend to the doves, son. I can't sit around squawking with you all day," she teased.

"I want to write again," he blurted, stumbling over his own words. He even shocked himself.

His mother stopped putting away the baskets and looked him straight in the eyes. Was that disappointment or concern he saw in her gaze? He should have asked her a question instead of admitting what he wanted to do with his life.

"Writing doesn't help Zaidu with his mounting responsibilities. It also doesn't help Ur become greater. Shipping and merchant work brings our city status, Taku. You know this." She pointed her finger at him. "It shouldn't matter what you want to do, Taku. You must do the work to keep order in Ur and even in Dilmun."

Then, she headed back to attend to her beloved doves, leaving him behind.

His mother was right; his desires didn't matter in this situation. Ur needed him to send shipments, and to be honest, he did enjoy helping Zaidu. He even liked shipping Miu's ideas across the waters.

Still, something inside him knew he had more to offer the gods. Maybe he would write during his trips across the waters. It wouldn't take away from the work the gods had him doing already. Then he could see if the gods were pleased with his words. Then he thought of his mother; he didn't want to disappoint her.

"If I could write something the gods would honor, Mother would understand," he said to himself, taking a step outside into the sunshine. "Until then, I will help Zaidu and Miu's shipments."

He took a deep breath. A walk would help him. Maybe he would head out and buy a new tunic today, one to celebrate his decision to put his ideas onto tablets. He'd celebrate that he finally decided to keep looking. But where would he look?

"Where?" he said out loud.

"Abram."

The voice hit Taku like a stack of tablets across his chest. Scanning his surroundings, he saw no one. It was the same voice he had been hearing; however, today's voice carried a weight of authority he had not heard before. A sense of urgency.

Taku needed to speak to Abram. Nothing else he'd ever done mattered more than this.

THE TEMPLE ziggurat cast a shadow across Taku's neighborhood. The sun had a way of creeping across Ur slowly, then pummeling the city with unbearable heat. Its blistering rays hadn't made their way over the temple yet to scorch the streets with its heat, so Taku, like many others, tried to run his errands in the morning. It was the only time in the day to do so, because once the sun's full power came into being, it was insufferable to walk the streets.

In Taku's frustration, he knew the wool must be purchased at the ziggurat, and he dreaded this part. The temple and its surrounding area were more crowded than the docks he called home. Priests and merchants argued over prices, while common people argued over the prices they had to pay the temple. Taku was thankful he had eaten at his mother's house because the price of food and items only grew the closer he got to the temple.

His mother was shocked he even mentioned going to the temple today, because she knew he only went for two reasons. The first was to accompany Zaidu as he made his sacrifice for a safe crossing. And even if they hadn't crossed safely, Zaidu would insist on making an offering for a successful crossing in the future.

The second reason was to purchase wool. Wool was rationed by the government in Ur, and then purchases were managed by the priests. If wool was to be produced privately by local shepherds, it was sent across the seas to places like Dilmun or even Egypt.

As the streets flooded with more people, he began to wonder

why he chose a day off to purchase wool instead of waiting until a day he was already there with Zaidu. But his hopes were high, and he had a mission to complete: find Abram, or at least someone who knew him.

Taku knew he needed to speak to the merchants in the tents. They were the ones who knew where people were during the day and kept up with the latest gossip. Pulling his shoulders back, he walked up to a weaver's tent.

"Excuse me, sir, have you seen or heard of Abram of Ur?" He noticed how shaky his voice was.

The merchant raised his eyebrows, and then took a long, slow look down Taku's body. The man had to know he was a sailor. His gaze then traveled back up Taku's torso and he met his gaze. "No." A smirk spread across his face.

Abram. Exalted Father. What a strange name for someone who was well known for having no children.

A line of giggling children bolted out of another tent, startling Taku out of his thoughts. Jara was passing out dried figs to each child.

When he was a boy, his mother had gotten very ill, and Jara was the only one who came to help his mother care for her beloved doves. Neighbors had feared the gods' curses on Taku's family, but Jara cared deeply for his mother and him.

Her smile and her pleasant voice reminded him of his childhood. "There, there, Taku. Just relax and listen to the cooing of the doves outside your window. They're happy and fed," Her knowing smile had spread across her face. "Now, Taku, come here."

Taku had walked toward her with hesitancy, unsure of why she would even speak to him as a young boy in the home.

"Put out your hand," she'd said, her dark eyes brightening as he did what she asked.

"Take these, and may the gods smile kindly upon you." She'd placed three dried figs in his hands.

He smiled, skipping away with joy that someone like Jara had noticed him.

Eventually, his mother recovered, all because of a little love from Jara, and Taku had never forgotten that moment.

Today, he couldn't pass her tent without speaking to her. Walking toward her tent beaming with joy, he wondered how a woman in business was successful with Ur's government. They had allowed for a few distinguished women to manage business tents. Taku was happy she was one of them.

"Taku!" Her tinted cheeks raised toward her eyes in a smile. She opened her arms, and he ran to them, feeling like a small boy again. Squeezing him and kissing him on both cheeks, she pulled back to stare at his face. "My how you've grown into a handsome man!"

Blushing, Taku tried to pull away.

She gripped his shoulders one last time before letting him go. "How are you? Please share how the gods have blessed you!"

"They've most certainly been good to me, Jara."

"Where are you working now? Still for the scribes?" She took a step back, still beaming with delight, as if staring at a long-lost son.

It had been a long time since seeing her. Taking a deep breath, he told her how he now traveled with Zaidu the sailor from Ur's port to Dilmun.

"Dilmun!" she said with shock. "The land of abundance, without disease, suffering, or death. I've always wanted to visit, Taku. Is it as beautiful as they say? Have you tried diving for pearls there?"

"Yes." He smiled hesitantly, remembering that the last time he was diving for pearls, Miu was flooding him with questions. "It can be quite profitable, but like everyone else, I also tried seeing what life was like as Gilgamesh."

She held her stomach, laughing. "Can you stay to eat, Taku? Or must you be on about your work?"

"I was on my way to buy wool for a new tunic. Zaidu has

given me a new shipping route to run myself." Taku tried not to sound too boastful.

She noticed his hesitation and leaned toward him, putting her hands on her hips. "Child, tell me why you're not filled with joy. You should celebrate!"

Taku put his head down, knowing Jara wouldn't let him get away with avoiding the question. She saw people. And today she saw Taku.

He wanted to tell her how much he wanted to write again. He wanted to say how much he had loved sneaking into the priest's homes and reading the tablets written to the gods. He wanted to tell her he was constantly making up stories in his mind to tell the gods.

But she'd tell him to stop making excuses, and for the gods' sake, stop letting Ur's priests and government tell him what he could and couldn't do. Hadn't Jara done it? Hadn't she broken all the rules?

Taku took a step back, creating distance between himself and Jara, nearly leaning against the side of her tent. Opening his mouth, he tried to speak, but the words lodged there like a thick piece of bread.

A piercing ache shot through his foot, as though something sharp had stung him. Looking down, he swatted at whatever it was while trying to ignore Jara's eyes. The pain didn't go away; it began radiating through his leg. It felt as if the chaos waters were now coursing through his blood. He rubbed his eyes, trying to take a deep breath, but the air was hard to find. Everything was blurry.

He said the only thing he could get to come out of his mouth. "Abram, do you know where ..."

Taku toppled backward, causing two jars holding lentils and barley to spill everywhere.

chapter
twenty-two

Once a month, Dilmun's finest soldiers took a training break and wandered through the streets singing and shouting. Their boisterous voices annoyed some while making others in Dilmun proud. The soldiers trained with intensity, so when they were allowed a night off, they made the most of it, often at Miu's tavern.

She was familiar with many of them by now, but more importantly, she knew their ration cards were ready to be filled with beer from her tavern.

Amah was the larger of the soldiers, and it was clear he was the one in charge. Every soldier walked behind him in respect. His tunic was always in place, and he carried himself with an air of confidence, which was useful in battle Miu was certain. Even when he smiled, his eyes remained hard, as if he had witnessed something that prevented the happiness from reaching his expression. He smelled of sweat and beer when he walked past Miu, and she noticed the girls in the back of the tavern giggle. Amah was clever, and men and women alike appreciated his humor.

"Tiame! Get to work," Miu shouted over the loud men, hoping she'd quit her idle giggles and direct the other girls.

Tiame rolled her eyes and pointed to the girls to get back to work.

Miu clenched her fists, holding back her anger toward the girl. Hulla flashed into her mind every time girls giggled at men. What was Hulla doing right now? Was she being forced into temple work as a priestess, or was she still at home annoying her mother with her desire for new tunics and jewelry? The latter option made Miu smile, just enough for her to relax and get back to work herself.

"Amah, thank you for honoring us with a visit today. How has training been for your men? Too hot?" Miu asked in the most professional voice she could muster.

His gaze left the table of men and looked toward her. "Got rid of that old hag that owned the place?" He ignored her questions.

Miu held his gaze for an uncomfortable amount of time, hoping to see a flicker of humor in his eyes. Nothing. His eyes were blank. Did he think she was guilty? She would not be thought of that way.

"Hashur made her own mistakes," she said as bluntly as she knew how.

"Do not cut off the neck of that which has had its neck cut off," Amah said with a slight grin spreading across his face, just missing his eyes. The soldiers roared with laughter. "Bring us another round, my lady."

Miu wasn't cutting off Hashur's neck, she was taking care of things Hashur couldn't. She scanned the faces of the men, seeing they didn't care what Miu's intentions were. She touched Amah's shoulder as she walked to the back to find Tiame. She would serve the men whatever they asked of her if they'd stop questioning her motives.

Pulling back the curtain, Miu found the girls stumbling around the kitchen trying to piece together ingredients for the new recipe for a spicy fish stew she had taught them. She'd tried to get Tiame and Didila to memorize it, since neither girl could read, but no luck. Frustrated with everyone's slow pace, she grabbed the newly imported spices from Tiame's hands.

"I'll do it myself later," Miu shouted. "Go serve the men outside and keep their rations flowing."

Out of sight out of mind was sometimes best for Miu. Dilmun was growing larger every day, especially with the rumors she'd been hearing about Ur. But if she didn't learn how to train these women to stay focused, how could she keep control? With the girls out of the back room and the soldiers being attended to, Miu sat down. The little ship Taku had carved her caught her eye, staring at her from the corner of the tent.

Taking deep breaths, she closed her eyes. Why was she still unhappy? She had gotten her tavern. She now had Didila to care for. She also ran a successful business as a woman. Sure, there were a few complications to work through, but wasn't this what she wanted? Why did freedom feel so lonely?

Looking at the ship again, she remembered asking Didila where she wanted to keep the ship since it was a gift to her. "Keep it in the kitchen. It will bring blessing there."

"Miu." Tiame bolted into the back. "Amah is asking for you. Come."

She took a deep breath; the silence never lasted long around here.

"Hello, Amah. How can I be of service?" She half smiled.

"Your girls. They're wandering around this tavern as if they were sheep without a shepherd. What is your plan to ensure they know what they're doing?" He pushed his chair back and turned to face her, shifting his sword further to his side.

Miu was flabbergasted. She knew they were out of hand sometimes, especially when soldiers were around, but she didn't think it was that bad.

"We aren't trained soldiers." Miu tried to tease him.

"It shows." He stared blankly at her, as if waiting for more of an answer.

Could she show her capability without admitting he was right? She needed more time to answer while trying to juggle the decision of asking for support from someone so close to the priests and the gods while also knowing she needed his help. She didn't have time with him staring at her. Instead, she chose honesty.

"May I sit?" She noticed a soldier eyeing Tiame. He stood quickly while she took his place. "You can go speak with Tiame, but you may not take her home."

He made eye contact with Amah and got silent permission. Then he left.

"Amah. You are just the person my girls need." She put a sparkle in her eye, hoping to win his good graces.

He held his blank stare. The flattery that worked with Zu and other men did not work with Amah.

Miu squirmed. How could she get his help with the girls while keeping her distance from the gods?

An idea came to her. "Since I moved here, the gods have shown their favor to me. We've started a new shipping route to Ur to get them a new type of traveling beer. We've won over this tavern from a lying woman. Now we can serve beer to patrons who only serve the king and priests. I've even watched the gods heal a girl."

She swallowed hard, trying to hide her doubt. "Heal her from a horrible sickness. Amah, the gods are showing us favor. You can join in and help us or be accused of ignoring the gods' blessings."

Now it was Amah who was shifting in his seat. "One cannot deny the power of the gods." He leaned forward and put his elbows on his knees.

Miu wanted to push a little harder to gain his support. "As an honored tavern owner, it is only fitting that the soldiers show their support for my endeavors, as the gods hold my establishment in high regard. What do you say?"

Two tavern girls sauntering by winked at Amah, and Miu waved them away. She didn't need flattery to win over this man. She also didn't want him distracted.

He stood, staring down at Miu and placing one hand on his hip and the other on his sword.

"If your girls can learn to follow directions, then my men will come by weekly to teach them how to be orderly. From what I can tell, the gods have blessed you with everything but order, and who am I to keep that from you?" Then he put two fingers between his lips and whistled a shrieking sound, halting all activity in the tent. "Men, let's head out."

When they had all shuffled out in an orderly fashion, Miu plopped in a seat and inhaled deeply. Had she held her breath that entire conversation? What were the chances she just talked a military general into teaching her girls how to work in an orderly fashion? She didn't have to use flattery or bribes. She spoke to him using his language.

Maybe she did have what it took to run this tavern. She'd do what she always had done, use her resources.

chapter

twenty-three

Gasping for air, Taku tried sitting up. His heart raced like horses in his chest. He heard soft whispers over him, and the air around him was thick and muggy. What happened to him? He had eaten breakfast with his mother this morning, but then what?

"He's waking up," a woman's soft voice whispered, her shadow darkening the light above his face.

Grabbing his stomach, an unbearable pain writhed through his body. He let out a deep groan, and another person hurried over to look down on him.

"His pain is manageable, but we're almost out of turmeric paste," a taller woman said with certainty.

How was this pain manageable? He couldn't sit still.

The quieter woman leaned down, putting her ear to his chest. "His heart must calm down, Jara," she mumbled.

That's right. He had been at Jara's tent. He'd been talking to her about Zaidu, and something had bitten him. Zaidu? Someone must tell him.

"Argh!" he groaned again as the quiet woman pressed on his stomach.

"Yes, his stomach is hard, and his face is yellowing. What can I do to help?"

"Go get Sarai," she said matter of factly. "And don't dawdle. His life depends on your ability to tell her what's happened. Now go!"

As Jara tended to his foot, he caught a whiff of damp earth, then came a searing pain. Then nothing.

TAKU WOKE UP AGAIN, this time with less pain. He still wasn't sure where he was. Was he still with Jara? Who was Sarai? Something was wrapped around his foot, and the smell of something cooking wafted across his nose. He wondered if he should try and touch his stomach. The last time he did, the tightness beneath his fingers scared him.

He tilted his head to the side of the pallet he was resting on. To his right was a woman drifting off to sleep in the corner; she looked like the quiet woman from earlier. Had she returned?

Turning his head to the other side took more effort than rowing Zaidu's boat. His head was heavy, but he needed to know what was going on. Streaks of sunlight peeked into the tent above, and then to the left, he saw two other women speaking in hushed voices to each other.

Placing his palms firmly on the pallet, he tried pushing himself up. Failing, he fell back to the mat in exhaustion. How long had he been on this pallet? What happened to him?

"Hello?" he tried to shout. Nothing came out. Wetting his lips, he tried again. "Hello?" he said firmer this time, though the sound was still not much louder than a whisper.

Two women came to his side, kneeling.

"What happened?" he tried to ask, his brow furrowing.

"You were bitten by a spider, Taku," Jara said.

Beads of sweat poured onto his upper lip and forehead as fear gripped his insides. His uncle had been bitten by a spider and died. He knew many people in Ur who had died from spiders, so how had he been saved from death? He tried lifting his head again to look the women in their eyes, but his head was overwhelmed with what sounded like pounding waves.

"We're taking care of you. You're healing well. Now rest," said a woman with the most beautiful eyes Taku had ever seen. He couldn't help but notice her beauty, despite her being older than his grandmother. Why was he thinking about an old woman's beauty at a time like this? Nonetheless, she was the most beautiful woman he had ever laid eyes on.

"Sarai, we've used the last of the turmeric treatment, can you show me how to make more?" Jara said.

"Sarai?" Taku said, a slow smile building. "Are you Abram's wife?"

If rumors were true, Sarai was the most beautiful woman in Ur. Men from everywhere told stories of her beauty and even tried to steal her from Abram. Even though she was barren, men wanted her for their harem.

But Abram stood his ground and protected her from the beasts in Ur. At least those were the stories Taku had heard at the docks. Sailors would spin any story. Sailors. Zaidu.

"Zaidu." Taku tried shouting, but a sharp pain seized his foot. "How long have I been here?"

"There, there." Sarai leaned down to touch his hand.

Taku tried to wriggle free, but the pain held him there.

"You've been here three days. We've told your mother. I'm sure she's told Zaidu."

Three days! He was supposed to leave for Dilmun today. Zaidu must be worried. Who would run the boats? He had just promised him he would lead his own shipment. He knew he shouldn't have taken on more responsibility.

"Drink this." Sarai leaned down with a clay bowl of what smelled like honey and peppermint. Taku tried to lift his head from the pallet but couldn't. The quiet woman from the corner came over and held his head so he could get a sip of the drink.

"The honey will help with the swelling in your stomach. The peppermint will help the pain," Sarai said.

She rambled on and on, but Taku couldn't get over her eyes. They pierced through his soul. He had been on his way to find this woman's husband when this spider bit him, right?

"We are leaving in a few moons, but may our god be with you to heal," she finished.

Their new god? Taku had been told to keep looking for what felt like one hundred moons. Here was his chance to ask her. "Can I ..." he tried. He tried with every bit of strength he had left. "Can ..." He wanted to speak to Abram. He needed to know about their god, but the one thing he was confident in using, words, had failed him.

"You rest. There is nothing this important right now, Taku." A tender smile swept across her face as just as light crept across the city of Ur. If he didn't know better, Sarai could have been a mother to hundreds of children. He saw it in her eyes.

And as quickly as he saw her maternal instincts come, a sadness chased it away. What was that? The joy erased by sorrow.

Taku's eyelids grew heavier, and then she squeezed his hand. Her presence didn't leave his side, and as much as he wanted to beg her not to leave until he could speak with Abram, maybe this was enough for now.

"Attention!" Amah roared at the girls.

As fast as goats being herded into a pen, the girls lined up at his command.

Miu tried to hide her smile, but this kind of order was good for the girls.

No one complained, especially not the customers. If anything, Amah's ordering of the tavern had brought in more customers. Was it the strict rules that had helped? Everyone knew their place. The girls knew if they were to stir barley or serve beer. Every girl knew if they were to clean the table after a customer left or right before they sat down.

Every girl except Tiame. Miu knew she had been by Hashur's side the longest of any tavern girl. She also knew she had been fiercely loyal to Miu. But she had questioned Amah's authority.

Two days ago, he asked all the girls to carry baskets to the well in Ur and back, to strengthen them he said. Then he'd asked the girls to balance water jugs on their heads as he watched the sun move to track their time, encouraging them to speed up.

Miu was excited to see her tavern in such order when Tiame pulled her aside.

"Does he really know what he's doing, Miu?" she had asked, gnawing on her lip.

"You can do this, Tiame," Miu encouraged. "You've been here longer than anyone. Your skin is tanned, and your muscles are strong. If you can't trust him, you can't trust me."

Tiame pressed her lips tight, lowered her head, and walked away. Miu knew she would have to get on board with the new structure and order. It was the way life was headed in Dilmun. The tavern was becoming too crowded for people to guess what their next move should be.

Sweat dripped down the girls' faces as they paraded into the tavern after Amah's training. Many of them were quiet, though a few still chattered away. Miu wondered if they'd be on their deathbed rambling away.

Rolling her eyes, she spoke up. "You can all rest for the afternoon. Your chores are caught up, and everything is ready for the evening. Be sure you're all back here by the time we open." Then she dismissed them to speak with Amah.

"How do you think it's going, Amah?" She tapped her foot.

"Stop your impatience. Order takes time. Especially in women." His face emitted no emotion.

She stared into his eyes, attempting to find insight, or feeling behind them. Nothing. She could read people well, but Amah was puzzling.

Miu tried a different angle to get information from him. "How have you learned to maintain such order, Amah? What part of the military have you led?" Miu hoped he'd share a piece of his story. A flicker of light. Was that what she saw? Was he excited to share?

"Spearmen." His tone sounded like there was more to it, but he hesitated.

Miu waited. She had a few hours before the tavern opened. She wanted to know what was behind this tough exterior.

Amah reached up to shift the turban on his head. "Hundreds of them, Miu. Men on the front lines of battle."

She nodded, not wanting to interrupt his thoughts. She had seen military men before coming home differently than they left.

The deep crevices in his face and the darkness in his mood high-lighted to Miu that Amah had seen more than most men.

"Do you know how Dilmun attacks their enemies?" A darkness behind his eyes set in.

"We serve our god, Nanna, by protecting our city." She hoped he didn't hear the cringe in her tone. "And King Sargon represents Nanna himself, which means our warfare is always just and right. The battles we fight maintain order. Which is what I see you doing here as well, Amah."

Now he did smile. Not a large smile, still partially hidden, but there. She disagreed with the purpose of war, but she saw a crack in his armor.

"I led hundreds of spearmen. We were the shock force that came upon an army first. We were some of the first men to use the new composite bow, crafted with layers of wood and bone, often using different types of trees. Miu, we were the first army to use these bows. They had greater strength and further reach. Because of this, I had a greater responsibility to Nanna. I drilled my men, kept them in proper formation, and led them. Among myself as a leader were musicians and—"

Miu interrupted him. "Musicians? What does music do?"

"My voice and commands can only be heard across a short distance, especially in battle. The musicians, drummers, and horn blasters keep the men maneuvering in close order. It was up to us to ensure the order was maintained." His chest stuck out a bit more with pride. He adjusted his tunic and placed his hand on his leather belt.

"That must have been difficult," Miu said.

"Behind us were slingers and other military soldiers. They buzzed behind us like angry bees, sending arrows and large projectiles into the enemy's formations. Behind them were the horse-drawn chariots carrying our supplies. It was in this chaos that order itself was formed. If you couldn't name each musician to direct the soldiers, your troops were doomed to the grave." His countenance fell.

"During my time in battle, Sargon replaced our local armies with his professional army. When he did this, he changed the way we moved into battle. Each group of soldiers stood in a closely packed formation, each holding a rectangular shield for protection. Then as we moved forward toward the enemy, my archers would open fire on them. Men fell all around us." Another hesitation, then he looked her straight in her eyes. "My men were brave, Miu."

"That doesn't seem as sad as you're making it. If you handle the women here as well as you handled the musicians and spearmen, you must have been good at your job." Miu touched his shoulder.

He flinched and took a step back.

At that moment, Didila bolted into the room, startling Amah even more out of his remembrance. He looked down at the girl as if she were a wild animal. He hadn't liked her running around the tavern; he didn't know what to do with children. He was used to men who took orders and women who obeyed commands. She was a child who laughed at his mustache and when he looked too serious.

"Tiame said she was taking the tools to get them sharpened." Didila's cheeks were bright as pomegranates.

"Thank you, Didila. Can you say hello to Amah?" Miu encouraged.

"Hi," she said in a tone sweet as honey.

Amah nodded, softening only slightly.

"Now run along, see if your friends can play for the afternoon. The girls here are resting," Miu said.

Amah watched her skip away.

"What is it, Amah?" Miu seemed to have interrupted his thoughts.

"I don't understand children. You can't order them. What's their function in Dilmun? Why did the gods not create us to be fully adults?" A real smile spread across his face.

"For that." Miu pointed to his face. "For smiles and for joy. I understand being concerned about keeping this tavern controlled, but then I remember the gods also enjoy life. The gods almost took her. But she fought hard for her life. She's strong and brave, a real soldier, Amah. But she's also full of smiles."

Amah's smile faded, and he began fidgeting, looking as if he were holding back emotions. "It's time for me to go. The soldiers have bow practice today, and I must oversee it." He stood and began to walk away.

"May I walk you as far as the sunflower fields?" Miu held her hands loosely behind her back. She did not want to come across as threatening, even though she would push Amah to tell more than he wanted to share. But she needed to know more about what made this man so strong, unlike her father who bent over backward for any man willing to give him status.

He also wasn't like Zu, in need of the pleasures of life to satisfy his every craving. Amah was grounded and secure in who he was, at least on the outside. Now that Miu was in control of the tavern, she wanted to learn how to control her emotions, especially her anger. Would Amah teach her?

He nodded before he continued walking, his head high and chest out. A slow pace, but a steady one.

Together they walked past a few tents with dwindling customers. The sun was high, and it was too hot for people to be out and about. Miu was determined not to waste the day.

"How do you stay so brave?" she questioned.

He paused, seemingly shocked by her question. He turned his body to face her, then turned and continued his pace down the dirt path.

"I remember what the dust tasted like between my teeth. That day it was as if the sun moved slower in the sky." The lump in his throat moved up and down. "Word reached us that a piece of irrigated land outside of Dilmun had been compromised. Someone had moved the stone boundary line back and claimed that land for Uruk, stealing it from Dilmun."

"Our shepherds depend on our irrigated land for the survival of their flocks." Miu exclaimed, ready to go to war herself over stealing something so priceless. Usually, her outburst caused men to either quiet down or get angry, and this stoked Amah's anger.

"Yes, Miu. This is true. This is why we chose to go to war that day. Here our land is valuable, but the land doesn't function without water. By moving this boundary line, Uruk broke the will of the gods. It was our responsibility to maintain the gods' order. We called our men to battle outside the city walls. It was a one-day walk from the city to the fields of the shepherds, and there we gathered our chariots and our supplies. Men were shouting, women were crying. It was a day I was thankful to the gods I had never been given a wife."

A group of children ran by them, disturbing the conversation. Miu looked at Amah, trying to discern his frustration with children.

"It was during that battle for water that I learned to be brave." Amah clenched his jaw. They walked on in silence for a few minutes, the sunflowers up ahead. Their conversation would be over soon.

"What happened in that battle specifically, Amah?" Miu knew she was pushing him.

He folded his arms and sighed heavily. "If I tell you about the battle, will you just take orders and leave me alone at the tavern?"

Miu wasn't sure she could commit to that. "I promise not to ask you more war stories."

Amah unfolded his arms. "As I said before, I still taste the dirt from the land that day. The smell of sweat filled the air as we neared the boundary line. Then the smell of water reached our noses, and our men's anger was stoked. That was it. The moment we saw Uruk's army coming out to taunt us."

The skin on the back of Miu's neck chilled. She nodded, trying not to interrupt him.

"I gave the orders to the musicians. The archers began shooting, the sound stinging our ears as if bees were flying past us. The smell of blood replaced the smell of fresh water. The shouting of men in agony replaced the sound of marching." Amah squinted, looking as if he was holding back the memories. "As we progressed across our boundary line, we dodged spears and rocks from slingshots. We marched across fallen men. Our own men."

He paused, pain spreading across his stoic face. He looked out toward the open road. "Open wounds in their skulls and in their sides. The worst was our chariots needed to advance over the fallen men. The battle felt intense, sometimes clear and focused, while other times the world around me was blurry, and I couldn't see where we were going. It was as if I was walking through a valley and couldn't see either side of me. I could only see forward."

"It was the death of your own men that gave you bravery? Didn't you want to run away?" Miu asked. Fear must have mounted in his chest as it did for her the day she saw her brother die, so how did Amah stay? How did he continue marching forward across men he cared for, men he loved?

When he squeezed his eyes shut, Miu could tell he didn't want to relive this pain. "You don't have to tell me more." Miu wanted to reach out and touch his hand.

"I have known chaos and order. I have known war and peace. I sought the face of the gods, and I have learned that to bear the gods' burden is all there is. And Miu." He paused as they reached the sunflowers. He reached up and placed both hands on her shoulders, waiting for her eyes to meet his. "He who keeps fleeing, flees their own past. One day you must face your own."

Now it was Miu who wanted to avoid the conversation. Did he know she was running from something?

He dropped his hands from her shoulders, then his eyes from her face. Before Miu could defend herself, Amah was walking away, rounding the corner from the sunflower field.

chapter
twenty-five

> In Ur, the linking place of heaven with
> earth,
> Let us create humankind from the gods'
> blood.
> Humans' labor will be labor for us;
> To maintain the boundary ditch for all
> time,
> To set the pickaxe and workbasket in their
> hands,
> 'To make the great dwelling of the gods.

Taku lay on the pallet listening to the calming voice of Jara telling Ur's story of creation. A time when heaven and earth overlapped, and the gods came and went as they pleased. A time when the gods decided to make the humans slaves for their enjoyment.

People spoke of that time as if it were an honor, and Taku guessed it could be ... sometimes. It was only an honor when the gods blessed humans with abundance for working for them. But when men lay down at night, their minds wrestled for peace and

joy. Abandonment of the gods felt real when the darkness spread over the mind like a heavy blanket, unwilling to move, suffocating any thread of peace they clung to during the sunlight hours.

Even the gods struggled with peace. Creating man from the dirt wasn't the plan they had thought it would be. Men and gods. Gods and gods. Someone was always at war.

Taku never did like the war, with all the anger and fighting. He despised arguing with Miu, much less an entire city. He tried sitting up, but the pressure in his head caused his eyes to squeeze shut from pain. Rubbing the back of his neck, he tried opening them again.

How he missed the open waters and the way the tension in his body eased up as they rowed away from shore. He had to get better. Zaidu needed him. He couldn't just lay here while Zaidu worried about him. When everyone else abandoned him, Zaidu was there for him. He had given him the job that now let him travel the waters.

Jara finished her story, and then walked across the tent to check on him. "You sat up on your own, Taku. I'm so proud of the progress you're making!" A smile spread across her face.

"I need to speak with Zaidu." He crossed his legs and propped his elbows on his knees. He was sure his hair was a mess without his leather band to keep it back.

"He said he'd be by to visit today." She handed him a clay bowl to drink from.

After he took the cool liquid from her hands and guzzled it down, his muscles relaxed a little. If Zaidu came to see him, he would see if he was stressed without him.

Just as he was about to take another sip from the bowl, a tall shadow darkened the doorway of the tent. The bright sun peeked around the man, hurting Taku's eyes enough to lift his forearm to block the bright rays.

"Who is this boy who takes my wife from me?" a voice brimming with life asked. Taku could hear the smile behind the question.

Jara jumped up from Taku's mat, then bowed at the waist to the man as he entered the room.

As Taku's eyes adjusted, he saw a man much taller than Jara with a beard that was just beginning to gray. Then the man made eye contact with Taku, who noticed the nets of wrinkles lining this man's hopeful eyes.

"How's the boy doing?" The man's voice filled the tent, sounding like waters pouring into a clay pot, smooth and life giving.

Taku swallowed hard; it was Abram. He tried standing, but he couldn't.

"I'm getting stronger every day," he piped up, not willing to be overlooked this time.

Abram turned to look at him as he surveyed his desire to stand. "My wife tells me even a spider won't stop your persistent questions." He chuckled. Why was there such youth in his hands and his face, and yet he still looked like the years had aged him?

"That is correct. I've been waiting for days to speak with you, sir." Taku held his breath. He would *keep looking* ... and asking.

Abram's head turned slightly to the side as if Taku had piqued his curiosity. "You had questions for me? Many things have been said about me, child. You must not believe everything you're told. What's your name again?"

"Taku, sir." Taku scratched the back of his neck as he struggled to find the right words. If he said the wrong thing or asked the wrong question, Abram could walk away, and he'd lose his opportunity.

"Then speak up, Taku. What have you been told about me?" Abram replied.

Jara brought over some beer and a plate of apricots and dates.

Abram reached over for a date, biting off a little piece and waiting for Taku to gain the courage.

"Why would a god ask you to leave everything, Abram? You're well known here in Ur. People know your wisdom in business. Even your father used to make sacrifices in our city. If you leave Ur, that means you leave your great name and your possessions behind. Abram, you lose your safety." Taku felt like something sucked the air out of him. Then heat rose in his cheeks, as he hoped he wasn't too forward with this stranger.

Abram's eyes softened even more as he leaned toward Taku. Lowering his voice, he waited for Taku to look at him. "He spoke to me, Taku. When you hear his voice, you follow. There was no doubt what we should do when we heard him." Then he lowered his head.

Was that reverence Taku saw? Taku looked around; he didn't have any gods he brought in with him. Why did he bow his head? There was not an idol of a god inside the tent.

"What did he say to you?" Taku softened his voice with wonder.

"Go out of your country with your family, and come to the land I will show you."

"That's it?" Taku announced, raising his eyebrows.

Abram chuckled.

"You're leaving everything just because a god asks?" Taku pressed.

Jara came over, placing her hand on his shoulder. She hated to see him get irritated, but he was invested in the conversation now. He shrugged her off while fixing his gaze on his fidgeting hands. How insane could a god be? Taku was hoping he'd hear more details than what he heard in the streets. The rumors were true ... or worse.

"When do you leave?" Taku asked with a shaky voice. He hoped Abram wasn't leaving soon. He'd wanted to learn about this god, but now he was more hesitant. Would this god ask Taku to leave everything behind ... blindly?

"We have a few things to get in order. We've put in orders with the tentmakers. We will now be a wandering tribe, but we will leave after the next full moon."

"Why are you following this god who is asking you to leave Ur? Why him? Isn't Nanna enough?" Taku already knew the answer. Nanna had never been enough. Everyone in Ur was still searching for the peace that lay behind Abram's quiet eyes. People used Nanna's name to make their own name great, or they lived in such fear they never wondered if Ur's gods were honorable or worthy of worship.

"In Ur, people are an afterthought. We are just another part of the world that helps the gods do as they please. They need us for food, for their own security, and for pleasure. Without us, Ur falls apart. We must fight our way for the gods to see us, or to care for us. Would you say this is true, Taku?"

Taku nodded, wondering why Abram was stating what everyone knew to be true.

Abram continued with a boldness in his voice. "Yahweh who has asked me to leave Ur does not need me to keep the world supported on its pillars, nor does he need people to keep the nations at peace. He is outside of all creation. He is not sun or moon. He is not waters or dry land. He is the creator of these things. Taku, Yahweh doesn't need us but has decided to dwell with us. He created the land we live on for people to function and create order so we can walk with him, as they did when the world was first created. And his invitation to dwell with him is why we are leaving. For us to dwell with him, in the land he will show us."

Taku couldn't move. He could hear his breathing in his ears. He tried looking around, but his vision was blurry. Maybe he needed a drink. Abram was the craziest man he'd ever met. And so was this god ... Yahweh was it? One single god in control of how the world works? A single god that didn't need people or other gods?

But this god was just crazy enough to stoke something inside Taku's gut, begging him to learn more.

"May I tell you something now?" Taku felt his insides turn.

"Sure." Abram waited with sincere patience.

"I think someone from your god has been speaking to me. I first heard him when I was sitting in a hammock in Dilmun, a day I was questioning their gods. I've heard him again when I travel across the chaos waters. I wonder ..." He hesitated then continued in a whisper. "... if the gods we worship have any power. The more I doubt them, the louder this voice tells me to, '*Keep Looking.*'" Taku dropped his head, embarrassed to speak his story out loud.

In the corner of his eye, he saw Jara shifted on her pallet. She wouldn't interrupt, but he would have to answer to her once Abram left. He'd deal with that later.

"So, what do you do with that?" Abram asked in a fatherly tone.

"I've wandered around continuing to ask the same questions to myself, but it wasn't until I landed back in Ur two weeks ago that I heard about your encounter with this god. I knew I had to ask you. Something was different in the way people spoke about him, calling you crazy. It's what I had been feeling. Then I got bit by that spider, and I didn't know if I'd ever reach you."

Jara spoke up. "He kept asking for you Abram. I didn't know what to tell Sarai or if I should bother you since you're trying to get your household in order before you move."

"You've done well." He patted her on her hand. "Thank you."

"What do I do with this god now that you've explained him, Abram? My work with Zaidu is growing. My responsibilities are a lot. He's asked me to run my own trade route from here to Dilmun. I can't follow your god without leaving Zaidu without help."

Taku's heart quickened. He couldn't ignore this god after what he'd heard, but he also couldn't ignore his friend and mentor either. A god that wanted to be with him, not use him? This was unheard of. A god that was not like humans. A god that was faithful to do what he said?

The gods he knew and experienced caused the flood for the simple reason that humans annoyed them. The gods he knew destroyed people because of their neediness.

"You have a choice to make, Taku." Abram stood to leave.

"You're leaving?" Taku tried to hide his desperation. If he left, how would Taku find him again? How could he tell him if he wanted to follow this god as well?

"I will come again in two days. Jara here will continue to take good care of you. That should give you time to decide if you want your own trade route or if you want to follow us to where Yahweh shows us."

As Abram turned to leave, Taku reached out to touch his gold-hemmed tunic. "Wait. Please. I have one more thing to share."

Abram turned to face him.

Jara shook her head, pulling his hand away. His rudeness had shocked her, he could tell.

Abram noticed her face and smiled and nodded toward her as if to say he understood.

"Years ago, I trained to become a scribe for the priests. I tried writing my own hymns to the gods, and the priests refused to let me return ..."A grimace spread across his face.

But Abram's look of horror met Taku's pause. It was unclear to him which the other man viewed as worse: Taku's role as a scribe or his habit of writing his own stories. The shock wore off almost immediately, and then Abram burst into laughter, high-lighting the laugh lines around his eyes.

Had Taku said the wrong thing? He knew he'd be laughed at again for his desire to write. Hanging his head, he started to lie down.

"Taku, we need someone to write down the stories Yahweh will show us on our journey."

Taku bolted up, looking this wild man in the eyes.

Abram continued, "I have faith he will do more than we imagine as we continue to walk to the land he will show us. But I know we need someone skilled to write his great works down. We need a scribe. If you choose Yahweh and have the faith and the courage to leave your family and friends behind, I believe you will see great things following him."

Taku's mouth fell open in shock. A scribe for a new god?

Then his brow furrowed, pondering Abram's request while also wondering what Abram meant by "seeing great things." What else did he know? Taku's mind raced with ideas … then fears.

"A good thing is to find it; a bad thing is to lose it." Abram quoted the phrase Taku heard often in the streets of Ur. Today those words held more meaning to him. Had he found what he was looking for? If he chose this with Abram, would the voice stop?

"You're right, sir." Taku nodded. "Thank you for visiting with me. I will have an answer when you come back."

Abram turned to leave, but this time Taku knew he'd see him again. Although this time, his heart raced with a different purpose. How could he leave Ur? How could he talk to Zaidu?

Then another thought flooded his mind. It felt so heavy he slumped back onto his pallet.

How could he tell Miu?

chapter
twenty-six

Miu wiped the sweat from her brow. The sun was rising, and it was already proving to be hotter than yester-day. Laboring over her own numbers for the tavern was more rewarding than doing the same thing for her father, but the heat was causing her to lose focus. A sense of pride kept her going while also pushing her, knowing she alone was holding it all together.

Sure, she had needed Amah to help bring order, but she wouldn't need him for long. Sure she needed Zu for connections, but she kept her own freedom by saying when and where the beer loaves could travel. She used the leather tie to gain control of her hair that kept falling out of the tight braid. Throwing the braid behind her back, she wrote down the last of the inventory.

The open office gave her more freedom than her father's small back office had. She was glad to be away from his firm grip; he only wanted her to pursue numbers and business so he could gain his own prosperity.

If he could get her settled into the business, her sister, Hulla, could become a priestess. Then he would be well positioned for the gods' blessings. Hulla in the temple with her connection to the men of Ur.

Miu's shoulders felt heavy. Who could carry such a burden? No wonder freedom tasted so sweet.

She could hear his voice now. "When the gods created us, they couldn't do without us. It's an honor to create beautiful jewelry for the temple. You should hold your head high, Miu."

"No wonder people treat each other as if they can just be thrown out of the city. If the gods use people, people use people," she had spewed back at him.

"Get your work done, Miu," he'd roared, slamming his large, calloused hands down on the table, shattering two tablets of her work.

Miu shrugged off the memory; she couldn't sit any longer looking at the clay tablets in her office. With him out of her mind, the memory of her sister stayed. She stood to leave. Maybe she'd walk down to the water or go to the sunflowers, pretend Taku was in his hammock.

What was he up to these days? She didn't realize how difficult it would be to run this tavern without his support or his friendship. On her way out, she saw Tiame, her face flushed from the sun. But there was something else hidden behind her eyes.

"Did you get the baskets and tools to Zu?" Miu asked.

"Yes, ma'am." Tiame fidgeted with her tunic.

Tiame's weak answer infuriated Miu. Why must everyone be so weak? She wouldn't hesitate to put Tiame on the street if the girl was up to something.

"Look me in the face when I'm speaking to you," Miu said directly. As the girl obeyed, Miu saw a tear in her eye, but that didn't stop her interrogation. "My tavern needs strong women. Speak up when you're spoken to, Tiame. Do you want to be controlled by the men around here? Do you want them to tell you how to live and what to do? If you can't handle it, I'll send you to Amah's men. You know what they do to women."

Without a word, Tiame's face jerked away, then she put her head down and retreated quickly down the street, away from Miu's harsh accusations.

Flinching, Miu refused to watch the girl run away. She hated how quickly her anger bubbled up inside her and then poured over those nearest. She used anger to keep people away when she worked with her father; it was what he taught her. She'd spew anger at him or at other businessmen asking for too much from her.

But now, every time she saw that stupid ship Taku carved, she remembered how her anger harmed those she loved. And she hated it. But how else could she push people to do better? If she didn't yell, then they just stood there, staring at her.

She knew Tiame had the skills to run the women and the tavern, so why didn't she do it? Why was she so timid in front of Miu?

Her father's voice followed her everywhere she went today. Escaping the inventory for the day hadn't helped. Her response to Tiame was the same way she'd seen her father yell at her brother. Was she any better than he was?

A thought came to mind, halting her walk. *What if I go find Tiame?* What if she tried again instead of letting her run away? The thought was so profound and so new, she wasn't sure where it came from. She just knew she couldn't lose her like she lost Taku, or even worse, like she lost her brother.

Returning to the tavern, she began searching for Tiame. The tavern girls were swatting at the birds on the roof. At least they were doing what they were supposed to be doing.

Cupping her hands to her face, she shouted toward the roof, "Have you seen Tiame?"

All the girls shook their heads in a quick no, put their heads down, and kept working. "Are they scared of me as well?" she asked out loud.

Continuing her search for Tiame, she went to the kitchen. It wasn't the best place to search for the girl this time of day, but maybe Tiame was flustered enough to hide out here. Where would she have gone?

Pausing to retrace the girl's day, Miu realized Tiame had been spending a lot of time with Zu for errands. But she just came from there. Her stomach turned. Should she search for her there?

Throwing her shoulders back, Miu vowed that the girl wouldn't run from her, and she wouldn't let her stay gone. Even if she wanted to check on Tiame, she wouldn't let her run away. It was settled. She could make it to Zu's house and back before the evening rush.

THE PATH to Zu's was well worn, dirt packed tight by travelers' sandals and horses' hooves. Small puddles were drying due to the high sun, and shimmering heat waves rising from the ground. Miu's heart raced inside her chest as she trudged the path. Placing her hand on her chest, she tried to match her incessant breathing with her footsteps.

She swore again to herself that freedom was worth never running away again. But now that she was building a name for herself here in Dilmun, it was hard to watch those she cared about run away from her.

"I'm not my father," she mumbled to herself.

She would never be him. She'd never murder the innocent. But she also wasn't allowing the innocent that worked for her to live either. She quickened her pace, hoping that if Tiame wasn't at Zu's he would at least know where she was headed. Either way, it would be nice to check in on him.

Zu had been putting together the last connections for Miu's beer loaves to head across to Ur. The first trip had seen great success, and Miu was already tracking new inventory. She knew she needed to grow more barley next year for the demand.

Zu had been helpful with this new shipment and used every contact he had to ensure the beer loaves' future success. He even sent his own girls to worship at the temple in Dilmun, begging for the blessing from the gods.

Having Zu fight for her success reminded her of Jara. How

she missed her. She welcomed the memories flooding her mind of Jara as she continued the walk toward Zu's.

She saw herself at eight years old, running away from home again. Why did she always run? She had been nearly running with her eyes shut from the tears of anger pouring down her face and had run right into Jara on the street. The look of surprise had scared Miu into trying to collect herself. She hadn't wanted Jara to see her cry.

"Jara." Miu had wiped a dirty hand through her tears. Inhaling deeply, she tried again. "Jara, I'm sorry. I didn't see you." Young girls could be punished for being so careless around merchants. The last thing she wanted was to be in trouble again. She waited with dread for her scolding from the woman.

Jara's gentle hands had reached down to wipe the hair away from Miu's face. "There, there child. What's wrong?"

Miu never experienced such gentleness and care before, not even from her own mother. With a little prodding, she'd told Jara how she'd worked really hard on a doll for her sister. Her father ripped it up. As she finished her story, she held the doll up to her with shaky hands.

"I made it just like Hulla would like it, Jara. I don't know why Father would do that. I don't know why he would take something from me or Hulla."

Jara bent down and told Miu they could make another doll together. And that's what they did that afternoon.

Miu was frightened about how her father would handle Jara overstepping his authority, but she assured Miu it would be fine. She discovered later that Jara had gone to her father to tell him how they had made the doll together, and that he couldn't take it away from such a sweet girl.

Her father never bowed down to anyone, especially a woman, but that day, Miu realized the influence Jara must have.

She wished she could go back to when it felt like her community was for her, not against her. Days when Jara showed her how real community was always there for each other. Days when she saw Jara look out for others before herself. Days when she saw Jara help other business owners with as much care as she'd helped Miu make a toy.

"Real community helps the hurting like you were hurting today, Miu," she'd whispered into her hair as they finished tying up the last bit of the doll, then placed it in Miu's small hands.

Today she wondered if she'd ever find someone she could trust like Jara. Too many people were like her father and Hashur for Miu to trust people. She'd resigned herself to believe she didn't need anyone to survive. Freedom in Dilmun or Ur was better than needing people. She'd find Tiame, not because she needed her, but because she would fight for her to be able to stand alone. Like she did with Didila. Like she hadn't been able to for her brother, Zigan.

She rounded the corner of the leather maker's tent and turned onto Zu's street. There was Tiame, clinging to Zu for dear life … sobbing.

"I'm sure Zu loves that," Miu mumbled to herself. Rolling her eyes, she made her way to them.

"Hello, Zu!" she shouted in a friendly tone, startling Tiame, as she hoped.

Tiame stepped back, wiping her eyes.

"Is my girl bothering you this afternoon?"

Tiame's gaze darted between Zu's face and Miu's. She clearly knew she'd done wrong by coming to see someone who was not her boss. Zu knew it as well, but no one would blame him for a woman clinging to him.

"Here's what's going to happen." Miu looked at Tiame, then glanced at Zu in a way that said for him to stay out of it.

He stiffened, then took a step back and turned to go into the house.

"Zu, I will need to speak to you as well."

"You can find me inside when you're done dealing with this overly emotional girl," he said with a wave of his hand.

Miu would handle him later, but she was not going to let

Tiame run away again. "Tiame, you can't just run away." Miu's past came rolling in waves over her heart and thoughts. Shaking it off, she needed to know why Tiame was running.

Calming her tone, she tried again. "Why do you run away from everything?"

This startled the girl enough that she opened her mouth to speak. Then something stopped her.

"I'm not usually here to listen to you. Normally we need to get a job done, but today I came to hear you," Miu encouraged.

"I think you're leaving." Tiame burst into tears. Miu wasn't sure what to think; this wasn't the response she'd expected. "You're going to leave and never come back."

"Why would you think that? I've just gotten the tavern under control. We have order, and you're doing a great job with the other girls." Miu attempted to calm the woman's tears while looking around to see if people were staring.

"I broke your gold-and-lapis lazuli necklace," Tiame stuttered then continued. "You've kicked people out for less than this, but Miu I can't lose this work, and I can't lose more people because of what I've done to others." Tiame fell to her knees, clinging to Miu's tunic.

Miu's toes curled in her sandals, gripping her feet and then her body, forcing her to stay. Maybe she had more in common with Tiame than she realized. Stooping down to touch the girl's long, braided hair, something in her wanted to know more about her. She didn't "need" Tiame around, but she did appreciate how she handled the girls in the tavern as well as her kindness toward Didila. Tiame wasn't going anywhere if Miu could help it.

"I'm not mad, Tiame. Things break." Then she swallowed hard at what was about to come out of her mouth. "I need you at the tavern."

Tiame still didn't move, her shoulders moving up and down with light sobs.

Did she hear her? She tried again, pushing back her own

pride. "Really, I need you at the tavern. It couldn't run without you."

After what felt like an entire phase of the moon passed, Tiame sat back on her heels and wiped her face. The dust on her face had pooled now into mud, streaking her cheeks and hands.

Tiame tried speaking. "When I was six years old, my family lived near the coast. One evening, a group of soldiers came by boat to see what they could steal from Dilmun." she hesitated, watching to see if Miu was listening. Then continued. "They raided our home first. The men stormed in and ripped our belongings to pieces. They shattered pottery, and my mother screamed for them to stop until one of the men slapped her so hard she fell silent on the floor."

Miu wiped under her eyes then took the girl's hands in her own. "You don't have to go on," she whispered.

But she continued, pouring out a story that had been buried since childhood. "After they stole everything of value in our home —our pearls, our tools for cooking, and our lapis lazuli—they fled the house like cowards." She exhaled.

There was pain behind her eyes as if she were still in her child-hood home. "That night two of my friends disappeared. Everyone believes those evil men took them away to be used for their own pleasures." Then the sobs began again, louder this time.

Miu tried picking the girl up to stand. She wanted to get her off the street. Maybe some of Zu's antics would be just what she needed. What did Miu know about helping a crying girl?

But she didn't budge.

"You were just a girl, Tiame. You couldn't have stopped those men if you tried," Miu suggested.

But the crying then turned into wailing. "I could have though! If I hadn't broken my mother's necklace of gold-and-lapis lazuli that day, this never would have happened. The gods hate me, Miu. They want me to be alone. It's why they stole my friends and Hashur and next will be you. I'm cursed by them." she wailed as she threw her head into Miu's lap.

Zu came out of the house, disturbed at the scene, but Miu had never felt more relieved. Waving him over without disturbing Tiame, she asked him to help pick the girl up.

A servant following Zu bent down, and Tiame didn't fight him. She had worn herself out. Tiame laid her head on the servant's neck, her entire body shaking with emotion.

"Take her to the room in the back of the house where she can see the garden from her window," Zu directed.

"Tiame, I will check on you in a little bit," Miu assured her. "I'm not going anywhere."

When she was out of hearing distance, Miu turned to look at Zu with eyes wide. "I don't know where any of that came from, Zu. Has she ever done anything like that before? Hashur never mentioned it. Why did she come to see you for this? You hate women who ruin your fun with their crying," Miu teased him.

"She brought me some things from the tavern you wanted to be fixed. All was good when she arrived. When she came, I was in conversation with a new merchant from Ur." He shrugged half-heartedly. "Then she left. When she came back, she was begging me to let her stay here, under the protection of a man or to send her away to Ur with the wealthy man she saw with me."

Miu felt anything but half-hearted after hearing this part of the story. A new merchant from Ur? Folding her arms, she tried keeping her own feelings under control.

"Tiame will be fine." Miu waved her hand, hoping Zu didn't notice her nerves. "Tell me about this new merchant. Was it a positive visit for upcoming shipments?"

"Let's go inside, Miu. I need beer and pigeon pies." He laughed. "My stomach only lets me talk business with food in hand."

As they walked up the steps toward Zu's house, he wrapped an arm around her shoulder and squeezed her. Was that a hug? She didn't have time to consider his fatherly affection before Zu began rattling on again.

"Miu, that merchant is a well-known lapis lazuli jeweler from

Ur. He might be just the connection we need with the temple there." Zu gave an excited wink, waving his other arm around in a grand gesture.

Panic surged through her, turning her bones into water as if the sun's heat melted them. A lapis lazuli jeweler? She knew of only one in Ur. One connected with the temple there.

Her father.

As her legs betrayed her, she heard Zu calling for one of his servants, and then the daylight went dark.

<h1>chapter
twenty-seven</h1>

Taku bent over, rubbing his knee. These evening walks with Jara had been healing his exhausted muscles, but they also healed something much deeper inside him.

"Two walks a day will help your muscles gain strength," she'd encouraged.

When they first started the walks, Taku could only make it to the door and back. Today he made it all the way to his mother's house. The asu had warned him that his right leg where the spider bit him would never fully heal, but he was doing better than anyone else Jara had ever seen with a bite like his.

When he limped into his mother's house, she welcomed him with open arms. Glancing around, he saw all was in order as he expected. The feeling of home washed over him.

"I'm so glad to see you're able to walk this far, Taku!" Her eyebrows danced. The smile on her face brought tears to his eyes. Oh, how he would miss her. He told her two days ago of his plans to follow Abram and this new god. He tried yesterday to explain what he knew.

"His name is Yahweh, Mother. No, he was never created; he only creates."

"How did he create the land, Taku, without first being created?" She rubbed her arms and then her neck.

"In the beginning, he created the skies and the land. The land was wild and waste, and darkness was over the watery deep, but the breath of God was hovering over those waters," Taku quoted the words Abram told him to memorize.

She didn't want to hear those words. Ur had a creation story. They didn't need another one to contradict everything Ur's priests taught. In Ur, the gods were part of the chaos, some even coming from the chaos.

But Abram's god ... he controlled the chaos. He ordered the chaos, putting it all in its place, just as Taku's mother did in her home.

The doubt lingered on his mother's face, but Taku had never been more certain of anything in his life. If there was a god that could contain the chaos, Taku would follow him to any land.

His mother's eyes were brighter than when he left her yesterday, her hug reminding him she loved him, no matter what choice he made.

"I came to tell you how far I've walked! I even have enough energy to walk back tonight," Taku exclaimed. "I can't stay for long, but I needed to see your face tonight, Mother. I will be taking a trip with Zaidu tomorrow, and I want to make sure you have whatever you need before I leave with Abram. You don't need my help, but ..."

He set his jaw, then continued, "You're a strong woman, and for that, I'm grateful for you. If you want to go with us, I can ask Abram if he needs help with his animals. I know how you love animals, Mother." He was rambling, he knew it.

Her smile wavered. "Taku, you're right. I don't need your help, but I will miss your friendship." A tear trickled down her dusty cheek. She turned to go tend to her birds.

She wouldn't want to be followed. He knew she was grateful he had stopped by, but leaving her with her birds was the best place he could imagine.

Exiting the house, Jara and Taku were silent as they turned toward Jara's tent.

"Can we go the way of the wildflowers?" Taku asked, knowing Jara never minded a detour. She nodded as they weaved their way between houses toward the wall of Ur. The wildflowers reminded him of Miu, wild and free ... untamable.

Jara broke the silence. "You say this god you're going to follow created everything? What does he look like? Where is his idol that we may know him?" Her posture was stiff.

It startled Taku. He'd never seen anything fluster her. He bristled, wanting to snap back at her that he didn't know the answers she was seeking. He needed time with Abram to learn. Nodding, he remembered she was learning as he was.

"I don't know, Jara." A lump choked his words. "You must speak to Abram to know. Or maybe ask Yahweh himself."

Her pace quickened, and Taku tried to keep up. She continued her rounds of questions as if Taku weren't there. "Then if he created the world and ordered the chaos, is he sky or land? Is he sun or moon? Wind or water? Tell me if you know, Taku," she demanded.

"He is none of those things, Jara. Not according to Abram," Taku pleaded. "He is not nature; he created nature. Look at these wildflowers."

The muscles in her jaw relaxed, so he continued. "The wildflowers are not god, but they were made by one god. A god who uses the sky and land, the sun and moon and the wind and water to display his strength. He uses these things to point to himself. I don't know him well, but I have seen his strength, and I have seen how he called Abram. I've seen the change on Abram's face of fear of the future of Ur into a peace that this god will guide him into greater things."

It was now Jara's turn to shed a tear, and Taku felt inadequate to help her. "I don't think I can believe all of this, Taku. If you choose to follow this god you call Yahweh, then you must deny the other gods. He's calling you to serve only him. Do you realize this? What if you lose their protection? What if he isn't as strong as Abram says? What if he leads you outside of Ur just to abandon you?"

Taku rubbed the back of his neck, feeling the weight of her questions and the loss he was risking. He had considered what she said, but he also knew the gods in Ur abandoned everyone at a whim.

"I've seen Abram's faith. That's enough for me. Plus, what has Ur ever given us? War? Division? Chaos? This god promises to make Abram's name great. If this god is who Abram declares him to be, I will follow him too. If Abram has found peace, it is peace I will follow."

Walking through the wildflowers, Taku gave her some space. As she steadied her pace, he wondered what she was thinking. If she wanted to share, she would. She slowed and bent down to pick a flower as red as their campfire last night. Twirling it in between her fingers, she continued walking.

"Taku, if you must leave with Abram, will you take one of Ur's gods with you?" She laid her hand on her heart. Was that pity in her eyes?

He didn't want her pity or to disappoint her. She'd saved his life. He owed her some peace of mind. "Sure," he consented. He wouldn't show Abram he had an idol in his belongings. He would travel with it and throw it out after they left the city.

Relief flooded her eyes as she took his hand and squeezed it. "Let's get you some dinner." She turned toward home and didn't look back.

After Taku had finished his lentil stew and fish cakes, he laid down on his pallet to rest. The smells from the leftover dishes wafted through his senses, and sleep would be a welcome friend tonight. The walk to and from his mother's house had left him feeling like he was on a boat. He hadn't been around that many people in weeks. His mother's hug had helped, but then the conversation with Jara had rattled him again.

Her interrogation shook the faith in a god he didn't know. But he also couldn't explain to anyone the peace that now rocked him to sleep at night. He couldn't explain the deep knowing Abram had of a god that created life, not chaos. He would give anything at this point to follow Abram. It didn't matter if Abram knew where he was going or not. He knew when Abram came tomorrow, Taku would tell him he would go with him.

People were an afterthought, he pondered; it was what he'd been told his entire life. The gods he knew made people do their bidding. The gods were weak and needed people to even feed them. What kind of god was that? They made rules for the humans to follow to support their happiness as if they couldn't create it themselves.

The god Abram described made a garden and placed people inside it for shelter, peace, provision, work, and to just be with Yahweh. The god Abram followed gave the people tools to rule the world. He wasn't lazy, and Abram said he wanted friendship with people. He made the world not just so humans could work but so they could work together. How strange.

If Taku didn't get his thoughts written down, he would never sleep tonight. "Jara, do you have clay and a stylus?".

"What are you planning on writing, Taku?" She pressed her lips together.

He couldn't make her happy, but her judgments would have to wait. Something was bubbling inside of him. A flow of sweet words bubbled from a well inside his heart, and he needed to dig the well to let it out.

"If you don't mind, I will show you when I'm finished," he said.

The words were too precious. Words he wasn't sure were his own.

Jara handed him the tools with a small nod and returned to preparing the tent for evening.

Yahweh needs no man. Creating man from dust.
Why would Yahweh bother to take notice of humanity and care
about our mere existence?
We are no greater than the dust from which we came.
Yahweh separated skies from land and hung the stars in the dome
above.

THE WRITING FLOWED through his fingers, and his heart raced. It felt as if everything he'd ever wanted to say about a deity was overflowing onto this tablet. Images flooded his mind as he pictured a world where a single deity had the strength to create everything around him, order the cosmos, rule it all, and never need help keeping it together. Today, his writing carried no shame, only relief.

Yahweh, you defeat the snake who lies in
wait to destroy us.
You guide me on paths to follow you away
from Ur, into a land you provide,
You guide me on paths of your choosing
As if it were a walk through the wildflowers
you've painted and planted.
As if it were calm seas to Dilmun.

EXHAUSTED, his hand cramping and dry from clay, Taku finally laid down his stylus. He went through every emotion while writing, everything pouring out onto the tablet. His breathing slowed, and his eyes felt heavy. Looking around, the world outside the tent was dark, while inside a slow-burning fire glowed. The crackling fire flooded his ears and lulled his mind as he almost drifted to sleep.

Until he remembered Dilmun. *Calm seas to Dilmun.* Those words had flowed from his own hands. Tomorrow he would speak to Zaidu. One more trip to help his friend, one more trip to tell Miu. If he never saw her again, then he needed to tell her about this god; even if she yelled at him to leave, or worse, even if she ignored him.

Would he have what it took to go back to Dilmun? Urgency stirred in his stomach. He must tell Miu. He felt a sensation in his legs, to get up, to do something. Standing to take a walk, he had to move. Pushing the tent door to the side, he stepped outside. Pulling his head back, he inhaled and looked up to see the stars moving across the dark dome above.

"How wondrous are the works of your hands," he whispered.

chapter
twenty-eight

Coiling up the lines, Taku watched Zaidu push off the docks at Ur. His insides felt like the line he was coiling, twisted and knotted. He had to tell Zaidu about leaving with Abram, but he needed the right time.

"Get on with it, boys," Zaidu yelled. The only time Taku ever heard Zaidu raise his voice was leaving the docks, keeping the men focused and moving to the sound of his voice.

The thought of Zaidu yelling at him made his stomach hurt. He needed something to calm his nerves. Leaning his hip on the side of the boat, he crossed his arms. The sky was filling with shades of orange and pink. His mother would love the colors, but for a sailor, it meant rough seas to Dilmun.

Bracing himself for the storm on the chaos waters and the potential storm with Zaidu, he meditated on the words he'd written to the god of Abram.

Yahweh, you defeat the snake who lies in
wait to destroy us.
You guide me on paths to follow you away
from Ur, into a land you provide,
You guide me on paths of your choosing

As if it were a walk through the wildflowers
you've painted and planted.
As if it were calm seas to Dilmun.

CALM SEAS TO DILMUN. And even if he bypassed the storms with Zaidu and the waters, another storm awaited him when he reached the shore. Miu.

"How are you feeling?" Zaidu slapped Taku on the shoulder, startling him out of his thoughts.

"Strong, sir." Taku kept his comments short. He wasn't ready to talk yet. He needed more time.

"Sun looks like it'll be menacing today, huh?" Zaidu said.

He was always observing the weather and knew more about it than the weathermen in Ur, at least from what Taku noticed. Two years ago, Zaidu knew a storm was coming three or four days ahead of time.

"The birds are on the move," Zaidu had told Taku then.

"Why does that matter?" Taku questioned.

"The birds know their maker, and they fly away when told. It's humans who don't listen to our gods."

Zaidu had shrugged his shoulders as if what he'd said wasn't profound. His wisdom surpassed that of kings and priests, in Taku's opinion. It was the same today; if Zaidu said today the waters would be hard to navigate, the waters would be hard to navigate.

Zaidu was nothing like the weather, which was hot and cold, unpredictable. He had his routine. He understood the world around him, and he walked in that understanding. He had strong opinions but never wavered when someone disagreed with them.

The slight ripples in the water moved in tandem with the rising of the sun. It was certain when the sun peeked its full face above the land that the ripples would turn to rolling waves.

Prepare the men, prepare the boat. That was Zaidu's order.

He'd lost a ship before, but not when he was captain. Rowing hard in calmer ripples of water meant gaining space toward Dilmun.

Taku walked the length of the boat handing out breakfast, a barley cake with apricot jam, filling enough for them to cross with strength in their bones.

Each man took his turn, pausing to eat their cakes while the rest of the crew rowed hard. Zaidu promised them all a jar of beer when they made it to Dilmun, always a motivator.

As the men finished their cakes, the warm rays of the sun emerged fully above the land, casting a bright light into their eyes. Concurrently, the rippling waters of the ocean began to stir, as if in response to the sun's awakening.

The rocking was steady at first, then the clouds began to cover the intense heat. The change would allow for better visibility, but worse control of the oars. The air temperature dropped suddenly, leaving a cooling breeze that gave Taku chills. He took a breath, the fresh air smelling of rain.

"Alright men, have heart!" Taku shouted. He prepared the boat, checking every crate and bin. Every man's oar. Every plank. The dove Zaidu brought flapped its wings and cooed incessantly, grating on Taku's bones.

The boat glided through the water like a bird through the wind. There was no room for a man to be seasick. The waves grew as the wind picked up speed, blowing any remaining lines the boat had around in the air.

"We must row faster!" Zaidu shouted, forcing the men's speed. "One, two, three."

"One, two, three." The counting kept their minds on a rhythm and off the storm raging around them.

A large wave splashed over the side of the boat, but the men continued counting along Zaidu.

Gripping the side of the boat, Taku watched Zaidu. He had no fear on these waters and always knew just what to say. "A beer is on the line, men!"

Taku went to the bow of the boat to see if he could find the sun. Which direction were they headed? With the sun gone, and no heavenly beings in the sky, it was impossible to know.

He was desperate to find their direction as another wave smacked him off the bow into the belly of the boat. On his back, he only saw the dark skies above. His strength had returned, but this storm would tire even the healthiest of men. A gust of wind blew across the boat, spinning it in a circle, leaving Taku ready to spill his barley cake.

"Yahweh, god of all gods, make way for calm seas to Dilmun," Taku prayed. He didn't know what else to do. If the god of Abram was real, then he created the watering skies and the winds. If he was real, he could guide their boat on his own waters. The waters were not a threat to him, but a creation of his. "Yahweh, god of all gods, make way for calm seas to Dilmun."

The wind ceased. The waves stilled. The clouds began to part as the sun came out in full force. Taku stood breathless and not from his fall.

Standing to see if it was real, he looked at the men. They were staring over the sides of the boat. What happened? Did Abram's god really hear his prayer? Did he really make a safe way to Dilmun? Taku's mouth fell open. Even the dove was resting in his crate. A god of peace.

Zaidu looked more shocked than any of the men. He was silenced.

"Keep rowing! Calm seas to Dilmun!" Taku took control while Zaidu composed himself. As the men rerouted based on the sun's location in the skies, Taku couldn't stop smiling, a smile that broke into a childlike giggle.

"What are you laughing at?" Zaidu asked. "That was the strangest thing I've ever seen. I didn't predict that. We were certain to get off course and lose our cargo."

Taku knew he couldn't keep quiet about this god any longer. Zaidu needed to know him too. He didn't care if Zaidu ignored him, dismissed him, or laughed at him. This god was powerful.

"Zaidu, we have to talk. I won't be able to lead the new shipping route for you."

AT THE TAVERN, the men guzzled beer at an abnormal rate. The ruckus would soon begin. Taku was anxious he'd run into Miu, but Tiame said she was at Zu's for the evening.

Zaidu finished paying his portion of the beer he promised the men and came to sit beside Taku.

"You really think this god of yours calmed the waves and the wind?"

"I do." Taku looked around, wishing they could speak somewhere quieter.

"If he was able to get us out of that storm and safely to Dilmun, you can have my dove for sacrifice to him," he said then paused. "Where do you sacrifice to this god, Taku? He doesn't reside in a temple. You cannot travel to the heavens and meet with him for offerings."

Taku hadn't considered this, but it was true. Every god required sacrifices of some kind. He tucked the question away to ask Abram when he saw him.

"I'm not sure, Zaidu. I will speak with Abram." He rubbed his sweaty palms on his thighs then continued. "I'm sorry I cannot keep my promise of running a trade route for you,"

"If you're following a god that can do what I just saw, then you must do just that. I've also heard there is strife in Ur and that the rains will cease soon. Our great Ur will not be what it once was."

Zaidu looked down at his hands and then put them on the table open-faced. "Taku, men like me have served Ur for years. My callouses have hardened from the building of Ur's walls and temples. These hands have traversed many chaos waters so Ur can enjoy the sweet waters from the land. I am set in my ways. I am committed to serving Ur's gods until its destruction or its greatness."

Taku started to speak, but Zaidu raised his hand as if to quiet him and then continued. "You, Taku, have been given a gift. A new way to see the world. You can experience new lands while being guided by a powerful god. You have my blessing."

Then his calloused hands pushed him up from the table, and he turned to leave. He paused and turned to face Taku, "You're welcome to travel home with us, and you're also welcome on any of my boats at any time." With a nod of his head, he left.

Inhaling deeply, Taku didn't know what to say. Yahweh had done the work. Zaidu saw with his own eyes what he had done, and there was no room for doubt. Taku was free to follow Abram!

"This place is running as smooth as ever," came a voice through the tent's curtains.

Taku's cheeks flushed. Time to tell Miu. Turning around to face her, she caught his eye. He'd never seen her speechless before, and it made him laugh.

"What are you doing here?" A smile crept across her face. She ran to him, throwing her arms around his neck and squeezing as if she'd never let him go.

Not expecting such a welcome, Taku stumbled backward, falling into another tavern girl and spilling beer on everything. Himself. Miu. The girl. The floor. Another patron. He knew Miu would get up shouting, but she didn't. She politely asked the tavern girl to get some things to clean up.

"Taku, I need to change my tunic now. Meet me in the kitchen, I'll be right back. It's so good to see you!" Then she left.

Walking toward the kitchen, Taku wasn't sure what had happened. He thought after he'd left that Miu would never want to speak to him again. Women. He'd never understand them.

Pushing the curtains back to the kitchen, he walked into the most smoothly-operating place he'd ever seen. Every girl had a station for chopping food, kneading dough, or stirring a pot over the fire. The sounds that would normally deafen him today sounded like a melody, everyone moving to the same notes.

Shocked again, he wasn't sure what other surprises he would encounter. Sitting down in a seat in the corner, he bumped his head on something. Rubbing his head with a scowl, he turned to see what it was.

"My ship!" he whispered. She'd found it. How had she ...? It had been for Didila.

"I asked Didila where she wanted to keep the ship you made for her, and she said in the kitchen." Miu slowly walked into the room. She looked hesitant. Something had changed in this girl.

Taku rolled the wood around in his hand, remembering the hours he spent crafting a ship to remind Didila of his trade route. The one he no longer would be doing.

"Why did she choose the kitchen?" His tone was uncertain.

"She said it's where we all will see it. It's the busiest place in the entire tavern. She wanted to remember your kindness."

Was that a tear in Miu's eye? Surely not.

"Where is she? I'd love to see her," Taku asked.

"She is just getting ready for bed. I can get her for you." She stood to leave again.

"No, wait. I want to see her, but there's something I need to tell you first." He bit his lip.

Miu stared. Was she wondering why he was back?

"Do you need money? I hear things are getting bad in Ur, is there something wrong?" She was clearly worried for him.

Taku stood to reassure her, forgetting he was the one with something to say.

"Speak up, Taku, What's wrong?"

"Nothing is wrong. I just ..." Was this the right thing to do? Should he invite her to leave the tavern? She'd just laugh him out of the tavern. She despised the gods. Here he was, a crazy man asking her to leave everything to follow the one thing she wanted freedom from.

She tapped her foot, and he realized his thoughts weren't helping him speak. "Do you remember Abram? From Ur?"

"Of course. Everyone knows him. Old man, rich, no kids." She folded her arms.

He was dragging this out and refused to give in, even a little. "I've encountered a new god," he blurted out. "One who Abram knows, and who knows Abram. One who created the whole world without help. One who supports the pillars of the earth by his own hand. One who brought us safely through a storm from Ur to Dilmun today. You can ask any of the—"

"Heaven and earth, Taku," she cut him off. "You of all people know how the gods use us. Every sailor says the gods bring them home from a storm. Your god is nothing new. He's no different." She turned to leave the kitchen. "I'm going to get Didila. She'll be happy to see you."

Taku dropped his head in defeat. Would he ever be able to get through to her? Did Yahweh hear prayers like this? Could he ask Yahweh to speak to her?

Miu laid down on her pallet. The girls were finishing up in the kitchen, putting the pots in their places and letting down the curtains with a swoosh to close off the tavern. She felt her muscles relax, finally with a sense of peace for the first time since Taku had left.

She understood why he did. Miu was controlling and never listened to him. Leaving Ur was the best decision for her, and she'd chased freedom from the gods and her father for what now felt like many seasons, but Taku had grounded her in a way she hadn't expected. Sure, he infuriated her, but he also challenged her. Like with this new idea of a "new god."

Miu rolled over onto her back in frustration, wishing she was staring at the stars. She slammed her fists down on her pallet. Didila coughed and rolled away from her.

Then she remembered the community she'd been building here. A smile pulled at the corner of her mouth. Taku simplified life and brought peace. Didila brought joy to any hardship. Zu trusted her and gave her the ability to dream. Was this what life was supposed to be about? Less about the gods' demands and more about people who loved her? If Taku would promise to stay, she'd finally feel as if she could cut all ties to Ur. She'd finally be able to let go of her dreaded father and run her tavern, be able to show the people of Dilmun the strength they needed. Together they'd be able to let go of this false promise of the gods and live in freedom to do whatever they wanted to do.

She leaned over to rub stray hairs from Didila's brow, smiling to herself. The only thing stopping her was Taku's new belief in this god of Abram. It was absurd, as all gods were. A god he could pray to that heard him? Wasn't that the same as every other god?

"He calmed the storm to Dilmun," he'd told her over dinner.

She'd wanted to send Didila off to play, protecting her from wild dreams of the gods.

"Don't fill her head with dumb ideas, Taku."

"The chaos waters were raging. The men were going to be slung overboard. I myself was at the bottom of the boat, and I cried out to him. He heard me. He cared enough to stop the chaos waters, Miu." He pleaded with her to believe him.

And she'd wanted to. She was scared to lose him in Dilmun, but more afraid to lose him to worshipping a god.

"How do you know your god is real?" Didila asked as she looked up into Taku's eyes. He stopped bouncing her on his knee and turned her to face him.

"I wrote a poem about him. Would you like to read it?" Taku glanced at Miu's face with what she guessed was apprehension.

She'd nodded at him to go ahead. She didn't want to stop his writing; he'd worked hard for the freedom to write.

He pulled a clay tablet from his leather pouch and let the little girl's maturing hands take it. They weren't pudgy any longer, but were losing the little dimples in her knuckles and growing longer.

"Can you read it, or do you need me to help?" Taku asked.

"Can we do it together?" excited to practice reading the way Miu had taught her recently.

*Yahweh, you defeat the snake who lies in
wait to destroy us.*

*You guide me on paths to follow you away
from Ur, into a land you provide,
You guide me on paths of your choosing
As if it were a walk through the wildflowers
you've painted and planted.
As if it were calm seas to Dilmun.*

MIU WAS STUNNED. Defeating a snake? Paths away from Ur? Wildflowers he painted? Calm seas to Dilmun? Trying to calm her own nerves, she looked at Didila's face and saw a tear in her eye. The words spoke to them both, just obviously in a different way.

"That was beautiful, Taku. Your god made your seas calm all the way here to tell us about him." And then Didila jumped down from his lap. She walked over to kiss Miu on the cheek and bounced off to bed, leaving silence in her wake. What was Miu supposed to do with that?

"Miu, I know you don't want to believe in the gods of Ur and Dilmun. Then don't. But Abram says this god is one of peace. He's a god that brings families together. He's called Abram to leave Ur and its gods. I came to see if you'd follow us." More silence followed his question.

"How dare you ask me to leave everything." She waved her arm around the kitchen. "I can't leave Didila, Tiame, or Zu. Dilmun needs me."

"I'm leaving Dilmun tomorrow, and when I do, I won't be coming back, Miu."

She could tell he meant it. His voice held more determination than she'd ever heard.

"When we get back to Ur, Abram has tents to be made. Then in a few moons, we will be leaving for a land Yahweh will show us. I hope you will be with us when we do. I will come by in the morning." Then he stood and left the kitchen.

She could see how trusting only a few close friends was valuable, but she'd never leave a friend just to follow a god. Now, she needed to decide if Dilmun, Zu, Didila, Tiame, the tavern, and her beer loaves business were more important than Taku. Her breathing slowed as her muscles grew heavier.

Now as she lay on her mat thinking of their conversation, she wrestled with sleep and the decision she had to make tomorrow.

Didila and Miu were running with abandon through the wildflowers of Ur, the wind blowing in her face and the giggles of the sweet girl in her ears. She put her hands out to her side letting the flowers tickle her fingertips. Miu had never felt a happier moment. The air was fresh and crisp, different than normal.

Why was she in Ur? She looked around, and then came to an abrupt stop. From the field, she saw the city that raised her engulfed in war. Blood was pouring down the walls of the city in LARGE amounts. She could hear the screams of children, and she even thought she heard her brother, Zigan.

In dread, she began reaching for Didila, not knowing if she should run away or toward this city of death, but she couldn't find her hand. Prying her eyes away from Ur's walls, she searched for the girl. When she couldn't see her, she yelled ...

Nothing came out; her voice choked. Trying again, still without sound. Frantic, she began running through the flowers that had once held hope, in circles at first, then back and forth through the field.

Putting her hands on her knees she paused to catch her breath.

That's when the petals came into clear view. Each one contained letters, and each flower held a word inside. She tried to decipher the words. Rubbing her eyes, she looked again. Touching a delicate yellow flower, she saw it read *control*. A red one read *leadership*. A bright blue flower read *peace*. The last word she saw was on an orange flower bearing the word *freedom*.

The flowers were inscribed with her dreams. She frantically picked each flower, holding them to her chest as she kept trying to call to Didila. Exhausted and clinging to her bouquet of dreams, she fell to the ground.

She sensed something near her head; was it her sweet girl? Fear gripping her insides she tried opening her eyes.

A black snake, a dragon in nature, slithered toward her, smelling her with its forked tongue. As it came closer, she realized it was eating all the orange flowers in its path. Heat was coursing through her body. She clutched the flowers tightly as the snake drew closer, stripping away her remaining freedom.

She had nothing left to fight with, and she began to crawl away. Squirming, her arms and legs felt like iron attached to her, not moving, not giving her any freedom to run. She looked down at her chest, hoping not to drop the dreams she had left, but they were gone. Turned to dust.

Hot tears were pricking her eyes and then falling to her cheeks, the wildflowers crumbling as she frantically tried to hold any tiny fragments in her fingers.

Startling awake, Miu found she couldn't breathe. She sat up, sweat pouring from her brow, and checked on Didila. She checked her hands for dust but found nothing. It had been a dream. Her body wouldn't sit still; she had to move.

Careful not to disturb Didila, she got up and walked to the front of the tavern. She passed the tables that held patrons who respected her. She passed pots and barrels of beer she'd learned how to brew, which meant freedom to her. The ability to run a tavern that was her own. She'd gotten rid of Hashur and Alor. She'd earned respect from Amar. She'd gained control, leadership, peace, and freedom here in Dilmun.

Would a snake steal it all?

Opening the tavern's main curtain, she walked outside. The

sun was just beginning to light up the sky. She needed stability. It felt like the ground was shaking beneath her.

"Zu," she whispered. He'd promised he'd be there for her. He'd looked her in the eye and told her, "Your interests are my interests. I have fought hard for you, to ensure your name is known as the creator behind this invention. If I've gone to these great lengths, you have to trust me."

And she had. She'd trusted him to care for her shipments and connections. She'd trusted him to help her gain control of the tavern. She'd trusted him to help her keep her dreams. He'd given her freedom and control all at the same time. He'd know what to do with this dream.

⁂

MIU THREW OPEN the door to Zu's mansion. She'd been here enough to feel like family. She looked around the empty entrance room; maybe he was still asleep from a party he'd had the night before. No worries, she'd wait. She'd go to the back patio and see if someone would bring her some breakfast. Hands still shaking from the dream and feet still sure of her confidence in Zu, she opened the doors to walk outside.

There he was. Even with his back to her, she recognized her father. He stood taller than ever. Fear coursed through her, but she willed herself to stay. She was safe with Zu. Her body temperature rose as she tried to speak, just as in her dream.

"You snake," she mumbled.

It was enough sound for him to turn to face her. A smirk spread across his face as he took one small step in her direction.

Miu held her ground. Today she would not run. She braced herself.

"You're a murderer. I saw you kill Zigan," she spewed as unexpected tears pricked her eyes. Pushing them back, she continued. "His sickness plagued your success. You couldn't handle it, and you took his life. You snake!"

Anger crept up her father's face like a treacherous wave over a ship, immediate and sudden. He stepped toward her and grabbed her arm.

His breath was on her face, but she clamped her mouth shut, refusing to let him see her fear.

"The law states you still belong to me." His voice sounded like rolling thunder, ready to explode. "Whatever little party you think you've created here is over; you're coming with me."

He began to drag her out, but Miu held onto the fact that they were in Zu's house.

"Zu!" she shouted, her voice not failing this time. "Zu!"

"He won't save you, child. You are the daughter of Badak. No one can save you." His laugh was dark as he dragged her out of the back patio and into the main entrance.

Miu fought him the whole way. She kicked, but his grip became tighter. He pulled her down a hallway toward the front door. There he was.

"Zu," Miu said, relieved when she saw him. "This man thinks I belong to him. Tell him I'm under your protection."

Zu looked at her then at her father. Taking a step back, he said, "She's simply a servant. If you must have her, you can take her."

Miu tried making eye contact with him as her father grabbed her by her elbows and dragged her closer to the front door.

"Zu, you promised! You said my interests are your interests. What are you allowing?" she wailed.

Zu never looked up as her father dragged her out the front door and down the stairs, his firm grip never relenting.

Good morning!" Didila ran and jumped on Taku's stomach.

"Umph!" Taku smiled as he tried to sit up, and the little girl toppled off his stomach onto the floor. "You're up early." he smiled.

"Come on, Taku. Miu is gone, and I want to hear more about your god." Her eyes were wide with expectation.

He couldn't tell her no, unless Miu came in. She deserved to know about the kindness of this god.

"God said, 'Let there be light' and there was light, and God saw that the light was good; and God separated the light from the darkness, and God called the light 'day,' and the darkness he called 'night.'" Taku quoted Abram's words to her.

As he continued, Didila's eyes lit up as light illuminates darkness. "This God is not like us, Didila. He doesn't struggle to keep the light separated from darkness. Because of his strength, he holds all creation in place. Just as he holds you in his hands." He smiled and poked her in her stomach, causing a giggle to rise from her mouth to her cheeks and into those dark eyes of hers.

How did children hear of a god like this and want more, yet Miu heard the same words only to run farther away? Taku didn't understand.

He needed to find her anyway. She left the conversation last night looking worried. He'd offered her a way out of her fight for freedom and independence, but she craved that more than anything. He'd offered her a community of people who had a god who would dwell with them as they journeyed, and she'd run from that.

"Want to go look together? Or do you have chores?" Taku tilted his head to the side.

"I have chores." Her shoulders slumped.

"I'm proud of your honesty, Didila. Yahweh honors that!" Her shoulders lifted in pride as she turned to leave.

"I will come back to see you before I leave."

She nodded then she skipped away.

Miu had done a good job raising the little girl. She was responsible and curious. Even more though, she was kind. All traits Miu had encouraged in her. Smiling to himself, he turned to find Miu.

"WHAT DO YOU MEAN SHE LEFT?" Taku demanded, his nostrils flaring. His entire body was shaking, but he continued. "She would never leave Dilmun. We spoke about it last night. Tell me where she went."

Zu wouldn't look at him. He turned to smile at the woman on his arms. "Ladies, this man brings anger into our home. He should know we are here for pleasure. Someone from the temple in Ur named Badak came yesterday saying she belongs to him. Who am I to argue with the gods?" He laughed.

Falling to the ground, Taku let out a loud wail. Ripping his clothes, he sobbed.

Zu put his hand in the air as he walked away and snapped his fingers, indicating for the men to drag Taku away. Sadness was not welcome.

"You gorge yourselves on pleasures while others fade into the background. May Yahweh curse you and your household of women!" Taku pushed against the guards. When he stomped on a guard's foot, they released him. He ran down the front steps and into the streets. Stumbling from his hot tears, he headed toward Zaidu's boat. If Miu was in Ur, then he needed to find her.

TAKU'S FEET hit the docks in Ur, and he kept running. His mind hadn't stopped running the entire ship ride from Dilmun, and he'd worried Zaidu with his relentless pacing. He'd worried the doves too. They barely stopped squawking for the journey across either. He related to them. The ship had never crossed so slowly; he was sure he could have swum faster.

Feeling his feet on the dry ground again gave him another boost of energy he needed. On the slow trip across, he'd made up his mind to go to Abram first. He could try to find Badak and Miu on his own, but he lacked authority in town; he wouldn't convince Badak of anything.

He reached Abram's home and paused. Putting his hands on his knees to catch his breath, he prayed. "Yahweh, go before me."

He knocked on the door, and Sarai answered. Her beauty was stunning, even in the state of shock he was in.

Her eyes pierced through his panic. "Oh, Taku." She ushered him into the house. "You look as if you've encountered death itself."

"I need to speak with Abram," he announced.

Her kind smile calmed him. "He's with the tentmakers preparing for our journey. It seems as if Yahweh is encouraging some of them to leave their tent work and follow us from Ur."

"May I find him there?"

"Why don't you pause for some food first? Bread? Cheese?" Her eyes were hopeful.

"I can take some to go." He was sure she wouldn't let him

leave without it. Even without children she was naturally motherlike.

Making his way to Abram, he tore off a piece of bread and chewed it. Sarai was right, he did need the food. How was this god Yahweh already making a new family for him? Smiling to himself, he picked up the pace to reach Abram and the tentmakers.

Organized rows of weavers, women and men, were seated at their looms singing. Together, they joined in a song about the slaying of the chaos waters, a dream Taku had had himself. One day the waters would not flood their cities or capture their ships. Was it possible to believe that one day the waters would be tamed like a wild horse honoring its master?

The delight in their voices cast out any hesitation Taku had about following a man like Abram. They worked together, with one goal in mind. Their hands may have been calloused from work, but their hearts were soft with expectation.

"Taku!" The now-familiar voice called his name. To his left, Abram walked toward him with open arms.

For a moment, he forgot his mother, Zaidu, and even Miu. He let himself embrace this strange yet welcoming man.

"What brings you here?" Abram held him at an arm's distance.

"They took my friend." The weight of everything over the last couple of days immediately weighed on Taku.

Abram waited in silence, but his presence never wavered.

Taku raised his head to meet Abram's gaze, and all he saw was compassion. Clenching his fists at his sides, he tried again. "My friend Miu used to live in Ur. Her father is a jewler for the temple there, specializing in lapis lazuli. Miu escaped him and ran. All the way to Dilmun. It's there where I met her. Now she runs a successful tavern there and raises a little ..."

"Raises a what, Taku?" Abram pushed.

"I left in such a hurry. Didila has no one!"

"Taku, calm down, son. Who is Didila?" Abram asked.

"Miu's father met a man in Dilmun and discovered Miu was

there in town. He came to take her back. She's now here in Ur. If her father is half as evil as she described, then he likely has her being prostituted at the temple." His story was getting attention from the weavers.

"Continue your work." Abram smiled. "We leave as soon as these tents are completed. To Yahweh be glory." Then he guided Taku out of earshot of the weavers.

"Tell me now, who again is Didila?" he asked.

"Miu adopted a young girl from the evil woman who owned the tavern in Dilmun. She's all alone there. Her mother is in jail. I left in such a hurry to rescue Miu that I left Didila."

"I will send word to a trusted man in Dilmun. He will find her. Now tell me about how to find your friend Miu." He smiled.

TOGETHER ABRAM and Taku walked back to Abram's home and discussed Miu's predicament. The bricks beneath their feet became a pathway in joining their hearts together. They had the same goal: Yahweh. And in the heart of Yahweh, they knew he was a creator. A creator of new paths, new friendships, and a creator of order.

Miu lost in the temple of prostitution or under her father's strong hand was not the way of Yahweh. They both knew it. They'd both experienced Yahweh's hand of protection and strength. They'd both seen how Yahweh had pursued them, and so they now would pursue Miu.

Clearing his throat, Taku wanted to be honest with Abram about Miu. "She doesn't even want to believe in Yahweh." His ears got hot. Would Abram only want to rescue someone who wanted to follow Yahweh?

"Taku, I spent my entire life not following Yahweh. We all think the gods of Ur are all there are. It wasn't until Yahweh showed himself to me that I understood. We will find your friend and see if she's willing to go with us or not." Abram smiled as if it were that simple.

"You don't know her, Abram." Taku fidgeted with his tunic, hoping he didn't sound rude. "She's her own god. And she's not afraid of authority. It's what got her to lead her own tavern. If only she'd realize she needed other people and her Creator."

The ziggurat loomed in front of them. Inside was all the evil she'd been fighting since he met her. It was also the same evil he'd fought, the one that told him to keep his voice silent. The priests said he was made to mimic their words, not ones that bubbled up inside of him. Especially not the words that flowed today to a god who wanted to lead them outside of these walls and into a place to dwell with him. The same god that created the skies and filled them with birds, who created the land and filled it with creatures that actually wanted to dwell with him, and Abram, and all those tentmakers. Those willing to leave behind a land of chaos into a land he would show them.

Abram let Taku sit with his thoughts for a while as they continued their walk, but it wasn't until they neared his home that he asked him a question. "Taku, what would it take for Miu to leave Ur and come with us?"

He pinched his lips together, willing the tears in his eyes to stay put. He'd asked himself the same question all the way from Dilmun to Ur. "Miu believes the gods are unreliable and that she has to hold it together with her own strength. It's why she fights so hard for people. It's why she took care of Didila and every person at that tavern.

"But she doesn't have the strength to hold everyone afloat. Her strength rises and falls like the tides of the chaos waters. She doesn't have to be strong all the time. But Abram, if she could understand there's someone who made not only the chaos waters but also the tides, she'd stop trying to be the strong one. She'd fight for others and let them ride her waves, knowing she was strengthened and supported by the Almighty One in a sea of waves, each wave in community with the other. Each wave bringing life to the next one."

He thought he saw a tear in Abram's eye as he opened the door to their house to go inside.

Sarai smiled when she saw them both and came to kiss her husband on his cheek, ready to be the next wave to his day. "How long until we're ready, Abram?" she asked.

"Not long now, but we have a problem we must fix while we wait." He nodded toward Taku.

"Taku, what kind of trouble have you gotten into this time?" Sarai teased, winking at him.

"You have no idea," Abram said, still smiling. "We have a war to fight before we ever leave Ur, my sweet Sarai. Tomorrow I must speak with Badak."

Sarai's lighthearted smile faded as she searched Abram's eyes for answers.

He gave no further words as they sat down together to share a meal of pigeon pies, melon, and fresh cheese. But Taku felt a sense of peace knowing that Abram of Ur would help him get Miu back.

Miu's eyes ached from the tears that fell as they crossed the chaos waters. She wasn't fearful of this crossing, because what was there to lose? If her father had thrown her overboard and let her body fall to the grave, what would it matter? He had her and she had nothing.

She'd mourned the loss of her tavern and the girls at the tavern, especially Tiame. She'd lost her breakfast over the side of the ship crossing when she remembered the look on Zu's face as her father dragged her out of his house. He'd had the power to keep her in Dilmun, but he had walked away.

But her greatest loss was Didila. As her father's men carried her down the streets of Dilmun, she went back and forth in her mind on whether she should demand they go get the girl. Was she safer if Tiame took care of her? Was she better without ever knowing the hands of Badak?

Rubbing her sore cheek from the punch of a guard, she looked up, squinting. There was the city of Ur in all its glory.

After they pulled up to the docks, she took a guard's hand to step foot on her homeland soil. At least her father hadn't bound her hands for the ride home, leaving her some small freedom.

She'd resigned herself to Ur. Walking in a single file line behind her father, with men in front of him and behind her, they marched through the city. In Dilmun, she'd imagined Ur to flourish and grow more. As a little girl, it felt as if the city grew every time she opened her eyes from her pallet, something new to explore and see being built. The hope she once felt in Ur was now condensed into this single moment of shame, walking to her father's house.

As they passed by the little houses, children played in the doorways and women kneaded bread in time for dinner. Families. Together, the way they were supposed to be. The smell of dinner wafting through the streets hit her mind, taking her back to Dilmun. Tiame must be preparing the girls for customers. If her timing was right, they'd be lining up for their hair inspection, making sure each strand was properly in place. Was the tavern even running? Why did every memory make her feel like she was breaking into a thousand pieces?

They neared the place where she used to play as a little girl. She'd weave wildflowers into crowns for her sister's hair, giggling. "For you, Queen Hulla." She'd place the wreath of blues, oranges, and yellow onto her head.

Her father's house was coming up, and she dared to speak. "Father, did Mother know you were coming for me?"

Silence.

He'd refused to speak to her since he stole her from Dilmun. Maybe her mother would answer questions for her, although she never went against him in the past. Seeing her childhood home in the distance, she wondered if her sister was still there. Was she still as happy as Miu had last seen her at the festival, bouncing hair and joy bubbling up? Her father's workshop was in the back of the house, and she remembered the years she'd spent trying to keep him successful, trying to keep his finances in order so the city would honor him. Not her.

Resentment built in her bones; the house was right beside their troop of people. But instead of stopping, her father kept marching. Where were they going? What was happening?

Squirming, she tried shoving her way toward him. "Where are we going?" she demanded.

Silence.

A guard jerked her back into her place in line, leaving an immediate bruise on her muscled arms. She refused to show pain. Her arms had carried children. They'd carried pots of beer and baskets of barley. She'd not grown weak in Dilmun. Why was he not taking her home?

Then they turned the corner, and she saw.

Shoulders curling forward and her chest caving in, she knew. Looming in the distance just in direct view was the temple. She knew the atrocities that happened to women there. He wouldn't do to her what he'd done to her brother. She wasn't worth it to the gods. But she would bring a decent amount of silver to him as a temple prostitute.

She no longer had to fight her father, now she was up against the gods. She'd avoided their control in Dilmun. How could she do the same here? The temple was too large. The power was too strong.

"This way," Her father barked at the men.

Miu and the men followed him up the flight of stairs to where heaven and earth met. They were going to the highest place, where women gave themselves to be inhabited by gods, or priests to a god, as an offering given in a detestable exchange. Bodies for blessings. Honor for humiliation. Control and freedom for shackles and bondage.

Miu knew her father well, and this was his form of punishment for her. He hadn't been able to control her then, so he would have the gods do it for him. He'd have the priests use her again and again while she wasted away to nothing.

Reaching the top sanctuary of the ziggurat, Miu refused to show how winded she was from the stairs, while her father's men refused to show self-restraint while gawking at the sight of the half-dressed women lying around the walls.

"Nanna, keeper of time, do you wish to worship him?" their smooth, sultry voices cried out.

"Nanna inhabits his people through sacrifice of your seed. Lie with us, we give blessing," they chanted.

A smirk spread across her father's face as he turned to face her. "This will be your place."

"This is what you have to say to me? Years I toiled for you. Years I made *you* successful, and this is what you repay me with?" She spat on the bricks beneath her sandals. "You sacrificed—" The smack came hard, but she was expecting it.

"You will stay here." He motioned for one of the guards to grab her arms.

Reluctantly, the guard took his eyes off the women making their way toward him and obediently took Miu's arms.

Those were the last words he said before he sacrificed Zigan. She had no fight left in her. Falling to her knees, she wailed, ripping her hair and her clothes.

Her father never turned around.

THE DAYS WENT by slower and slower, and as they passed, Miu's restrictions grew tighter. The head priestess watched her like a hawk to a mouse. Any freedom she had was between patrons. She was allowed to eat her meals on a corner of the ziggurat lined with gardens. She'd stand and look out at the city of Ur with anger, knowing that just beyond the city walls was her beloved wildflower patch.

She'd daydream of frolicking there with Didila, and even Taku. Dream of the freedom to do whatever she pleased. Maybe the gods had won in her secret game. They'd given her father the wisdom to find her and drag her back here. Maybe they'd simply waited until she got back to finally have their way with her.

If the gods were real, and if they carried this much power, she'd rather be dead.

And then she remembered something. What was that Taku had told her the night before she was found? He'd been fixated on his new god that night, filling Didila's head with all kinds of absurd ideas.

But were they? He'd told her, "I cried out to him. He heard me. He cared enough to stop the chaos waters."

What gods heard a prayer and then decided they cared? Sure, the gods in Ur heard their women screaming as men desecrated their bodies. Sure, the gods heard the cries for freedom and then responded with stealing it away.

But what god heard their people and then responded in love? A god who saw, heard, and responded?

She'd ignored Taku that evening, because she'd had her freedom. She'd had everything she wanted in Dilmun, except peace. She'd watched his face that night in wonder. When she met Taku, he'd been too scared to say hello, but that last night in Dilmun he was bold. He came back to Dilmun, not because he needed her, but to tell her about his new god that wanted to dwell with people.

If she wanted anything, she wanted independence. But what had that gotten her? Only a fight for survival and being used as a temple priestess.

"No, it's not worth it," she whispered to herself. "What if Taku's god would see me? A god who can take a weak man and give him boldness." She glanced at the wildflowers and whispered, "Yahweh, lead me in your way."

Fiddling with her jewelry, she tried to show little emotion. She just prayed to an unseen god. As far as she knew, the god didn't have any images to worship or bow down to, so a prayer spoken toward the skies would have to work.

Taku would have gotten a laugh out of that. Smiling to herself for the first time since being dragged to Ur, she turned to head back to work.

The head priestess was coming her way, two men behind her.

That wasn't how this worked. She was supposed to sit at the

wall and men chose her. Men never followed the head priestess. Something was wrong.

"Here we go." She rolled her eyes and squared her shoulders.

The sun was high in the sky, blinding her as she glanced at men approaching her. Covering her eyes with her hand, she heard a gentle laugh.

"Taku?" Her ears were playing tricks on her. Squinting harder, she saw his face and ran to him, throwing her arms around him.

"You will act respectable in your priestess tunic." The head priestess slapped her arm.

Miu immediately recoiled and bowed her head.

Taku's eyes went wide.

"Miu, this is Abram." Taku introduced them.

Lifting her head, she snuck a glance at the man beside him. She waited. The head priestess waited. She knew Taku was gathering his thoughts.

But before he could say anything, the head priestess bowed to Abram, pulling Miu with her. "He is a man to be respected. He has acquired a god who is leading him from Ur. Abram and all his wealth will be gone," she whispered to Miu.

This man knew Yahweh. The god to whom she just prayed to for help. Had he heard her?

"Stand, Miu." Abram's voice overflowing from his lips like milk and honey. "We've come to pay your price for freedom. Twelve shekels of silver I have given to the high priestess."

"Freedom." Miu's voice was no louder than a whisper.

"Your freedom will be in the hands of Yahweh. He is the one who calls us out to a land we do not know." Turning to Taku, Abram placed his hand on his shoulder and smiled. "And it is Taku who wants you to go with us."

"So I am not getting my freedom?" she asked. "What about my father? He won't allow this. He's been known to travel the world; he found me and dragged me back here." She waved her arm at the women lying in clusters around them.

"I will handle Badak, Miu. It is you who must choose today. Do you want to serve the gods of Ur or become a tentmaker for Yahweh? You will not be free in the way you see freedom. But, you will be among our people. You will be committed to us and the ways Yahweh shows us. We have many tents yet to be made for our journey, and I'm paying for you to join in that work. Then you will go with us when we leave."

Had she heard him correctly? If she went with Abram and Taku, there wouldn't be freedom. It would be trading one man's wishes for another's. Her father had used her for his own gain. Zu had promised protection and instead, she lost everything she'd ever loved. And now here at the temple, she was used for men's pleasure and what they called worship. Going with Abram would be the same. More men using her. Tighter grips, less control.

But in her mind, she couldn't ignore that she had tried speaking to Taku's god, and now here they were.

"Miu, either you go with us now or stay in Ur." Taku finally spoke up. "I came to get you out of this, but you need to know that you can't run away once you're with us. You also can't belittle our god either. If you go with us, you must choose to follow what Yahweh shows us along the way."

Miu's resolve wavered, and then Didila flashed in her mind. Falling to her knees overwhelmed with grief, she knew her need to control everyone caused her to lose the only one she truly loved. She was no better than her father. She had clung tightly to her control and independence until they slipped away like sand through clenched fists.

Taku bent down beside her. She wanted to pull away or maybe even punch him. Instead, she blurted out, "I've lost everyone because I wasn't strong enough. I couldn't keep Didila or Tiame from harm. I wasn't strong enough for Zu to appreciate me. I don't have what you need to keep going, Taku. I can't be strong for you or Abram. I definitely can't be strong enough for this god you want me to follow."

Taku carefully took her chin in his hands and made her look

him directly in the eyes. She'd never seen strength in anyone's eyes like this. "You're finally understanding, Miu. Yahweh is almighty and has the strength we need. Sometimes our greatest act of strength is seen in our biggest display of weakness. Let us help you, Miu."

Miu nodded her head, giving up.

Abram took her by the elbow, helping her to her feet. As they walked away, he handed the head priestess the silver coins.

Miu didn't look back. Taku led the way down the long flights of stairs, away from the gods of Ur. Away from the control they had over her. Away from the control she had over herself. She wasn't sure what she agreed to with Yahweh, but she was done fighting.

To what do I owe this pleasure?" Badak stood from his workbench to face Abram and bowed at the waist.

"I've come to pay the price for your daughter," Abram looked Badak directly in the eyes, unflinching. "She will be my servant as I travel to the land Yahweh shows us. I heard she made a name for herself in Dilmun and is a hard worker. Your rights to her life are done. No need to pay her fees to the temple, I've taken care of that."

"Your god, Yahweh." He spit on the ground. "He has nothing on the gods of Ur and their power. Take my daughter. She was nothing to me. Worthless. Just like your god."

Abram turned to leave. A loud crash behind him startled him. He turned back.

Badak clutched his chest, eyes wide as he took his last breath.

"He what?" Miu demanded from Abram.

"He will no longer be a threat to you. He died on his workbench with his precious jewels scattered around his body. With my purchase of your freedom and his death, no one in Ur can threaten you any longer," Abram said.

Why was he always looking at her like that? Like he wanted to make sure she wasn't about to shatter into tiny pieces.

Miu wasn't sure if she should cry or shout for joy. She'd already grieved losing Dilmun. She'd fought to have Ur's chains released, and then Taku found her. And here was this man of Yahweh, looking in her eyes as if he saw her for who she was. As if he loved her even with the fight drained out of her.

"Let's go for a walk," Abram suggested.

Miu nodded. A walk always cleared her head. It at least kept her from punching or throwing things.

"Can we walk the way of the wildflowers?" she asked. One final walk through the wildflowers would be good for her.

Abram nodded and turned right, heading toward the wall where they could exit. The day's heat wasn't as oppressive as normal, and she thought she felt a breeze as they exited the walls.

Waving to two shepherds under a tree, Abram smiled.

"People think they're crazy and wild men. Shepherds, that is. But they must be strong. They fight wild animals to protect their flock from predators. Their life out here in the desert isn't easy," he said almost to himself.

"You have a flock that will travel with us, right?" Miu asked.

"Yes, along with other herds, but I have brought you on to help with tentmaking." He gazed upward as if he were also speaking to the sky.

"I've never made a tent. I've only lived in cities, Abram. Why would you think I can help?"

"I know the strength you showed in Dilmun. The tents are already being made, you will simply need to help where the ladies tell you. They're made of goat hair. The hair becomes porous when dry, but waterproof when wet, providing protection during travel in rainy weather. Then when the heat comes, we roll up the sides of the tent for shade." He checked her face for understanding.

"I understand. What I don't understand is your kindness," she said bluntly.

The field of wildflowers was ahead. Flashes of colors dancing in the breeze took Miu's breath away.

"I wish I were them," Miu whispered to herself.

"Who are you wishing your life to be like, Miu?"

"I wish I could have the freedom of the wildflowers. They grow wherever they please, wandering across the land." She smiled as she remembered how she felt crossing the chaotic waters and into Dilmun. How she felt as she finally was able to run the tavern away from Hashur and the freedom skipping through the sunflowers with Didila.

Purple and yellow coneflowers tickled her legs, and a breeze brushed her face. She bent down to pick one of the brightest purple flowers she'd ever seen, a tear in her eye.

"What if freedom isn't going wherever you please and doing whatever you want?" Abram's nose scrunched up, an irrepressible smile spilling onto his unwrinkled face.

"What are you talking about?" Miu snapped. Why was he smiling like that? She hated it when people laughed at her.

"Do the wildflowers grow everywhere, Miu?"

"They grow wherever they please. Look around, Abram. They have no boundary line. There is no one planting them in rows and cutting them off." Miu waved her arm toward the flowers. Thinking she'd proved her point, she put her hands on her hips, the flowers dangling from her fist.

"Look again. Do they grow everywhere?"

Miu was getting impatient, but she did as she was told for once in her life. She rolled her eyes to herself and turned to look around. The wildflowers did stop growing in some places.

"The shadow of Ur's walls. They aren't growing there."

"Where else?" Abram pushed.

She turned to look in the opposite direction of Ur. "They go on forever it seems, but they don't grow in the path of the shepherds. Nor do they grow where the flocks graze."

"Mmmhmm."

"Why does that matter?" She rubbed her chin, still looking for places where the colors were missing from the landscape.

"Can you think of any other places where the wildflowers aren't growing?"

Frustrated, she looked around one more time. She saw the chaos waters gleaming far in the distance. "The flowers do not grow on the bank of the waters." She sighed. "Are you done yet?"

"Miu, the wildflowers hold a secret." He responded to her curt tone with gentleness, as that smile began to spread to his eyes.

"Then tell me!" she demanded, and threw the flowers in her hand to the ground. Covering her mouth, she tried to quiet herself to show respect.

"The wildflowers weren't created to grow in the chaos waters, so they don't. They weren't created to grow in the shade of a city, so they don't. They were created to grow in the open, drinking in the sunshine. If they creep outside of those boundaries their roots are strangled or drowned. The wildflowers' secret is that they live within their boundaries, Miu." He paused to look around at the field beneath their feet. "We are no different."

The anger in her calmed for the first time in her life. She didn't feel the need to punch or throw something. The peace radiated through her like sunshine. Where was that coming from?

"Yahweh has given us boundaries in which we should live. When we stray to the bank of the chaos waters or hide in the shadow of someone's approval, then our roots are drowned or choked out. When we live within the rules Yahweh gives us, they bring life to us. It is only then that we can leave a city and follow him to places we don't know. It is only then that we can run taverns and lead people, Miu. It is his love and his correction that guide us to places where freedom grows. It is not freedom to do as we wish, but it becomes freedom to do what we were created to do."

A tear slipped down her cheek, and this time she didn't wipe it away. She stepped toward Abram and wrapped her arms around him.

Abram chuckled.

She pulled away, and now it was her turn to look Abram directly in the eyes. "I've fought against the gods since I can remember, but I've also fought hard against other people. I didn't think I needed them. But it wasn't until I encountered you, Abram, that I realized we need each other. We need to know more about this Yahweh, because it's his love that changes us."

"Yes, we are all made in his image. We don't need stone or clay images of the gods of Ur. You, Miu, were made in Yahweh's image. Just as the images in Ur are made to reflect the presence and the revelation of the gods, as humans we were created to reflect Yahweh's presence and revelation to others. There is coming a day, Miu, when Yahweh will dwell with us once again; until then we follow him in faith where he leads, not where we lead ourselves."

Miu knew he was right. She let his words wash over her need for control and desire to push people over with her demands.

And then she remembered Taku. She needed to apologize. She wanted him to know she believed in the goodness of Yahweh. She finally saw how, unlike the gods of Ur, Yahweh didn't need her or use her to survive, but Yahweh wanted her. And that changed everything.

"Can we find Taku?" She wiped another tear from her eye and smiled. "I'd like to take him some wildflowers."

chapter
thirty-three

Miu woke early as she always did, long before any of Abram's people did. She loved watching the tent-makers come to life while their children ran circles around their feet. The hustle and bustle within Abram's people was different from what she'd observed in Ur or Dilmun. There was joy in their work. They weren't fighting for the best seat or the best goat hair to make the tents. They were all working with one mind and one goal: to follow Yahweh to the city He would show them. There was something peaceful in that. There was something that lacked the striving she'd done since her birth.

The sounds of bleating sheep and goats reminded her of the hard work they had ahead. Shepherds didn't have an easy life of frills like Zu or an adventurous life like Zaidu. They had a dedicated life, and dedication and fidelity were often boring. However, Miu was content with boring if she kept the peace of Yahweh for the journey.

Sitting down beside Sarai, she studied how the older woman's hands moved. Nimble. Dedicated. She wondered how she moved so quickly. She wanted to take the needles from her to learn it herself, but something held her hands in place. She didn't need to push someone out of the way; they were working together.

Sarai turned to catch her eye, a smile on her face.

"Are you laughing at me?" Miu asked.

"No, I'm watching you learn to control yourself." Sarai laughed softly. "You're used to leading, aren't you?'

"I am, but I want to learn the way of your people." Miu put her hands up in defeat.

"New tents are rarely made," Sarai continued, that mothering tone hidden in her voice. "Usually new tents are only made when a young groom and his bride move to a new location apart from the groom's family. And since we are following Abram and Yahweh, many new tents must be made."

"Show me how it's done," Miu said, shocked at her own ability to listen.

"Usually, we gather clippings from goat hair. We take these strips, join them together to create the tent itself. As our family grows larger or as his wealth grows, we will enlarge his existing tent. Remember how your father built onto his home and added the jewelry workshop? It is the same with the tents. We will take the goats' hair, because after it becomes wet with rain, it shrinks and tightens up to create a dry living space below."

A group of young girls ran through the tentmakers' area giggling. Miu tensed. If this had been her tavern or Zu's home, the children would be silenced. She darted her gaze to Sarai. How would she handle the children? She had no children of her own, and Miu's experience led her to believe that made women grumpier around children.

"Hello, Miriam. Hello, Milkah," Sarai giggled back. She reached into her pocket and pulled out two dried apricots, giving one to each of the girls. "Now run along."

"You didn't scold them?" Miu's brow furrowed. "How do you expect to finish the task Yahweh has given you if they're in your way?"

"Oh, Miu." Sarai put her needles into her lap and turned to face Miu. "Children are not in the way of the work we do. Children need to learn the way of Yahweh. They must see us work with joy for him. They must watch us make mistakes and love each other anyway." Then she picked her needles up and went back to work.

Miu saw she had her own set of needles on her stool. She picked them up awkwardly.

Without saying a word, Sarai held the needles between her forefinger and thumb and waited for Miu to do the same. Together they took the sewing step by step, Miu learning and Sarai waiting with patience.

Miu looked up from her work to see Taku standing beside her.

"Look! I made this all by myself!" Miu exclaimed.

Taku dropped his shoulders and let out an exaggerated sigh.

"What?" Miu asked.

Clearing his throat, he asked, "You did this all by yourself?"

Miu looked around. All the tentmakers were watching her. Sarai stopped her work and smiled like a mother would her own child.

"I was able to make this piece of the tent because Sarai taught me to sew. I was able to make this piece of the tent because Abram brought in the goat hair. I was able to do all of this because Yahweh gives me breath. Now, are you happy?" She laughed.

"Yep." He beamed, waving her on to follow him. "Now are you ready for some lunch?"

Together they grabbed some food that one of Abram's people had put together for them: a handful of almonds, goat cheese, and barley cakes. They walked to sit under a tree, and Miu felt the peace again, the same peace she'd felt when they left the temple.

"I told you Abram was different." Taku broke the silence.

"Yeah, but it's because he's encountered Yahweh," Miu pushed back.

Taku threw his head back in laughter. "You have changed, but you're still the Miu I met on Zaidu's boat. Full of life and argumentative."

"I don't argue, Taku. I state what's right." She placed her hands on her hips.

Taku laughed as he sank comfortably against a large tree. Watching everyone work together to follow Yahweh was more than Miu ever knew she needed. Running away from her father and then fighting for control drained any desire for a different life she might have been holding onto. There was contentment found in learning from others while also using her talents to help the people of Yahweh thrive.

"I'm sorry," Taku blurted out as he popped a few almonds in his mouth.

"What are you talking about?"

"I'm sorry you had to leave Didila." He quickly wiped a tear from his eye.

They sat in silence for a moment, feeling the grief of losing a little girl they'd both wanted to protect and love.

"Tiame too," Miu said. "I miss her. I said I'd take care of her. I told her promises that I couldn't keep. I pray to Yahweh for his provision of them both. I pray he will lead us to Dilmun so we can take them with us." Now it was Miu's turn for a tear to fall from her eye, but she didn't wipe it away. Instead, she sat still as it fell down her cheek and onto her barley cake.

"One day I hope Yahweh comes to rid the world of the snake," she whispered.

"The snake?" Taku asked.

"Yes, in all my bad dreams there is a snake. It comes to destroy Ur, my family, my friends, and especially my peace." She played with the almonds in her other hand as she thought about it. "If Yahweh truly comes and destroys that snake, we all can dwell with him again. Not in these tents made of goat's hair, but in a permanent location."

A smile swept across her face, and she stood. "Taku, Yahweh will lead us to a place where he can make his own name great. He will lead us where Abram's family will make a great nation, and every family on earth will be blessed by him."

"Yahweh did tell Abram that," Taku said.

"Do you believe that though? Do you believe that we get to be a part of this promise from Yahweh? The god that calmed your way to Dilmun. The god that gave my restless heart peace to live in community. Do you know what that means?" She jumped up and down.

"It means we need to get back to work on those tents," Taku teased her.

But this time, Miu wasn't worried about Taku telling her what to do, or Sarai being a better tentmaker than her, nor was she worried that Abram would ever try to control her. Yahweh would be her God, and she would be one of his people.

Two weeks later

"Today is the day!" Sarai shouted. All of Abram's people were standing around in expectation of what Yahweh might say on their first day of leaving. Men with graying beards held hands with barefoot children. Aging women locked arms with younger ones.

Looking across the crowd, Miu thought she saw Jara. What seemed like years ago, she remembered wanting to be like her, independent of man and blessed by the gods. Today she was blessed by the one true and faithful Yahweh. And she didn't need independence any longer. She needed people. She needed community. She'd miss Jara, with her worn hands and her strength, but she'd gained much more.

"Anna, are you ready? Have you gotten all our tents onto our cart? If not, do you need my help to do so?"

Anna nodded. And Miu wrapped her arm around her shoulder and squeezed. She saw something in Anna the first day she joined Sarai in tentmaking. Every time Anna would make a stitch, she'd need someone's approval. Every time she prepared her lunch, she'd ask if she'd done it at the wrong time.

Miu saw her dear friend Tiame in Anna. Instead of yelling at her, Miu stood with her. She had asked Sarai if she could give Anna pointers, promising to take responsibility for her errors.

"If you're responsible for her, then you can." Sarai nodded approval. From that day on, Miu had taken responsibility for three other girls, catching herself when she wanted to push them harder than they were capable. She could lead without fear, for she was led by someone greater.

"Miu!" Taku came running up behind her. Turning to look, her heart leaped. Bubbling up from her was a shout of joy.

"Tiame, Didila!" She covered her mouth with her hands. "How did you find us? What are you doing here?"

"We went to find you at Zu's house, and he said you'd left for a trip to Ur. Then we went to find Zaidu, and he had left with Taku. All we knew was something was wrong. You wouldn't leave without us," Tiame said.

Embracing Tiame, she noticed Didila standing back, fear in her eyes. She'd lost her mother and then Miu in a short time span. No wonder she was hesitant.

Pulling away from Tiame's embrace, Miu bent down to look the young girl in the eyes. Oh, how she'd changed and grown. She'd overcome sickness and near death, losing her mother, and now a trip across the chaos waters.

"Didila." Miu took her hands with tenderness. They were no longer pudgy but growing more slender and feminine. "My sweet apricot." The words stuck in her throat. "Thank you for finding us." She waited, not wanting to push her, and Didila noticed.

Lifting her head, the young girl wiped a tear away. "I thought you left me. Tiame said you didn't leave people. She said you'd never run away." She sniffled, and Miu could see a little girl still hiding behind her eyes.

"I would never run away. But I want to tell you about someone I met. Do you remember Taku telling us about Yahweh?"

Her dark eyes got bright with anticipation as she nodded, hope brimming.

"All the times I pushed you. All the times I scared you. All the time other people have left you. Yahweh will not. I've met him. And my sweet girl, I want to tell you about him. The one who will never leave you. A god who will never abandon you. He created you to love you. And Didila ..."

She nodded again, wiping her hands on her tunic.

"We no longer need to fight for control of a tavern or wrestle with someone for our freedom. We are free to be who he has made us to be because He is Yahweh, and he holds the skies, the land, and even the chaos waters in his right hand. And guess what?"

Didila now had a smile spread across her face, and she began to jump up and down.

"You've made it just in time. Today, we all get to leave Ur and grow like the wildflowers. Free to bloom in the way Yahweh made us."

"Do I get to ride a donkey?" Didila giggled.

Miu looked toward Taku and Tiame as everyone laughed.

"Of course you can ride a donkey." She smiled. Taking Didila's hand, they headed toward the crowds of people leaving Ur.

As they passed the field of wildflowers, Miu glanced back one last time. She no longer craved running free or running away. She was blooming among her people, right where Yahweh planted her.

author's note

Dear reader,

This book was never meant to be written—a year before writing the book, I adamantly declared that I would never write a book.

But God ...

He has a funny sense of humor. The idea for this book began when I started a study through the Bible Project in Genesis. Little did I know at the time, it would spark my curiosity in ways I've never experienced. I was blown away when I saw the attention to detail the author(s) of Genesis used to craft the first few chapters of the Bible's creation narrative.

I then came across other creation stories such as Gilgamesh and Enuma Elish that have similar themes to the biblical one. I saw how scholars pointed out that Genesis was written to an Ancient Near Eastern set of beliefs and not written to my preconceived ideas. I read about the creation stories of Israel's neighbors, which were drastically different, yet similar. In the neighboring stories, they told how the gods created humans to be slaves to work the garden and provide them with food, whereas the biblical narrative tells of God creating the garden for humans to flourish. I saw how the other creation narratives told of the gods creating the world through violence and struggle, and then I saw in such contrast how the God of the Bible spoke words and separated light from dark. No violence at all, in fact it was all labeled good. What I saw staring me in the face was a contrast between gods who needed people and a God who wanted a relationship with his creation.

> *The framers of creation in the Bible inherited a treasure trove of venerable traditions from their cultural neighbors. Instead of creating their accounts ex nihilo, the composers of Scripture developed their traditions in dialogue with some of the great religious traditions of the surrounding cultures, particularly those originating from Mesopotamia and Egypt, as well as those of their more immediate Canaanite neighbors.*

> William Brown, *Seven Pillars of Creation:*
> *The Bible, Science, and the Ecology of*
> *Wonder*

It was from these ideas that *Secrets of the Wildflowers* was birthed. I began to imagine a girl who grew up in a world where gods were capricious, the seas were chaotic and unknowable. I wondered how her fear of the world around her would shape her thinking. In her world, the gods were no better than humans; they either weakly yielded to human requests or fiercely fought them back. What would she struggle with? What questions would she have about the world she lived in? What would it be like to wonder what God was like?

It was through this lens that I realized today we aren't much different than Miu or Taku. My goal was for people to see how personal and loving God is, while also emphasizing the importance of trusting God's boundaries.

The wonder of exploring Genesis has led me to a profound realization of the immense effort God put in to ensure that we never have to doubt His true nature, his goodness, and his love. He made it crystal clear. And it is through this book I pray you can see glimpses of his deep love for you, and I hope it will inspire you to bloom like the wildflowers, no matter where life takes you.

resources

1. Ur of the Chaldeans
https://www.christianstudylibrary.org/article/ur-chaldeans

2. Ur of the Chaldeans
https://www.jstage.jst.go.jp/article/orient/51/0/51_63/_pdf/-char/en

3. Mesopotamia: Social Structure
https://factsanddetails.com/world/cat56/sub402/entry-6396.html

4. Mesopotamia
https://www.historyonthenet.com/mesopotamia

5. What Did Ancient Mesopotamians Eat?
https://www.historyonthenet.com/what-did-ancient-mesopotamians-eat

6. Jacobsen, Thorkild. 1973. *The Treasures of Darkness: A History of Mesopotamian Religion*. P.122

7. Medicine in Ancient Mesopotamia
https://scholarworks.gvsu.edu/cgi/viewcontent.cgi?article=1056&context=gvjh#:~:text=Mesopotamia%20were%20methodically%20trained%2C%20had,asu%20physicians%20in%20ancient%20Mesopotamia

8. The History of Pearling in Bahrain
https://www.wanderlust.co.uk/content/bahrain-pearling-history/

9. John Walton. *Ancient Near Eastern Thought and the Old Testament* (2nd Edition)
http://bakerpublishinggroup.com/books/ancient-near-eastern-thought-and-the-old-testament-2nd-edition/230844

10. A Hymn to Ninkas
https://etcsl.orinst.ox.ac.uk/section4/tr4231.htm

11. Health Care in Ancient Mesopotamia
https://www.worldhistory.org/article/687/health-care-in-ancient-mesopotamia/

12. Toxicology Rounds: Opium, from Ancient Sumeria to Modern America
https://journals.lww.com/em-news/fulltext/2013/04000/toxicology_round
	s__opium,_from_ancient_sumeria_to.14.aspx

13. In Praise of the Pickax
http://realhistoryww.com/world_history/ancient/Misc/Sumer/Hymns2.htm

14. Abraham the Habiru
https://ready4eternity.com/abraham-the-habiru/

15. Why Did Terah Leave the City of Ur?
https://www.genesisforordinarypeople.com/faq/why-did-terah-leave-the-city-of-
	ur

acknowledgments

A huge thank you to those whose unwavering support and encouragement have played a pivotal role in bringing this book to fruition.

First and foremost, a heartfelt thank you to Ben, my amazing husband and steadfast supporter since the age of 13. Your belief in my abilities, even when I doubted myself, has been a secure foundation in my journey.

To my incredible children, who never wavered in their belief that Mom could achieve this feat—your unwavering faith fueled my determination.

Dara, Sarah, and Carrie, your constant stream of uplifting text messages served as a source of motivation during both triumphs and challenges. Your encouragement made every step of this journey more meaningful.

A special acknowledgment goes to Jennifer Crosswhite, my editor and book coach. Your wise counsel and generous support have been instrumental in refining and shaping this manuscript into its best form. I also want to thank my proofreader, Debbie Guerrant, and my cover designer, Alexander von Ness of Nessgraphica.

Lastly, I extend my appreciation to the Bible Project for their invaluable Classroom, which not only inspired ideas but also introduced me to the rich tapestry of ancient Near Eastern beliefs. Their teachings guided me to approach the Scriptures as a respectful tourist, avoiding the imposition of modern beliefs onto ancient contexts while seeing the Bible as a unified story that leads to Jesus. Also, to John Walton for his pioneering research and studies—your work has paved the way for many of us, providing invaluable insights to navigate historical settings with respect and authenticity.

about the author

Sarah Talbert is an enthusiastic storyteller who loves to explore the complexities of faith. She uses her creative writing to inspire others in their own spiritual journey.

She has a deep passion for making God famous. By using her gifts as a historical fiction author and poet, Sarah shares powerful stories that honor the beauty of humanity while pointing readers toward a deeper relationship with Jesus.

She is passionate about building community through discipleship, hospitality, and practical evangelism. Married to her middle school sweetheart, she and her spouse manage their own businesses while navigating the joys of raising three children and chasing the Florida sunshine by boat whenever they can find a moment to escape.

Learn more about Sarah here: www.sarahtalbert.com

www.ingramcontent.com/pod-product-compliance
Lightning Source LLC
Chambersburg PA
CBHW021229310726
48971CB00006B/1744